The Ones That Walked

by

Daniel Oliver Bradshaw

Printed in the United States of America
First Edition, 2025

ISBN 979-8-9996832-0-5

Published by MindMaze Publishing
www.mindmazepublishing.com

To Dad

and

for those who wander in search of meaning

[CH.01]

INITIAL CONDITIONS

He opened his eyes. A surge of blood rushed to his head, the fog of a blackout still clinging to him. He inhaled sharply and lumbered to his feet. The sound of running water bounced around in absolute darkness. Thick. Total. He could see nothing.

"Hello? Is anyone there? HELLO!" Only an echo returned as he stumbled forward, feet splashing. Reaching out, he brushed his fingertips against what felt like brick. Damp. Cold. A shiver moved through him.

He shuffled right and felt the other side. Only an arm's length away, the wall was continuous and concave.

A tunnel?

He leaned against the brick and tried to think of where he could be. With no light and no memory of how he had arrived, thinking was difficult. He crouched and pressed his hand into the finger-deep water. It was greasy and dense. The current pulled behind him. He stood and walked with it.

After what felt like an eternity, a dim light appeared ahead. Faint. Pulsating. He stood still, pulled by it, until it peered down at him like an eye. He ran toward it. Feet kicked water. Pants soaked through. A godawful smell attached itself to him.

Please don't be a sewer, I'm already in some shit!

As he neared the blinking light, he saw someone. A woman. Semi-unconscious and dressed in climbing gear. A flashlight was clipped to the strap of a backpack slung over her right shoulder.

"Hey," he gently poked her, "Hey, you okay?"

Her eyes fluttered open and locked onto his. She threw herself back into the stream.

"What's going on? GET AWAY FROM ME!"

"Shh—hey look, calm down. My name is James. I mean… at least I think it is."

She doesn't seem dangerous. Maybe she knows something.

He offered his hand. Under the strobing light she could make out his face. Only for a moment, before it disappeared again and again.

On. Off. On. Off.

Short brown hair. Blue eyes. Pale skin. Broad shoulders. She stitched together a picture from flashes of light and impulse. She decided he wasn't a threat.

She unclipped the flashlight and smacked it once. The beam held steady. Her eyes traced his fingers, his palm, up his arm. He looked rugged —dirt streaking his face, clothes damp, knuckles dark with grime.

"M-my name is Ashley." She rested her palm in his, locked it tight, and recovered.

James pulled her to her feet. "Ashley. Okay, mind telling me where we are?"

"I don't know." She shook her head. "What did you mean by, you think your name is?"

"I-I don't really remember anything."

"What about a last name?"

"Nope."

James sat down across from her and rested his head against the mossy brick. He exhaled. She had long brown hair wrapped in a ponytail, hazel eyes, a straight face. He found her attractive. The thought passed quickly.

What's someone like her doing in a place like this? Why am I here? Why are we both here?

Ashley's flashlight flickered.

"No!" he said, fearing the dark.

She smacked it three times. "Lucky flashlight." The beam steadied.

"Lucky flashlight, right." James rubbed his temple. Between the light and his soaked pants, a headache was forming. "Sorry if I startled you. Like I said, I don't know what's going on."

"Clearly." She swept the torch around. The tunnel walls were spotted with green slime, the water below brown and milky. Neither of them had time to think about how unpleasant it was. Their minds were cloudy. Trying to remember anything hurt.

"I think we should stick with the current," she said. "Maybe it leads somewhere."

"Sure, can I tie my shoes first?"

She nodded and held the light on him. James used the moment to take stock of himself—blue striped long-sleeve shirt, boots, khakis. He checked his pockets. Some change. A phone. He pressed the power button.

Dead. Why did I think that'd work.

Ashley checked herself too. Red Henley, cargo pants, hiking boots. Her small blue backpack held a pair of batteries, a pocketknife, a climbing course map, and a water bottle. Attached to the side: a coiled rope, three carabiners, a belay device, and sunscreen.

James noticed the watch on her wrist. "What time is it?"

"Well according to this, it's ten in the morning."

"Is that right?"

"I don't know."

"How do you not know? Don't you remember what you were doing?"

"Obviously I was climbing." She gestured at her clothes with a small laugh.

How can she laugh at a time like this?

She was relaxed, something James couldn't be.

"I don't remember what was happening before," she said calmly, "and it doesn't matter. We need to find a way out."

"What do you mean, doesn't matter?"

"You don't remember anything either." She met his eyes. "So focus on what's in front of us."

He exhaled through his nose. She was right, and he didn't like it.

"We both remember our names," she added.

That's strange. But why only names? Was it even my name?

He let it go.

"You really can't remember anything?" Ashley studied him.

"I woke up in pitch black." He looked at his feet. "I followed the water thinking it would lead out, and saw your light." Pressing his palm against his forehead, he grunted.

"Then we have a direction." She pointed downstream and tightened her backpack straps.

"What are you doing?"

"We're leaving." Ashley started walking.

He followed her lead.

Then—a sharp, high-pitched noise rattled the hall. A scream. The sound skipped along the brick, vibrations thick enough to take shape in the air. He felt blood move out of his ears. He dropped to his knees, clamping his hands over them, his body folding inward.

"AH! WHAT IS THAT?"

Ashley collapsed in the water beside him, hands pressed to her head. Veins pushed through her skin and fanned outward in dark webs across her face. James saw the same happening to himself—black, spreading, wrong. The sound had paralyzed them both.

Then it stopped.

James coughed hard, throat raw. Clear phlegm hit the air. The black veins faded as quickly as they'd come. Ashley fought to stand.

"Wh-what was that?" he rasped.

"I don't know. But we need to go—now!" She grabbed his arm and pulled.

He picked up the pace. Eyes locked on the flashlight ahead—the only thing in the dark he was certain of. James wasn't going to lose sight of it.

[CH.02]

THE
DESCENT

"How long have we been walking?" James asked.

Ashley glanced at her watch. "Just past eleven."

"An hour and we haven't seen an exit? We haven't even turned!"

"I wouldn't be so sure about that." She swept the light left, revealing a subtle curve in the tunnel walls. It was only a slight bend. Any change felt like a victory. "Don't worry so much, James. It doesn't help."

"How can you say that in a situation like this?"

Twenty more steps around the curve.

"Because-" Ashley pushed the beam forward. "-look!"

Dead ahead, a metal grate jutted from the tunnel wall, bolted to brick and bordered by a three-foot railing. Water rained through the floor holes, smacking into a pool below and echoing through the cavern.

Definitely man-made. I wonder who could be down here.

She gripped the oily railing and cast the light outward. The balcony was four feet across, hanging fifty feet above the bottom. Massive gray-brick walls rose around them, crusted with the same green slime from the tunnel. Chains hung sparsely from the stone. The flashlight swept left, right, up, then below—darkness swallowing the beam before it reached the floor.

"This place looks medieval," James said scanning the area.

"Medieval? You a history buff?"

"I don't know." He laughed once. *I really don't!*

"Hey check this out!" Ashley dropped the beam left, landing on a steel ladder descending into shadow. The metal was tarnished, slick with moisture.

"You sure it's safe?" He had a good reason to question its integrity.

"I don't know. Why don't you check it out first?" She extended her arm toward it.

James stared at her. He had genuinely expected her to go first.

"Who, me?" He really didn't want to go.

Hazel eyes answered.

"Fine." He climbed over the railing and stepped cautiously onto the ladder. His hands clutched each freezing rung. "This place is seriously creepy, huh Ash?"

Okay, just play it cool.

He descended slowly, gripping each frigid rung. Ashley followed above, her pace quicker than his.

I don't want to give her any reason to doubt me. She's the best chance I've got of getting out of here.

Between the damp clothes and the dropping temperature, he fought off every urge to spiral. His hands twitched. He had to pry them from each frozen rung.

"You're calling me Ash now?"

"Yeah, why not?"

"I don't know, I just—"

CLACK!

His foot slipped. On reflex he flung his left arm up and caught the rung.

"You okay?" Ashley peered down.

She'd clipped the flashlight back to her bag for the climb. Squinting, she shifted her head around her shoulder and looked below. He was near the bottom, hanging a few feet from the floor.

"I-I'm okay. I think."

He dropped the last few feet and steadied himself.

A red glow bloomed in the air.

"What the hell—" He reached toward it, moving his hands through the hue as though he could catch it. Dark but real. From nowhere visible.

"Ashley, are you seeing this?"

She reached the bottom and her head swept the room. No bulbs. No fire. Just a glowing presence, bathing everything in soft, eerie red.

"It's luminescent."

"Luma-what?"

"I don't understand it either." She pocketed the flashlight.

The glow strengthened, saturating the space. It revealed a square room, exactly symmetrical. Three tunnels branched from the one behind them —left, center, right.

"You don't want to keep using the light?"

"Well, if we can see, then maybe we should save the battery."

James nodded. With the faintest dilation of his pupils, his head kicked back—like something clicked—and in an instant, the room sharpened around him. A rush of clarity broke through. Until now it had all felt like a dream—instinct carrying him forward without thought. Now he could see everything.

This is real! There's no way two people wake up down here by accident. I don't know her. Who is she? Were we left here to die? Why can't I remember anything?

"Ashley, why can't you remember anything?" he asked.

She frowned. "We talked about this."

"Yeah, but think about it—two strangers, both trapped underground, both with memory loss? That's not a coincidence."

"And you expect me to explain it?"

He gestured at the tunnels, "Why have we only gone straight until now? And that noise earlier?"

"What are you getting at?"

He stopped himself.

Keep it together. She's not thinking this through yet.

"So… which way?" she pointed.

"Don't ask me!"

"I say straight then."

"Why?"

"Why not?" She was already moving. James followed. The red hue lit about fifty feet ahead—not ideal, but better than total darkness.

She's different.

Her wit kept him in his place, whatever that place was.

"Can I have some water?" he asked.

Ashley stopped and pulled out a plastic bottle from her pack, "Water break it is!"

He locked his lips to the opening and drank deeply.

"Hey!" she shoved his shoulder. "Don't drink it all!"

He handed it back. "Sorry, I was thirsty."

"We have to conserve!" She looked at him until he looked away. "Look, I wanna get out of here just as much as you okay but we have to work together. And that means taking it slow. I want to find out what's going on, but we have to get out of here first! And that requires keeping our heads straight. Got it?"

He saw her differently for a moment. Strong. Sharp. A subtle accent—Southern, maybe Midwest.

Midwest. Is that a place? Am I from that place?

He stepped back and caught himself on the wall, left hand sinking into something slick running down the brick.

"UGH! This smells like shit!" James flicked his wrist, slinging the goo away. "Yuck!"

Ashley laughed.

"Hey, it's not funny! This could be poison," he protested vehemently.

"Would you calm down?" Her amusement was clear.

He shook his hand—then stopped. It was glowing.

Ashley stared. "How is it doing that?"

"It's… acting like a light," he said.

"Does your hand hurt?"

"No, I don't feel anything." He held it up, fingers spread. A green tint lay across his skin, stopping at the wrist, casting a few inches before dissolving into the red hue around them.

They watched it fade. Then it was gone.

The noise hit without warning. The floor shook. The walls shivered. Another vivid scream. Harder than before, it knocked them both down. They clutched their skulls, pulsating black veins pushing through their skin again, coiling outward. Eyes bulging. Then it stopped.

James pulled himself up. Ashley was already on her feet.

"Come on! We need to move!" She grabbed his arm.

Adrenaline reached his legs as he caught up. Clutching his head, he followed close behind. The sound subsided. Their panic, however, grew. Running further and further, faster and faster, he began to trail. The walls grew bare and dry. The redness—too slow—was swallowed by night.

Neither of them looked back. As the thin red light faded, Ashley dissolved into the black ahead of him.

Thirty seconds later, Ashley stopped and caught her breath. Silence. No roar. No footsteps.

"James?" She swept the flashlight forward and back. "Which way did we come from?" she whispered to herself. "Shit, James! Where are you?"

Again she swept the light back and forth. The light ricocheted off the barren walls. Confusion set in as she lost her way. Trying to get her bearings, she called out once more. "James!"

Nothing. No reply.

She stood there without any thought. Was he lost? Dead? She didn't want to think it into existence.

A soft wail whisked through the air. The hairs on her neck struck upright. Cutting the flashlight off, she tuned into her senses. The slightest clamor rippled through the air. Now panting, a wet sliver crept down her forehead. Time was valuable. Once more, she waited. Then, again, it came. A pitch too distant to place, and yet she acknowledged it.

Immediately, she flicked on the flashlight and backtracked hastily. Keeping a steady jog, she kept her ears alert. She heard it clear as day.

"Ashley? HELP ME!"

Louder, the cry amplified. Her feet pounded harder.

"HEEEELLLLLPPPP!"

Ashley could see a good distance down the tunnel with the flashlight but still couldn't place the cry for help. She called out, "Where are you?"

She stopped. Everything was still.

"THE WALL!" An extremely muffled voice, somehow, made its way through the impenetrable walls. She pressed her fingers against the stone. Smacking on the right side of the barrier, she called out again. "WHERE?"

Quickly moving to the left, she signaled her light to an awkward spot on the brick. "One single brick covered in moss? That's unusual."

Without further thought, she drove her fist into the solid slab. Then—*click!* A small noise followed by weightlessness. Ashley looked down to find her feet hanging over an abyss. In shock, the flashlight dropped first, accompanied by her. Expecting a deadly fall, her body tightened. She gripped herself. Falling. Falling faster.

YANK!

Swaying, Ashley lifted her arms away from her face to find herself vertical, hanging upside down. Her backpack snagged on a rope dangling from the rock ceiling. Looking down, she saw her lucky flashlight, sparkling yet again from the floor.

"Oh, that's not good. I must be sixty feet from the ground. Lucky flashlight survived that fall."

Adding the height upwards, the total fall was roughly one hundred feet. Something that would've surely ended Ashley. Unfortunately, death missed its chance.

14

Still swaying in the air, she carefully attached a carabiner from the rope to the backpack. Then she shuffled out of her shoulder straps quickly, catching them as she dropped down. There she was, suspended in the air, holding onto a couple of backpack straps.

Feet dangled. Eyes scanned the vast cavern below. "This is definitely not the tunnel anymore," she mumbled.

The cavern around her breathed silence. Ashley cinched a harness from her gear with steady fingers, clipping it into the backup rope. "Step by step." The words left her mouth like a fading prayer.

As she rappelled, the flashlight beam below danced closer—until a sudden jerk stopped her momentum.

ZIP!

The rope kicked. Her heart seized.

SNAP!

She dropped. Then caught. Only three feet from the ground, her breath barely escaped. Eyes clenched. Muscles squeezed. Swaying side to side, her eyes fluttered open. She was face to face with the floor. "You've got to be ki-"

SNAP!

The final break flung her gear forward and she slammed into stone. Her head rattled as she took the force. Darkness spun. She gasped, checking herself for injury. Alive. Just sore. Dusting off, she sighed with relief then collected her equipment, which lay scattered nearby. After coiling up the rope, she clipped it to her pack and then pressed her fingers to her forehead. "Oh, please don't get a headache." Shaking it off, she spotted her flashlight up ahead.

The beam grew brighter. Impressed with herself, she hastened. She figured what had happened was the speed caused her carabiner to catch a tear in the rope. When the line pulled tight, the rope snagged and bounced her up, leaving her suspended for a moment. When the slack became taut on the way back down, her carabiner lost its grip and the rope slid through.

"Shit!" she collected the light. "Lucky flashlight. Lucky day."

The area was wide open and housed nothing but darkness. Even with the light reaching out as far as it could, the only thing she could see was the rock floor. She was in an ultimate abyss.

"James!" she cried out. A shout replied. She couldn't make it out and decided to wait for a moment. "It can't be him… unless I'm losing it too."

"HELP ME!"

She quickly spun and aimed her torch towards the call. As she advanced, it became more distinct. Definitely James. She sprinted further into the dark.

"Ashley! Ash is that you?"

"James! James, I'm right here okay," Ashley reassured him. Just ahead, in the sticky blackness that engulfed her, she saw more rope like the one hanging from the ceiling. Except this one was intertwined. She made out a blue striped shirt caught between the lines.

"Ah, what took you so long," James' body lay curled up sideways in a surely uncomfortable position.

"Sorry it just took me a while to find the stairs," Ashley felt a little relieved. "How did you get in this thing?"

"I have no idea! It got dark and I lost sight of you. Next thing I know I feel like I'm floating. Then I land in this thing."

She looked in her bag as he spoke.

"I thought I was screwed. Worse, dead!" He noticed her pull something from her bag. "Oh, the knife, perfect!"

She cut him free and his body landed.

"Ouch!" He rubbed his shoulder as he stood up. "How are we supposed to get out of here now?"

"I don't know James, you tell me."

He took a deep breath remaining in place. "Let me see your torch."

She gave him the light and he led the way.

"Where are you going?" she asked.

"I'm looking around."

The further he pushed them into the abyss, the more confused they became. Everything about this place seemed asymmetrical. Nothing made sense. James couldn't help but think about it.

Why are we underground? Maybe we really are dead and this is hell.

When Ashley fell, the area was a void. However, each step they took, it closed in. They could finally make out the enclosure, but this time there were no brick walls, no tunnels. This time they were surrounded by straight jagged rocks, like the cave before. Although with each step it appeared to change.

Metal structures materialized, integrated here and there, floating, anchored to the stone with giant bolts. "Look at this place," he said, tilting his head up. "It's really something. We must be beneath some… thing?"

"What's gotten into you?" Ashley was thrown off by his new course of action. Little did she know. Fear is funny like that.

The thoughts from moments ago resurfaced in his mind.

Shit! I'm fucked. How do I expect to get out of this net? What is this? What did I do to deserve this? I have to call for help. Maybe Ashley will save me. If she did then she'd definitely be trustworthy. But what if she doesn't trust me? I have to make her trust me. I have to show her I can act.

The thoughts soon passed.

"What do you think it is?" Ashley said attending to his side.

"I have no idea, maybe like a mine or something." Again, he swept the light around staying straight. The further he went the narrower it became. He saw more metal infrastructure bolted to the environment. "Maybe we're below the foundation of whatever it is." He kept moving the light at every angle.

"How do you know all that?"

"Just a guess, I think. I mean I'm not sure. It's hard to comprehend anything. Like I can think to myself but I-I can't *remember* anything."

"I've been feeling the same way. Like amnesia or something."

"Yeah. Just like that."

The light lingered around, side to side, in an attempt to reveal anything, anything at all that could guide them.

After a few minutes, James noticed something in the distance. He pushed the torch in front of him. A light flashed, then faded away.

"Wait! Did you see that?" He pushed even deeper into the dark. Again, a little flicker in the distance. "Hello?"

"Give me that!" she snatched the torch out of his hand and steadily aimed it forward.

The light had returned from afar.

"It's a reflection, not a person."

"Oh." He went numb.

Idiot!

"Come on." Ashley led the way this time. About two hundred feet ahead, she saw clean stainless-steel. "What the hell? It's another ladder."

"It looks like someone just put it here."

"Yeah, it does, doesn't it? That's not creepy at all."

"This whole place is creepy."

Ashley's eyes cut deep into him, giving the usual look.

"What? Me first, again? Seriously."

As they approached the vertical steps, they traced its length only to find something more odd. It didn't go up, it went down.

"Down. But… how?" He stepped back, as though a sudden gust of icy wind had pierced his skin.

This can't be right.

The hairs on his arm struck upright.

"There's no way we can go down there."

"Do we really have a choice?"

"That's not weird to you? This isn't fucking normal."

"What do you mean?"

He cut himself off, remembering to hold out on saying it.

This has to be intentional.

"Forget it," James waved his arms.

"You don't want to tell me?" She pressed.

"Look, just forget it. I'll go first." The thought of saying it out loud scared him more than the ladder did. "Let me see the flashlight."

Descending into darkness, he squeezed the torch hard enough his knuckles popped. Any direction he aimed it, the night swallowed it.

I'm starting to think this stupid thing is pointless.

They descended further and further. This ladder was much longer than the one before. After what felt like two minutes, they broke from the dark into light.

It was like stepping through a portal into a new world. The steel steps led down through a ceiling. James looked between his feet on the rung. Light pierced upward. Clear and pristine. Actual visibility. Their eyes adjusted by the time they reached the bottom. The light was coming from panels on the walls.

These panels were huge white tiles that made up everything. The floor. The sides. The ceiling. Even more strange were the torches that hung sparsely around, an imbalance to the main theme of the room. Though unlit, Ashley could smell the coals in each one, blended with a bleach-like aroma that filled the area.

When James looked up into the small entryway, it closed. The ladder was useless now. Instantaneously, the torches burst into flames and two human-sized cages slowly slithered down from new openings in the ceiling, steel chains feeding them in.

Inside these miniature prisons were two individuals who were unconscious and constrained. One had on a sleek black suit and the other, plain blue jeans and a brown leather jacket.

"What the fuck is this?" James clutched the torch tight.

The room vibrated and the spaces between the tiles on the floor began to radiate.

"Woah Ash, you feel that? Do you see what the floor is doing right now?"

Then her eyes caught something even worse. The floor was beginning to separate underneath the two enclosures. As James and Ashley scrambled to figure out what to do, two pedestals rose from the floor in front of them. On each plinth lay a rusty key. With the prisoners waking up, James and Ashley felt that their lives were in jeopardy.

"What do we do?"

"I-I don't know!"

The rumbling grew stronger, and the prisoners came to. The scent of black smoke tickled their noses, furthering hesitation. Sweat rolled into one of James' eyes. He wrestled to clear it out.

"Help! Somebody, please? Get me out of here!" a panicked voice shrieked through the barred cage.

The two of them stood motionless, wide-eyed and breathless—bewildered, untethered. Caught in the chaos.

What do we do? Help, leave, should I ask her? What the fuck is going on!?

He had to come up with something. Ashley stood speechless, more or less, overwhelmed by the situation. The set up. The engineering. James snapped his head left then right, taking note of the keys on the podiums. He took off, running to each pedestal, grabbing both.

"Here, take this and open that one," James pointed left.

Bolting into action, they sprang onto each cage, holding on with one hand and trying to unlock the cells with the other. Hovering over the pit below, the cages rocked back and forth. Each rescuer wrestling the iron locks. Smoke enveloped the open room as the fires below them thickened.

"Hurry!" shouted the man in the leather jacket, straining against the bars. James fumbled with the mechanism, while Ashley worked to free the man in the suit.

"I have a family, please," sobbed the man in the suit. "We don't have much time!"

"I-I can't get the key in," she called out.

James coughed as the smoke thickened, swallowing the room in haze. He jammed his key into the lock just before Ashley, ripped the door open, and seized the prisoner's jacket.

Leaning back with all his might, he tore the man free from the cage.

The second cage jolted, swinging violently. Inside, the man gripped the bars, eyes wide and glistening. "Please… hel—"

The mechanism released.

Ashley stumbled backward as it dropped.

The impact shook the floor. In a burst of flame, both cages were consumed—the second man swallowed whole by fire.

His holler pierced the air like a blade, slicing through the choking smog. It echoed downward, long after he was gone. The walls shivered and a rising fireball followed.

Embers of flesh glistened in the smoke. The smell of burning skin persisted, torturing all senses. Still coughing, all three lay there, rolling back and forth unable to process the experience.

"What was all that?" she said climbing to her feet.

"Fuck! What happened to the other guy?" James knew what happened. He couldn't accept it.

"I couldn't get it open! That's not my fault, I tried," she cried.

The newcomer freed himself from the rope binding his wrists. Having just witnessed all of this from what could've been a coma, he simply leaned against one of the stands.

James put his hands behind his head and howled, kicking the other pedestal down in his rant. The shriek hadn't left his ears, and he knew he'd never forget it. The one he saved was here. The other was ashes. As the gray pedestal shattered, the ceiling above them opened and released the smoke in the room, restoring visibility and fresh air.

"What the…"

The stranger caught his breath. "It was… set up. Like one of us had to die. I don't know how I know that. I just do."

James crept toward him, "What do you mean?"

The stranger coughed, still trying to catch his breath, "I mean you had to choose."

Ashley looked over at James. Red-faced, he marched toward the stranger, grabbing him by the collar. Slicked-back black hair grazed the man's shoulders as James tugged on his jacket. "You knew?" James threw the man down.

"James, stop!" Ashley rushed to intervene. For the first time, she learned something about him. He had a temper.

"You fucking bastard!" A tight fist hung in the air.

"James! STOP. IT. Stop it right now." Her demanding voice reset his focus.

He exhaled. The fist lowered. He released the man's jacket at the same time with the other hand.

She wrapped her arms around him and held him at bay. The beaten man didn't dare move.

"It's not what you think," the man composed himself, still coughing. "It's a bit more complicated."

Pacing about, James disregarded him.

"How did you get here?" Ashley took charge.

"Sean, my name is Sean."

"Okay Sean, what were you doing in th-that *thing*?"

"I don't know."

"Well then what did you mean by choose?" James interjected.

"I-I mean. I don't—"

"What did you mean?" Ashley asked.

"Isn't it kind of obvious? The second my cage opened the other fell. Only one of us was going to make it out," Sean said, already pacing.

James threw his hands up and walked away. Sean stood there trying to recollect. "Everything is a blur. AH!" Running fingers through his greasy hair, he too, tried to think. "It's so hard to form a thought. One second I think I know, now…"

Ashley crouched beside him and put her hand on his shoulder. "Please, try to remember."

Sean's attempt to contemplate failed, just as it had for them before.

"So he remembers his name." James regrouped, a little calmer.

"So do you dickhead," Sean countered.

"Look Sean, we just woke up here a couple hours ago, in some tunnels. This is James. He found me before we made it here. Neither of us know what's going on."

"You don't remember?" Sean clenched his jaw. He had a strong chin, shadowed by dark stubble, and wore a taut leather jacket that stretched over his broad shoulders. Clean blue jeans. Suede shoes. He looked different from the other two.

Taking in the now smokeless air, they all lingered. There was nowhere to go. No exit. No entrance. Until.

CREAK! CREAK! CREAK!

"Quick, move to the sides," James called out, fearing the floor would open again.

"Look!" Ashley pointed to the left wall.

Five panels on the wall, starting from the bottom up, cascaded into the floor.

"What *is* this place?" James tiptoed, nearing the breach, the other end dark. Typical.

"Guess we're back to the flashlight," Ashley stated.

Venturing into darkness again, Ashley led the troupe. This time she played with the light. It danced around, allowing each of them to make out details of the hall.

"At least it's not a tunnel this time," she said, relieved.

The light skimmed over white tiles like from the room before, except these were turned off. Just perfect square tiles. Clean. Exact.

They crept farther down, the light still emitting from the previous room before dissipating. The wall behind them closed itself off. Now they had returned to darkness.

How are the walls doing that? Is someone controlling this?

James kept his thoughts to himself.

"You think we're in a building?" Sean asked as he kept pulling his hair back.

"I'm not sure there is even an answer to that," James said as they kept their pace. "I mean we are definitely underground, but the way everything keeps changing, there's no logic to it. One minute we're in a tunnel the next, a thoroughly constructed, futuristic, torture chamber."

"What are you trying to say?" Ashley asked, intrigued. She stopped walking and returned that same look to James. "You're holding out James. I can see it in your eyes. Tell me."

They all stood together, casually stepping closer to one another. The darkness pressured them into a huddle.

Leaning in, James opened up. "I—" he exhaled, "I'm saying this has to be intentional. All of this. We all have amnesia. We all woke up randomly. I mean… the cages, the room itself, the walls shifting on their own! You seriously don't think someone's behind this? Doors don't just open themselves. The lights turning on? The ladder?"

"But who woul—"

"Guys? Um Guys!" Sean interrupted, waving his hands.

"What is it?" Ashley aimed her flashlight at him.

"Turn that off. Get down!" Sean nudged her hand to the floor and crouched. The others followed suit.

"What's going on?" James tried to see.

"Shh get down!"

"Where do you think you're going? You're not getting away from me."

Someone was yelling and they didn't sound so happy.

"Who is that?" Ashley whispered.

"Footsteps. Shh!" Sean pulled her back.

BANG!

A gunshot echoed through the passageway.

"Turn off the flashlight!" Sean smacked her shoulder.

"Maybe we should turn back," James advised.

BANG!

Each shot grew louder, amplified by the hall.

"Is he getting closer?" Ashley took a step back.

"Wait," Sean motioned. "We don't want to let him know where we are. Be quiet."

The shooting stopped and it grew uncomfortably quiet. Their own heartbeats pushed through their shirts as they remained, crouched in the pitch-black.

"What's th—"

"Hush!" Sean wasn't taking any chances.

The sound of metal dragging the cold hard floor sliced their eardrums. "He's coming this way!" James latched onto Ashley. Sean concentrated on the footsteps.

PAT! PAT! PAT!

Each step came slower than the one before.

"Shit! What do we do?"

"Shh!" Sean removed his finger from his mouth and motioned them to the other side of the hall.

Pressing his back flush against the tiles, he gestured to them to do the same. Everyone leaned over. Hands over mouths. Cowering. Still. The footsteps were only a few meters away. Each pat came closer and slower. Not a breath. Not a scrape. Even the air felt like it had paused.

"I know someone's here. I can smell it." A heavy silhouette loomed at the edge of their vision, metal glinting in one hand, eyes—maybe eyes—scanning the dark. "I'm going to find you."

[CH.03]

THREE
THROUGH
THE
HALLS

James held his breath. In the lightless hall, a man roamed. A weapon clicked as it reloaded somewhere in the dark. Only going off audio cues, the trio knew he hadn't moved. Their stillness persisted.

Maybe if I just run for it. I can't leave Ashley behind though. Would she get mad if we bailed on Sean? What if I got shot? It's a gun, too deadly. But distance… and the dark? He can't see me, can he?

James began devising a plan while Ashley and Sean waited with no inclination to move.

"I'll get you!" Another slug, restocked.

Is he ever going to run out of bullets? I can't hold my breath forever.

The man took four long, deliberate steps. He positioned in front of Sean, who was on the far right. Ashley sat next to him on the left.

"I will find you!" The shotgun blared once more.

BANG!

The muzzle flash exposed the shooter, only for an instant. Something refracted light. James' eyes flared, his body straining for the next breath. He couldn't make out every detail, but with that single flash, he could see one thing.

A badge? What the hell?

Another four steps. Now they were clear, at least by a couple feet.

ENOUGH!

James reached far right and palmed Sean's shoulder, giving him a slight push. Ample enough to suggest it was time to leave. Ashley, between them, felt the middle of an arm. She knew.

BANG!

James pounced, not even a second after the shot. Letting out a battle cry, he blindly tackled where he thought the man was, only to collide with the wall. Ashley and Sean jumped to their feet and ran the other way.

BANG!

The muzzle flashed again, sparing James another glimpse. He pounced once more, grabbing the hot barrel with his left hand and roping his right arm around the man's neck. He grappled him to the ground, and without thinking the rest through, he took off behind Ashley and Sean.

They were probably thirty feet ahead when James caught up. No one stopped running. Still in the dark, all they could do was hear each other.

"Guys!" James rushed to reconvene. Only their dissipating footsteps replied.

Where are they going?!

BANG!

James ducked and heard the buckshot hit the wall. He quickly patted himself down. He was unscathed. Knowing the man couldn't see, he called out once more.

"Where'd you go?"

Keep running. Just keep running.

James distanced himself from the shooter.

I *did it! I got to find Ashley.*

Losing his breath, he held back on his sprint. Darkness, once again, pressuring him into stillness. He called out carefully this time.

"Ashley where ar—" He was interrupted. A beam of light emanated from the left.

He turned his head. Another hall? Not quite. When the light flashed there were many halls. He was at an intersection.

Are we inside now?

"Psst," someone rattled behind the light, "Come on."

James hurried over. His breath finally caught up to him. "Are you guys alright?"

"Yeah. Are they gone?" Ashley crouched, pupils ping-ponged. The torch held steadfast against the floor. She didn't want anyone to notice.

"I ran," James said, "What else was I supposed to do?"

"You didn't get the gun?!" Sean violently hissed.

James raised his tone. "He was fucking shooting at me! What do you want me to do about it?"

Sean's angered whisper remained. "Not a good idea to be so loud when the guy still has the gun in his hands."

"Hey, both of you, calm down!" Ashley's vigor persuaded them to settle. Then she spoke deliberately. Soft. Forceful. "Did-he-follow-you?"

James felt her intention. "I don't think so. I didn't hear any screaming or shooting after a while. He might have gone the other way."

Ashley didn't buy that suggestion, but nonetheless, she kept her cool. Sean was on edge. Tightening his fists, he started to think of all the possibilities of why, or even how, all this was happening.

"Goddammit. We need to get out of here," he hissed.

Ashley pulled her flashlight to the right. There was Sean coiled up, hands raking through his slick black hair. Unnerved. The light continued to dance around the halls. The white tiles that made up the concourse were interrupted with solid white doors and silver knobs, patterned down the distant passageway.

"We're in the building now," James mused out loud.

"It looks like it," Ashley gripped her flashlight tighter.

Sean sprang up and played with one of the door handles. It wouldn't budge. He tried another. Nothing. The next door. Locked again.

"What are you up to?" James was always so full of questions.

"You don't want to know what's in any of these rooms?" Sean reached into his pocket. Fingers digging, he retrieved a small bobby pin. Then he added, "I want to know what's in these rooms."

James and Ashley watched as he worked the bobby pin inside the doorknob. Grinding metal to metal, he raked the pin back and forth.

CLICK!

The door cracked open. James stood amazed. Ashley, impressed. Sean hurried inside and they followed behind. The flashlight bounced around the confined space. Surprisingly, it was an indifferent room. The walls were smooth concrete. Simple. Plain. There were rectangular metal desks and chairs spread about. Six to be exact, paired and patterned around the area. The seats were white with kind of curvy backs. The desks were broad and stiff.

Nothing else was in this bland space. The ceiling was made up of the same white tiles from in the hall, same as the floor.

Why does everything have to be so dark around here?

James struggled to detect anything. Maybe it was shock. It was definitely shock. Despite his prior remarks, his ears had been ringing the entire time, like a bee was taped inside the canal. His mind was still heavy.

I wish I could remember something, anything! All those freaking gunshots gave me a headache! Should I tell them what I saw?

After a bit of pacing, James took a seat, rocking the chair back and forth.

Ashley was still playing with the flashlight. Sean, using it the best he could, rummaged through the desk drawers. James watched him.

"So, what made you do that back there?" Ashley asked James.

James' pupils retracted as the flashlight swooped across his eyes. "I-I don't know."

He grew serious and leaned back. Ashley pretended to ignore him and shined some light on Sean. Sean's fingers were sifting through papers filed in the drawers.

"I think you do know James." Her flashlight, suspended on Sean, reflected off the metal table and filled the room. Eventually, after all their eyes dilated, they could see. Just not very well.

"He was pissing me off with that shotgun. It was too loud." James witnessed Sean pull some papers out and throw them on the desk.

"You got a hidden temper you don't know about?" Ashley pondered out loud.

"Hey look at these." Sean pointed at the papers, signaling the other two to join him.

Ashley's torch hovered directly over the papers like a spotlight. The top of their heads bumped into one another as they peered down at the messily arranged sheets. Paragraphs of fine ink spread across each piece revealing pictures of strange plants, one on each page at the bottom.

"What do you think this is?"

"Looks like someone was studying plants." Ashley picked up a sheet and examined it a little further. "Strange thing to find in a place like this."

The paper was yellowed and brittle, edges curled like old leaves. A sketch of roots ran across the page—sharp, angular lines branching into strange symbols that didn't quite resemble any known language.

It read:

FULIGO SEPTICA

Plasmodial; slime mold   *Myxomycetes*

Multinucleate mass   Cell Integrity:86%   Cell Count:97%
                              Composition:58%   Degeneration:15%

White, Grey, Yellow
  (Yellow Common)   Lab results conclude acidum boricum counters
                             spore growth at a degeneration rate of 15%
                             Lepisma saccharina found carrying spores in
                             cave systems were unaffected by the composite
                             acid used on sample. More testing required
                             for efficient results. NOTE: Metal Resistant

SAMPLE#1567089-2A

SAMPLE PICTURE ATTACHED BELOW

"That looks like vomit," Sean said, glimpsing at the photo. The image revealed a fibrous yellow sponge, mucus bleeding off it in watery strands.

"Sort of looks like what we saw in the tunnels, doesn't it?" Ashley said, handing the paper to James.

"Kinda, just not green. And I can't smell it." James pulled the paper closer to his face.

"Why would they be studying plants down here?" Sean asked.

"Maybe we worked here or something?" James was being *very* open-minded.

"Freak accident?" Sean humored him.

"This room doesn't look like any kind of lab." Ashley resumed swinging her torch around.

"Need I remind you of the metal cages. The desks could explode for all we know! It wouldn't surprise me if this was some secret botanist lair." James was feeling agitated.

The more he didn't know, the more he grew angry. He kept circling back, trying to find a connection. Sean stood up and tried another desk. Same thing. Plant papers. Nothing in this room was going to help. Maybe if they locked the doors and stayed quiet, someone would find them? No. No use. Ever since Ashley and James woke up, they knew no one was going to find them, and now, staring at pictures of fungus, Sean was beginning to think the same thing.

"Maybe we should try a different room," Ashley suggested.

"Think it'll help?"

Sean pushed out through the doorway, back into the dark. He appeared to have no problem with being blind. The others could hear him already picking another lock. Following Ashley's light, James filed behind her.

"You trying again Sean?" she asked.

"What other choice do I have?" Again, another click and the door was ajar.

"Where did you learn to do that?" James interrupted, stepping in front of Ashley to get into the room behind Sean.

"Learn what?"

Is he serious? I just asked!

"The lock picking?"

Sean couldn't answer. "I don't know. I had a bobby pin and I… I just kind of did it."

James wanted to believe he could remember something. None of them could.

"Useful skill to have," Ashley said following in the back. Her light refracted off a mirror on the rear wall as she walked through the doorway, abruptly lighting up the whole room in a flash.

The mirror ran parallel with a bar, both of which ran down the entire wall. Five or so stools were clustered around it, though it was hard to tell. It was still so dark. A few metal tables were scattered here and there, partnered with the curvy white chairs like in the other room before. Another table was on the far right. Behind that, a sink and cabinets. Beside the cabinets stood a large white box. A handle rode down the top left corner to the bottom.

Arm extended, Ashley took a few careful steps towards the box, targeting the handle. Very slowly she gripped the rod and gently pulled back. As the door released, rays of blue light escaped. Door ajar, the three of them peered inside. It was a simple refrigerator, with three shelves. On each shelf, layers of vacuum-sealed bags lay flat with liquids bubbling up inside of them. Someone's stomach growled.

Please don't tell me this room is for experiments. I don't want to eat any cave sponges.

"Why is there a fridge in here?" James might have changed his mind about feasting on a cave sponge.

"This looks like an employee lounge," Ashley said.

"How do you know what that looks like?"

"I really don't know. It was an educated guess."

Sean pulled out a bag from the fridge and read the label. "Says here it's 100% beef."

"Beef?" James rubbed his stomach.

Food hadn't really been the subject of thought. Between not being able to see, tunnels, death cages descending into fire, and some crazy guy with a shotgun, food had been the *last* thing they thought about. But now? Now it was *all* they could think about. Ashley aimed her light right. Adjacent to the fridge was an oven.

"Do you think that still works?" She ran the light across the front end. It was all white and riddled with knobs and switches. It looked complicated. She started pushing each button and turning every knob. Nothing happened.

"Useless!" She was getting hungry.

Sean grabbed her shoulder. "Hey, keep it down. Maybe you don't know how it works."

"Maybe it doesn't have power," James said.

"True, but then why does the fridge work?" Ashley asked, eyebrows lifted.

Power was something none of them had considered. "Why would the room we found you in be lit up and not the rest of this place?" Ashley considered out loud. "These halls are pitch-black."

"Maybe there's just a switch inside the room," Sean replied.

The flashlight pranced around the walls; once around the square space, then twice. There really wasn't much of anything anywhere. It was out of place to see a fridge or even an oven. Every one of the rooms they entered inside this building was flat, square, tight, and sparse. No switches. No light bulbs. No buzzing electronics. No people.

Maybe this place is just abandoned and that's why no one's here. But what about the room that Sean was in? Someone had to have set that up, right? Dammit this doesn't make any sense.

Frustrated, James sat down and thought audibly.

"I woke up. Couldn't remember anything. Found Ashley. She can't remember. Found Sean. You can't remember." His words gained momentum. "No lights. No memory. No food. No power. It's fucking dark. There's a cop down here trying to kill us. We don't know where we are. We have to be dead. Is this purgatory?"

For a brief moment, Ashley assumed James was just breaking. However, for the four hours they had been together, she could only empathize. "Just calm down James."

"What's this about a cop?" Sean interjected.

"What?" James, in his rant, forgot what he was even talking about.

"You said there was a cop trying to kill us. What cop?"

Before he knew it, Sean was towering over him. James leaned back off his chair, attempting to create space from him. "I didn't tell you guys about that?"

Ashley's face turned sour, disappointed James left out that detail. "No, you didn't."

James looked at her, then Sean, then back to her, then back to him. "I-I don't know if he was a cop. But I saw somethi—"

"Saw what?" Sean barked, breaking his own rules. His explosive energy startled James.

"Cool it, Sean." Ashley jabbed with the flashlight like a dagger. "What did you see James?"

"Before I intervened, I mean, when he shot. I saw something during the muzzle flash—shiny gold, like a police badge or something. The rest of him was dark, like he could've been in a uniform. I don't know. I mean this could be my mind playing tricks on me, right? Why can I remember what a cop looks like but not remember what I did yesterday?" James stared at Ashley for reassurance.

Her smooth, thin eyebrows, arching in seriousness, pushed him back. Then, unanimously, they all started whispering to each other.

"That doesn't explain the officer."
             "Why would a cop be down here?"
"Maybe he was just looking for us!"
     "It was pitch-black. He couldn't see."
"That wouldn't explain him yelling threats."
     "He was obviously looking for someone."
"Where'd he get the gun?"
                         "He's a cop."
"Do you think he'd help us if he knew?"

"I think we should avoid him."

"Avoid him?"

"Yeah."

"Agreed."

POP! POP! POP!

A loud, pinching noise interrupted their hustle.

"Is that him?" James was poised in a running stance, ready to jet out through the door.

Sean crouched behind a table. "Sounds like a different kind of weapon. Shut the door and get down!"

Two people with guns? Great!

James pulled the door shut. A chair rolled across the flat tiled floor.

"Put that under the handle," Sean demanded.

Ashley lent him some light. James propped the chair under the handle and wrenched it down.

"Is that going to hold?" James took two steps back, staring at the rig, afraid it wasn't secure.

"Just come hide back here." Sean motioned them both over.

James and Ashley huddled behind the counter and waited near the fridge. Sean's fingers raked back through his slick hair—a nervous tic. If only he had forgotten about that. Ashley's fingers curled tighter around the flashlight and James thought, as he always did. He was always so full of reflections.

The only things we don't remember are about ourselves. Maybe something happened to us in here and we just forgot, so there's people

*looking for us and that's why there are people
with guns. The cop had to have been looking for
us, right? He just didn't know it was us.*

POP! POP!

Louder, another two rounds forced the three
into a cluster. Behind the counter, they
crouched, waiting for a sign or an all clear.
Their eyes wandered uselessly in the dark.
Muted, they remained stuck in their heads,
attempting to recall anything about their own
lives and why they might be there. For the time
being, no one spoke. As the flashlight made one
last lap around the room, Ashley returned it to
her lap and decided to shut it off.

[CH.04]

U N C A G E D

As darkness rested, the room felt uneasy and yet it settled in stillness. No walls. No sounds. No auras. Only this sense of endlessness.

"Ugh…"

Something rustled on the floor. It moaned.

"Ah… w-what…"

The man rolled onto his stomach. His palms pushed the floor away as he rolled back onto his knees. "Where's the light?" he said, voice hazy, as he stood. The blackness that had comforted him in sleep was now disorienting. His body wobbled as he clutched his left side.

Patting himself down, he tugged on a cylindrical metal object attached to his shoulder.

CLICK.

It came loose. His thumb slid up and flicked a switch. A light came on. His pupils contracted and his eyelids slammed shut,

44

wrestling to stay open. He'd been too long in the dark.

Thirty seconds passed before he could open his eyes again. The solid black steel flashlight in his right hand. He aimed it down, admiring his resting place. A shotgun lay on the cold concrete floor. Around him, alloy bars formed a vertical square—a cage, its purpose immediately clear.

He panned the light. Black stripes projected from the walls outside the cell. The room was entirely concrete except for the steel enclosure at its center. He paced, inspecting. His eyes found a door with a padlock. A quick tug confirmed it. Solid lock.

He patted himself down again. Nylon and metal. Beneath his shirt, an armored vest. Outside—a black buttoned polo, tactical pants. Attached to his right leg, a leather holster. His finger traced the imprints, up to a latch, onto smooth steel. A sidearm waited. His other hand found the nylon strap across his chest, lined with shotgun shells running shoulder to waist. He loaded a slug.

BANG.

The padlock exploded. The cage door swung open. Debris clinked around the small room. He lowered his weapon and stepped out of the cell. The light spun. One exit—opposite wall. He marched over and gripped the handle. It didn't budge. He jerked it up and down. Nothing.

He raised his shotgun to the knob, drew a breath, aimed—then lowered the weapon. Not worth the ammo. Instead he strapped the shotgun to his back, took ten steps from the door, and planted his feet. He positioned himself in a runner's stance, toes up, body coiled. Then he charged. Full momentum. He leaped, twisted mid-flight, and crashed into the barrier shoulder-first.

WHAM.

The door crashed to the floor outside. He rolled off it and came up with one hand on his right shoulder. Sprained, without doubt. He ignored it and panned the light forward.

A hallway of white tiles. The corridor was wrapped in the kind of dark that pressed against the eyelids like a blindfold. This didn't bother him. Eyes ahead, he marched.

Everything was the same. White tiled floors and walls hidden in darkness. The hallway stretched far but not wide. Doors patterned all the way down. No exit. No clues. He kept walking, clenching his fist. There was no need to check any of the doors or try to remember anything. He felt he was in the right place—that he would end up where he needed to be.

"Help!"

A cry pierced the dark. This man, who walked with inimical presence, stopped. He tilted his ear, testing it.

"God's sake, help me! Please."

He didn't blink.

"It hurts. Oh my God someone!"

This was real. Someone needed help. Where? He twisted around—behind?

"HELP ME!"

No. Dead ahead. He swung the flashlight and sprinted. Not a hundred feet away—a door on the right, handle missing. He palmed it. Locked. A trend that didn't amaze him. He didn't waste time. He reached for the shotgun without breaking stride, cocked, aimed, and fired.

A hole opened where the handle had been. The door swung wide. The room inside was black.

He drove his flashlight forward. Blood covered the walls. Cartilage and veins draped over scattered medical equipment. The light traced a wide trail to a gurney positioned upright against the wall. Strapped to it was a man, his legs were missing. The skin where his thighs should have been looked like string-cheese dripping with thick red liquid. Head down. Eyes bloodshot. Dead.

Beside it, another gurney. It restrained a man dressed in beige pants and a beige shirt, barefoot, covered in blood. On the left side of his shirt: a logo. Creedmoor Asylum. On the right, a name in bold: Dunn.

"Please get me outta here. I need to get out of here."

The armed man said nothing. He held his flashlight to Dunn's blood-drenched face. Dunn stared back, blinking rapidly, trying to see through the fluid dripping between his eyelashes. He took in the uniform, the gun, the emotionless face. There, strapped to a gurney beside a dismantled body, Dunn stopped shaking and grinned. He was convinced this cop wasn't here to help.

[CH.05]

THE

BLOOD

ROOM

The two men stared at each other in silence, the tension stretching thin between them. Dunn didn't bother calling for help anymore. He simply watched the officer, not the least bit surprised by his presence.

The cop returned the shotgun to his shoulder and took a step back.

Seeing him turn to leave, Dunn squirmed against the leather straps binding his chest and thighs. "No, no—wait! Come on, get me out of here!" He writhed, hoping the sight of his struggle would convince the brute to at least release him.

The officer had broad shoulders and biceps that strained against the fabric of his short-sleeved uniform. To most, he'd be intimidating. To Dunn, he looked like an angel in disguise. "Look, could you just help me out of here? Please? Come on."

The cop said nothing, unmoving in the doorway, eyes unreadable. Dunn kept pleading. After a long exhale, the officer stepped forward and reached to his belt. Dunn, squinting past the blood caked around his eyes, saw the glint of a clean, stainless-steel blade.

The clipped flashlight on the brute's chest reflected off the blade, forcing Dunn's eyes shut. When he opened them, the knife hovered two inches from his face, relentless and unwavering. Behind it, an emotionless expression.

"Now, now—no need for that. I'm not gonna do nothin'."

Gradually the knife lowered, and the cop began cutting the gurney straps. Once severed, Dunn crumpled to the floor, too weak to stand.

"That wasn't so hard, now was it." His voice calm, almost amused.

Struggling, Dunn wiped his face with his shirt, clearing enough blood to make out the officer's expression. The cloth spread streaks of red across his cheeks. "You wouldn't happen to know what's going on, would ya?"

The cop towered over him. Silent. He holstered the knife and reached for his shotgun.

Dunn was still cleaning his face when he heard the click of a shell chambering. He looked up, heart hammering—staring straight down the barrel.

"I was going to ask you the same thing."

Dunn raised his hands with measured caution. "Hey. It's okay now. Look here, no harm done, alright." He gestured toward the corpse with eviscerated legs. "I woke up here. I didn't do anything, I swear."

The officer didn't blink. Shotgun steady.

"I'm serious now," Dunn's eyes were dull, "I don't know nothin'."

After a long pause, the cop lowered his weapon. Dunn exhaled sharply.

Then—effortlessly—the brute grabbed him with one arm and hauled him to his feet.

"Well now. You're something special, aren't ya?"

Dunn, five-foot-six and barely a hundred and thirty pounds, looked like a twig compared to the mountain of a man standing next to him. His buzz-cut and skinny frame made him seem almost juvenile. His pants hardly clung to him, held up only by a drawstring. Standing next to the officer—at least six-foot-three and over two hundred pounds—he felt something close to safety, though he knew it was an illusion.

They locked eyes. Something familiar lingered between them—unspoken, buried deep. Dunn wore a half-smile. The cop, expressionless as ever, turned on his heel and walked out.

"Say, you don't mind if I tag along, do ya?" Dunn asked, trailing close behind.

The cop stopped and turned to glare at him. His gaze sliced through Dunn's flippant tone.

"Okay, okay, I get it. I'll shut up," Dunn said.

Without a word, the cop turned back and led him into the hallway.

The brute picked a bearing without delay. Dunn followed close behind like a loyal dog, though his gaze kept flicking to the holstered pistol at the officer's hip. A .45 ACP M1911. He didn't know how he knew that, but he did. The very sight of it made him smile.

The hallway was shrouded in darkness, identical to the others. Cold air clung to the tiled walls. The floor echoed faintly with their footsteps. The lawman scanned with his flashlight, the beam sweeping from side to side. Solid steel doors lined both sides, each with a polished silver knob. Everything was uniform. Immaculate. Pristine.

To the brute, it didn't feel abandoned. Someone was down here. Someone who knew exactly what they were doing.

Eventually, he stopped panning and focused the light straight ahead. The beam dissipated from the walls and embraced darkness. Then—a break in the pattern.

An intersection.

The first change in the long stretch of hallway. The officer stepped into the center, one foot still pointed toward his original path. He raised the flashlight and examined each branching corridor.

Left—nothing but still, dead air.

Right—another void.

He narrowed his eyes. Something was different.

"What is it? You see something?" Dunn asked, sensing the shift.

The officer didn't reply. He clicked off the flashlight.

"Hey, I think we need that," Dunn whined.

"Shh."

Eyes forward, the brute let his pupils adjust. And there it was—a faint sliver of light, scarcely visible, cutting across the floor in the far distance. Steady. Unmoving. Real.

It was enough.

Without a word, he marched down the right-hand hall. Dunn trailed behind, silent now.

On approach, the officer weighed his options. A subsequent party would be a hassle. One was enough; two too many. But his questions subsided as his need for answers grew. Even the strongest men surrender when desperation takes hold.

The glow intensified the closer they got. Not bright, but unmistakable. The light seeped from under one of the steel doors. Like the one Dunn had been locked behind, it had no handle.

"You think someone's behind there?" Dunn asked.

The cop didn't answer. His eyes were on the door.

Dunn's gaze drifted again to the .45.

As if sensing it, the officer spun around.

"Don't make me shoot you," he said.

Dunn held up his hands, grinning. "Alright, alright. I get it."

The brute brought his ear to the steel, straining to hear. No voices. No strange liquids. No shadows along the crack of light. Nothing but silence.

"I'm telling ya, no-"

"Shhh," the officer hissed.

He tuned out Dunn and focused. Slow and steady. His ear brushed the door. Suddenly, a flicker of shadow darted across the edge of his vision.

The shotgun swung up and the brute tore off into the abyss.

Dunn, startled, had seen none of it. He'd been fixed on the light under the door. He stayed behind, sliding down to sit with his back against the wall. Arms crossed. Eyes closed.

"Whatever," he muttered. "Go chase your ghost."

The officer was already gaining ground. The hallway swallowed his footsteps as he pursued the silhouette ahead. Too distant to identify. Close enough to shoot.

He raised the shotgun and squeezed the trigger.

BANG!

The blast lit up the hallway. The recoil did nothing to slow him. He charged forward.

"STOP! YOU WON'T GET AWAY!"

The flashlight clicked back on and swayed in rhythm with his stride. Another intersection approached. He passed through it. Then another. Or was it the same one?

The halls repeated like a loop—tiled walls, steel doors, identical in every way. As if the structure had no end. As if it was watching him, bending space beneath his boots.

BANG!

Another blast. The suspect gained ground. So did he.

Then—light.

A flicker in his peripheral. A sudden break in the darkness. A wide opening, sterile glow. Gone in an instant, swallowed by black.

His breath caught. He stepped back to the intersection. The light was gone. Something else remained. Voices woven into the darkness. Not words—murmurs. Fragments. Chatter among the mice.

He bolted towards the whispers, lungs burning.

"I'll find you!"

BANG!

From the left, a shape lunged.

Hands clawed for the shotgun.

BANG!

The muzzle flash revealed a face—brown hair, a striped shirt. For a split second, they locked eyes. It was a face he would not forget.

Then the man was on him—grappling, slamming them both to the floor.

The brute rolled, twisted, and shoved.

The pressure lifted.

He looked up. No one. The man had slipped away.

He scrambled to his feet and sprinted back, shotgun primed. The corridors were impossible to track. He retraced his steps as best he could.

Intersection after intersection. No suspect. No Dunn.

Then—weightlessness.

His foot struck a hollow tile. No time to react. The floor gave way and he dropped.

Elsewhere, Dunn still sat by the glowing slit. His legs stretched out, hands folded over his stomach. The sound of gunfire had stopped.

He smiled lazily. "Guess someone won."

The ground shifted—angled like a ramp. He yelped, arms flailing, the world tilting.

THUD!

He hit hard.

Rubbing his head, Dunn looked up just in time to see the brute land across from him in the small chamber.

SLAM!

The ceiling sealed. Gone was the hallway. Gone was the door.

"OW! What the hell did you do?" Dunn winced.

The officer rolled to his feet in one smooth motion. His flashlight snapped up and aimed at the sealed ceiling.

"Some kind of trapdoor." He thought out loud. Ten, maybe twelve feet—one level down.

Dunn stood, dusting himself off. "Where ya been? Looks like someone's playing games with us."

The brute's expressionless face darkened. Agitated now. A sure route to anger. He knew Dunn was right. Dunn noticed this. It pleased him. He had a permanent grin.

After a quick pat-down for injuries, both men took in their surroundings. Their nostrils flared at a familiar scent—foul, metallic, thick with decay. Rotten flesh. Dunn wrinkled his nose. "That again."

The officer swept the flashlight around the room. The beam cast over walls, floor, and ceiling. Blood smeared every surface. It dripped like paint. No furniture. No exit. Only rot and the stench of death.

The brute clipped his flashlight to his vest and reached for the shotgun.

The room lit up.

All at once, the white tiles blazed to life—blindingly bright. Both men staggered back. Dunn dropped to his knees, shielding his face. The officer stood his ground, gritting his teeth, blinking as his pupils contracted.

Clinical brightness—but the blood, the gore, and the red velvet smears were still there. Visible now in nauseating detail, scarlet stains running like veins along every surface.

Two bodies lay face down in the center of the room. One had his right hand severed, resting about two feet away. His torso was perforated with bullet wounds. A large section of his head was gone. Beside him, another body—less damaged, remarkably intact. Long matted hair soaked in fluid. The cop assumed it was a smaller bullet wound to the head.

The officer approached the second body cautiously.

As his boot nudged the man's side, Dunn called out from the far wall.

"Hey! Look at this."

The officer turned. Dunn pointed to a tile above his head. Letters scrawled in blood. Crude but clear.

"Charming," Dunn muttered, "Wonder who left that for us."

The officer didn't answer right away. He took a step closer before responding.

"Someone's watching us," he said flatly. His grip tightened on the shotgun.

Dunn laughed. "Watching us? Please. If anyone was down here, they'd be dead already."

"We've found three bodies so far," the officer growled. "Someone out there is still moving."

A sudden thud dropped the cop to the ground.

Dunn jumped.

From the floor, the officer looked up in time to see the second body was indeed alive. The seemingly intact corpse was now standing. Blood poured from his soaked hair and down his face. His eyes were wide—feral.

"сука!" The man snarled.

His right hand raised a pistol and he fired.

The cop rolled as the trigger pulled.

POP!

The bullet missed.

Still on the ground, the brute leveled his shotgun and aimed straight at the man's head.

Across the room, Dunn didn't flinch. That grin returned to his face—twisted, entertained.

The attacker didn't hesitate. He adjusted his aim for a second shot.

CLICK!

Empty.

The brute, now officially very mad, surged to his feet. His aim was persistent and exact; the shotgun didn't waver.

"Dunn! Grab his sidearm," he barked.

Before the sentence finished, Dunn was already walking towards the suspect. He darted behind the stranger and plucked the weapon from his hand.

"Makarov PM 9mm," he noted, inspecting it. "Definitely Russian."

"Russian?" the brute echoed, eyes slanted. "How do you know that?"

"I dunno," Dunn shrugged. "I just… do." He looked back at the stranger. "Oh, he called you a bitch by the way. The first thing he said."

The cop was still. His expression darkened. A flicker of something crossed his face—something cruel and familiar.

"Gun expert from an asylum, and a Russian mutilator." The brute's voice was low and bitter. "Great company."

He pressed the shotgun toward the man's chest. "Hands behind your head."

The stranger complied.

"So, he *does* understand. Good. Dunn, pat him down."

While the shotgun stayed steady, Dunn circled the man and began checking pockets and sleeves, searching for anything useful—any clues.

Nothing.

So they waited. Three men in a blood-soaked tomb, bound by confusion and suspicion. The brute burning for answers, Dunn smirking in silence, and the blood-drenched stranger concealing something—maybe everything.

[CH.06]

SUBMERGENCE

Dark. Still. Cold.

The defining traits of a dismal place that had become disturbingly familiar to its visitors. Outside of the conscious carnage lay another cube-shaped room, pitch-black and waiting for its need. At its base, a blanket of water shifted in hushed tones, crashing softly against tiled walls before folding back onto itself. A steady rhythm. A quiet swoosh.

The ceiling rumbled, breaking the water's tranquil pulse. Ripples darted across the liquid surface as four square tiles above screeched and slid back. The wavelets grew frantic.

Plip. Plip. Plip. Plip. Plip. Plip. Plip.

The final tile halted.

CLICK!

The water settled again. Still a second sound persisted—metallic, rhythmic, growing louder.

clank! clank! clank! Clank! Clank! Clank!
CLANK! CLANK! CLANK!

Two ceiling tiles lit up dimly, casting pale reflections across the surface. From above, four thick chains began their descent. Wrapped up in each, feet coiled and locked, were four unconscious men. Hanging upside down, they descended headfirst, arms stretched, weary and numb.

CLANK. CLANK. CLANK. CLANK.

There was maybe forty feet between the ceiling and the water, but no telling how deep the pool went. A quarter of the way down, each man dangled motionless, tethered to the one unyielding duty of the chain: bind and not be unbound. Every second brought their fingertips closer to the waiting surface.

Their red faces darkened as more blood rushed into their skulls. The possibility of regaining consciousness looked more dismal than the room itself. Until.

Ugh... uhh... ugh...

Wh-what's happening?

One of them stirred, trying to shake the blood from his eyes. As his vision returned, the situation became apparent.

Thirty feet left.

"HELP! HELP ME!" he shouted, twisting in place.

He jerked back and forth, uselessly. The chain resisted while he persisted—convulsing, pausing, squirming again. His body rotated halfway, revealing the other three.

"WAKE UP! EVERYONE WAKE UP!"

Now a little over halfway to turning into a dead buoy, panic rippled through his system. The more he moved, the worse the pounding in his head intensified. Eyes bulged, veins throbbed.

"WAKKKEEEE UUPPPP!"

And slowly, one by one, the others began to stir. Confusion. Then squeals. Then thrashing. All four squirmed like bait on hooks. They prayed there were no sharks in the water.

Fifteen feet left.

Okay. Think. THINK! What do I do?

His eyes scanned the room and locked on the water below where his reflection met him, wide-eyed and terrified. He flinched, jostling the chain.

CLACK!

Pain shot through his ankles. The chain had snapped back into place, digging in.

AH! What is… HAPPENING!?

He moaned as a bead of blood raced down his leg to his spine. His dangling body quivered as he felt warm blood trickling from his foot.

Back to thinking. Focus!

The pain blared louder than his thoughts.

MY ANKLES!

He clenched his core and raised his torso, folding upward toward his feet. His hands grabbed at the chain. It was better than hanging headfirst. If he were going to die, he'd be the last to go.

Seven feet left.

No slack. No give. Still, he felt along the damp metal. His fingers found something—square, solid, colder than the chain. Caressing the object, his digits traced a hook intersecting a chain link: a lock.

There's no way I can break this! Maybe I could float. No. Too heavy. Slack! I just need slack.

Gripping the chain tight, he took a few long breaths, readying himself for a bold move. One that required not only a bit of wit, but sheer core strength. His knuckles popped as his fingers gripped the chain with desperation.

Deep breath.

He climbed—hand over hand. Blood flowed back into his torso. Hope stirred. Near the top, the chain turned to bitter ice. A lifeless frost that clung to his skin and froze him in place.

Steadfast in his upright state, his feet took vigorous action. They kicked wildly. Side to side. Forward. Back. Somewhere, a foot had to break free.

His eyes caught the others, arms now grazing the water's surface.

DO SOMETHING!

He tossed his shoes with one hand and then flexed and hooked his big toe into a link in the chain. He pulled on his frozen hands, lurched up, and kicked out.

CRACK!

"OW! FUCK," he blared, clenching his eyes shut.

Three feet left.

His left toe was broken. A necessary sacrifice. The pain bought him slack. His right foot slipped free. He was loose. That frail sense of success was hastily dismissed when the cries of three other men—now thrashing, drowning—snatched it away.

He turned, selected the nearest man, and locked eyes with him. Then, with a sharp pull, he wrenched his hands free from the stiff chain. His body sank.

SPLASH!

His body hit the water hard, sending waves rolling in every direction. Around him, chaos. Three sets of flailing arms sloshed violently, desperate for breath. Each man struggled to keep his head above water as the chains halted, leaving them dangling just low enough to submerge their necks.

There was no final drop. No clean end. Only the agony of struggling to stay afloat.

"I'M COMING—HOLD ON! PULL YOUR HEAD UP!"

Nick—he would later remember that his name was Nick—swam to the nearest man. As he closed the gap, bubbles burst at the surface, muffling the frantic screams underneath. The prisoner thrashed wildly, arms crashing through the water, head jerking from side to side.

Nick dodged the lashing limbs. A battlefield of punches. He kicked harder to stay afloat, the broken toe wailing with every stroke. He positioned himself below the man and pushed up on his shoulders. The man's mouth broke the surface for a fleeting breath—wasted on another cry for help—before he slipped back under.

"CLIMB UP!" Nick shouted, fighting desperately to stay above water. He kicked again, harder, lifting the man's shoulders higher. "BREATHE AND CLIMB UP!"

As he forced the man's head out of the water once again, the man strained forward and grabbed at Nick's hair, trying to hold on. He was weak—lacking core strength. Coughing, he struggled to respond.

"Wh-what's… going… I-I can't bre-"

"JUST STAY UP! PULL UP!"

Relentlessly, each man struggled to do their part. The two became locked in a vicious rhythm: lift, gasp, slip. Again and again, Nick pushed the man toward air, only to be dragged down by exhaustion. Their gasps shredded against gurgled cries, clogged noses, and burning eyes as water climbed like vines curling around their lungs.

"STAY UP!" Nick bellowed, pulling with everything he had.

The other chains had gone still. No more splashing. No more screams. Just the hollow slap of water against the tile.

Nick glanced left. Arms hung limp. Heads bowed in defeat. The chains and the lifeless bodies remained.

He turned back to the man he held, still fighting and still breathing.

Why am I doing this? I don't even know who they are. Any of them. Do they deserve to die?

Concerns circled in his mind like the sharks they feared were still below. Unanswered. Unrelenting. For now, only one thing mattered.

Save this one.

SSSCCCHHHHHHH!

A hiss filled the chamber. The water began to recede.

The victim, still half-submerged, gasped as the level dropped. Inch by inch, the waterline fell past his chin, revealing more of his drenched form. Within seconds, the entire *ocean* was gone, drained through hidden slits in the floor. What remained was a glistening tile basin, the chains still hanging high above.

Both men stared at the wet floor in disbelief. The water had only been maybe seven feet deep.

"Is it… over?" the man in chains asked, panting heavily. He was calmer now. Shaken, but alive.

"I think so," Nick said. His voice was flat but steady. "Name's Nick."

The man looked down, still hanging awkwardly by the ankles. "Well, Nick… think you can get me out of this thing?"

"Yeah. Use my back. Push up." Nick crouched below the man, back turned.

The man reached down and braced himself, planting a hand on Nick's shoulders as he tried to hoist his legs up. Nick straightened, lifting him higher. The man gripped the chain above his feet and climbed. It wasn't graceful— there were grunts, slips, kicks—but finally, with a final tug and twist, he slid free and fell to the floor.

He started rubbing his ankles; Nick empathized with his pain, although he ignored his own broken toe for the time being.

"We've got to find a way out of here," Nick said, steadying his breath. "Can you stand?"

"I think so…"

Nick offered his hand. The man took it and pulled himself upright, unsteady but intact.

"Got a name?"

"Yeah, I-I think."

"You think?"

There was a pause as the two men glanced at each other. One unsure, the other indecisive.

"Ras-Raspberry."

Nick raised both eyebrows. "Raspberry?"

"Yes. Raspberry."

Nick repeated it deliberately, like trying out a strange flavor. The tension eased slightly. A moment of oddity in the aftermath of panic. With the feeling receding, he had time to absorb his surroundings in further detail.

Raspberry stood a few inches shorter than Nick, maybe five-foot-six, with a lean frame. His white dress shirt clung to him, soaked and slightly see through. A blue tie still fastened at the collar. Suede dress shoes, matching slacks. Clean-shaven face, slick hair flattened with moisture and pomade.

Even if Nick had no idea what was going on or where they were, intuitively he knew this man was either a businessman or a politician. However, this wasn't a time for formalities or backgrounds. After what just happened, it was about survival.

Nick glanced down at himself—black T-shirt with the word *Sculptor* scrawled across it. He also had blue jeans and bare feet. He had forgotten about his shoes in the moment he sacrificed his big toe. In his pocket, he found a slim, rectangular device. Not a phone. Something electronic. Something familiar.

Why do I feel like I should know what this is?

He tucked it away and noticed his water-logged sneakers across the room. Recovering them, he tightened the laces down and regrouped with the other survivor.

Raspberry broke the silence. "We should find a way out of here," he said pacing around the room, looking for an exit. His shoes squished as he paced across the moist floor.

In the center of the room was a drain grate, dark and silent.

"Hey Nick, come look at this," he motioned him over.

Nick approached. Together they peered down into the black hole. Raspberry grasped the metal square and gave it a solid tug. No budge.

"I don't think you're getting that up," Nick said.

"If the water went out this way, then it has to lead somewhere." Raspberry kept pulling on the grate to no avail.

"And what if it goes to another room just like this. What if it's a drop we can't survive?" Nick tried to reason with him.

"How would you know? Do you know where we are?" Raspberry snapped, jumping to his feet. "Is your name even Nick?"

"Hey, slow down mate." Nick raised his hands. "I woke up in the same way you did. And if it wasn't for me, you'd have ended up just like one of them!"

He gestured toward the two dangling bodies, still dripping from their chains.

"I don't know what the hell is going on either. And I'm not pretending to."

The room felt smaller, warmer. Raspberry's breath shortened. Sweat beaded on his brow, unsure if it came from the heat or the pressure.

Nick turned away. "We need to scope out the room. You saw how the panels opened, maybe there's a switch somewhere, we just don't see it," Nick said as he walked around the perimeter.

"You some kind of puzzle solver?" Raspberry trailed behind him.

"I didn't even know my name until the water dropped," Nick said as he brushed his fingertips against the damp white tiled wall. "I might be nobody."

Raspberry fell silent. He continued to follow along behind Nick. He noticed the room was not so different without the water, the clanking chains, or the sound of drowning.

Tethered to one another, they moved along the perimeter. The walls, still wet, gave off a soft chill. Nick's touch dragged across the white tiles, large and glowing. Electronic bricks that flickered with unseen intention. He'd seen rooms like this before. Or maybe… he hadn't. Memory was a fog. Instinct was the only compass.

CLICK!

A white tile sank into the wall. Both men stepped back in awe. A grin touched Nick's lips.

"Was that it?" Raspberry's eyes shot open.

"I think that was a switch Mr. Raspberry." Nick's eyes danced around the entire room looking for what changed.

From silence came a low rumble, growing steadily into a roar. The floor trembled. The sound held. Nick searched for something. Something that would at least get them away from the corpses. Then he saw it.

Across the room, a cluster of tiles slid open revealing a doorway.

"LOOK!" Raspberry shouted, but Nick was already moving, drawn not by the door, but the thing just beyond it.

[CH.07]

S T E P

B Y

S T E P

Only an hour or so had passed before the square room felt like a distant memory. Nick and Raspberry had walked through the exit into a pitch-black hallway, which led into another, and another. It was an underground maze of darkness without direction or hint of design.

Nick pressed on, trailing one hand along the wall, probing here and there in search of another hidden switch. The fact that he had made it this far without a sliver of light was a feat in its own right. Raspberry followed by sound alone, keeping up the pace just behind him.

"Do you think we're close?" Raspberry asked, shuffling behind Nick.

"Close to what?" Nick snapped—not cruelly, but firm. Assertive without venom.

What's with this guy?

Raspberry was annoying, sure, but Nick couldn't fault him. After everything they'd endured, anxiety was natural. Nick was just better at hiding it.

"An exit!" Raspberry said, hopeful.

"What? Again? What makes you think I would know where one is? You keep asking that like every five minutes."

"No look! I mean it's an exit!" Raspberry tapped on Nick's shoulder and pointed ahead. Even though Nick couldn't actually see his hand, he somehow knew where to look. A wordless rapport had formed between them, despite how Nick might have felt about the man.

"Up ahead. Look!" Raspberry insisted.

Far down the black hall, glistened a faint horizontal beam. Small and distant, barely visible—but there. Nick shook his head. After so long in the dark, his mind might've been inventing reality.

That can't be real… can it?

"We have to check it out," Raspberry said, drawn to the light like a child reaching for a star he'll never touch.

Nick had his reservations, but he knew Raspberry was right. He took one step ahead and led them both straight for it. The hall was midnight, like the light ahead was nothing more than a projection from their own eyes. As they closed the gap, it brightened the corridor just enough they could finally make out what they were in. Like the flooded square room before, the hallway was constructed of dormant white tiles. And even though Nick kept one hand brushing the sides, there were no switches. Nothing to turn on.

Such a dismal place. What's really going on? Where would such a place even exist?

The closer they drew to the light, the more real it became. After what felt like hours in total blackness, Nick moved on impulse. His body reacted before thoughts could catch up, until the faint illumination gave him enough energy to start thinking again. With contemplation came composure, even if only thinly veiled. Whether it was helping Raspberry, he didn't know.

"It's getting brighter. Let's not rush." Nick held his palm up to Raspberry, who was starting to outpace him.

Raspberry's wide eyes shimmered with unblinking awe. For the first time since they had met, his mouth was shut, not from calm, but reverence. Nick mistook it for fear.

At last, the hallway's end was fully revealed, just seven feet ahead. The source of the glow was clear. A simple door with a silver knob embedded between two large white tiles. Surreal at first glance, it was something real, something tangible. After so much darkness, that alone made it holy.

Was it a passage to the outside? Was it an exit? They didn't know. It was always just more puzzles waiting to be solved.

Raspberry's motion broke the silence as he leapt for the door, squeezing the knob with his right hand.

"Don't turn it yet!" Nick lunged, grabbing Raspberry's wrist. His voice was sharp but measured.

"What the hell do you mean," Raspberry barked, pulling back.

"Low! It could be a trap!"

"Low what!?"

"Keep your voice low. Just—shut up for a second!"

Raspberry didn't get it and didn't care. The light was too close, too tempting.

"Move out of the way!" Raspberry shouted, shoving Nick to the ground.

By the time Nick hit the floor, Raspberry had already thrown the door open. Nick scrambled and crawled into the threshold. On all fours in the doorframe, he peered in. There he saw Raspberry had stopped dead in his tracks. His tailored frame silhouetted by blinding white. Both their faces stretched wide. One smiling. The other grim.

At first, it looked like heaven. Endless radiance flooded the next room, stretching out in every aspect. Nick blinked. His eyes adjusted faster. Beyond the brilliance, he saw it clearly: a long hallway of the same bleak white tiles, only now gleaming.

It was not salvation. It was dread disguised as light.

This—this light—it is what Nick had been longing for. A chance to see. A chance to breathe again. Yet standing in that shining beacon of elation stood a heavy stone, doused with blood.

Within that glowing corridor stood a truth more terrifying than darkness. Blood. Coating the walls in thick, oil-like smears. Black-red streaks, viscous and wet, seeping into every seam between tiles. The scent hit next—iron and rot.

"RASPBERRY STOP!"

Nick's voice cracked the air like a whip.

The command sliced through Raspberry's trance. His neck stiffened. His skin prickled with electric fear. He blinked once, twice—then the illusion of heaven shattered.

Every wall was drenched—not just in blood, but in pieces. Scattered about were limbs and ligaments. Torsos and toes. Everything was too still. Too cleanly placed. As if the carnage had been arranged for them to find.

"Oh my god," Raspberry whispered, voice shrinking to a hush.

Nick climbed to his feet. "Don't move!"

Raspberry, rattled and awe-struck, took a single step back.

CLICK!

A metallic hiss—then pain.

A spike launched up through the floor, spearing clean through the arch of his foot. A solid, rust-colored rod, two inches wide, punched through skin, tendon, and bone.

"RAHHH!" Raspberry screamed, crumpling into a frozen half-split.

His body trembled as blood geysered from the wound, drenching the tiles beneath him in thick, arterial spray. The color spread rapidly, soaking into the joints of the floor.

His back leg, pinned, vibrated with every nerve-ending on fire.

"Don't move!" Nick continued to advise. *Does this guy ever listen?*

He pressed his back to the doorframe, spreading his arms for balance as he leaned forward into the hallway, eyes scanning with accuracy. He traced each tile with focus, cataloging shapes and measurements like a machine. Some were square. Others, narrow rectangles.

Four feet. Two feet. Square. Square again. Nick labeled each one to himself.

Each tile was a potential trap.

Measure. Map. Survive.

"HELP ME!" Raspberry's back leg continued to tremble, rattling the spike embedded in his foot. His blood pooled on the floor, merging with the crimson stains of those who came before him.

"STOP FUCKING MOVING!"

Raspberry ignored the command and took a knee. His shin dropped over the spike, driving it deeper into his leg.

"AH, MOTHER! HELP ME! HELP ME!"

Nick stopped giving him any more advice and focused instead on tuning out his cries. He had his own survival to worry about.

Raspberry's just another casualty waiting to happen.

His eyes scanned the floor, moving over each tile with precision. Something caught his attention further down the hall—a tile on the left with an odd bloodstain, a peculiar mark. Squinting, he tried to focus like he was using

76

binoculars. No matter how hard he adjusted, everything beyond ten tiles blurred.

I can't see it. I-I can't see it! Nick's eyes failed him at a distance. *I need glasses. Do I wear glasses?*

Unfortunately, now was not the time for remembering. He needed to see clearly. He needed Raspberry.

"Raspberry! I need you to tell me what you see on the left wall up ahead!"

Raspberry's cries softened, reduced to mere whimpers. He was kneeling on his injured foot with the other leg lunged out. His head was heavy from sobbing.

"Raspberry, look up! Come on!"

The brittle man stayed trembling, enduring the blood oozing out of his leg. Such an unfortunate circumstance to ruin such upscale slacks. His head tilted up.

"A2!" rasped Raspberry.

A2? Still perching into the hall, he ran the data through his mind. Eyes darting. *A2. A2. Okay, where's A1?* He paused, confused.

"Do you see anything else? Any number or letter?" Nick asked.

Raspberry groaned, turning his head slowly. The spike shifting deeper into bone with each tiny movement.

"C7! 5E! J... I THINK I SEE AN 8!"

"Good! Good! Keep looking around!"

Like a processor, he computed the information. *A2. C7. 5E. J8. A2. C7. 5E. J8.* He repeated it enough times that the pattern became a mantra.

What does it mean? Alphabetical? Numerical pattern?

He squinted again, eyes moving in time with his thoughts.

"HURRY!" Raspberry cried again, his voice frayed.

"Fuck it." Nick leaned back into the doorway and crouched, stretching out as far as he could without stepping on the tiles. He avoided the first square and looked left. It was a grotesque sight. Decaying on the adjacent block lay flesh, a severed leg in blue jeans still wearing a shoe.

With a tight grip on the doorframe, he stretched his fingers toward the limb, feeling the air around it as if playing invisible piano keys. Just inches away from brushing the pant leg, Nick's fingers had reached their limit. He shuffled left with his knees then tried again. Carefully, his arm stretched, and his middle finger dug in to secure the catch. Hands like a surgeon, he reeled in the severed leg.

It hovered over the tiled floor as he raised himself to his feet. Arm taut, he directed the cleaved ligament to the right adjacent tile. He held it upright and gently placed it down.

Click!

Raspberry flinched, but no pain followed. Instead, they were greeted with the same sound.

Click!

The once glowing white tile flickered to a sickly lime green. Nick exhaled in relief.

"Psh. Well. Now let's really try it," he muttered.

Nick stepped cautiously onto the next tile. No spikes. He was in.

"I'm in," he called, the excitement in his voice barely contained.

WHAM!

The door slammed shut behind them. Nick didn't bother to backtrack; he had made his decision. He knew what to do. His focus sharpened, repeating the sequence. *A2. C7. 5E. J8. A2. C7. 5E. J8.* He reached for the severed leg again, pulling it into his grasp.

This time, his target was three tiles ahead from his position. It was a risky move—no practice throw, no way to test judgment. But Nick wasn't about to second guess himself. With a swift motion, he tossed the limb diagonally six feet. Two clicks. Green light. *It worked!*

Taking a runner's stance, he lunged forward, landing on the next safe square. He wasn't out of danger yet. A river of blood trailed from Raspberry's leg, spreading across the floor. It was slick and treacherous. He couldn't stop now. Before moving again, he stepped in front of Raspberry, eyes darting to the path ahead.

"Grab my hand!" Nick called out, his voice calm but firm.

Despite the pain, Raspberry reached out, his left hand shaking as he grasped Nick's right. Nick immediately released him from the spike.

"RAH!" Raspberry jumped.

The jolt that shot through Nick's shoulder from Raspberry's impact was intense, but he held on, steadying the man. He had too much respect for his perseverance.

Teeth hardened with grit when Raspberry fell to his knees beside Nick. The two men, surrounded by blood, took a few seconds to themselves on this island tile.

"Th-th-thank you… N-Nick." Raspberry grew more fatigued by the minute.

"We're not out of this yet. Stay put," Nick replied, eyes surveying more tiles ahead.

He counted in his head. With a slate pinpointed, he grabbed the dismembered leg and threw it two tiles ahead. Two more clicks. Green light.

It's safe! Okay. I think I got this.

He took the jump to another oily tile, landing feet first, then dropped to his ass. The denim was now saturated with red.

"Come on! You need to jump!" Nick motivated Raspberry to continue.

Somehow, Raspberry had already made it back to his feet. Call it adrenaline. Nick had to admit, he was surprised. Considering the amount of blood loss, that man was tenacious. Raspberry put all of his weight on his good leg and hopped to the next safe tile. But the force of his movement sent him careening toward danger. Nick dove forward, catching his shirt collar just before he fell into the lethal trap.

Time seemed to stop in that second. As Nick's fingers curled deeper into the fabric, his eyes rose to see Raspberry's heels hovering above the next block. Nick noticed the once expensive suit now soaked in cartilage and gore. He could only stare in disbelief.

"Get. Me. OUT OF HERE!" Raspberry shrieked.

Nick pulled him back and the two crashed down. Safe—for now.

"Look. Right there!" Nick leaned beside the blood-covered man and pointed to a door just ahead. "That has to be a good ten feet wouldn't you say?"

The men had been so entranced by the light, severed corpses, blood, and adrenaline, they never took the time to notice just how long the hallway was. Had Nick had his glasses, he could've accounted for it sooner. It felt like miles in a panic. Now, the end was within reach.

"We're almost there. Just a couple more to go," he reassured Raspberry.

Nick pressed on, throwing the severed leg, checking his landing zone for reassurance. Another two clicks. Another green light. The jump was easy now. No time to wait.

Nick took a moment to himself after landing. He didn't want to end up like whoever had gone through this room. Those lifeless, cleaved bits of human flesh on the floor. Even though he might have entertained the thought of Raspberry's lifeless body, he couldn't manage to go through with seeing it. They *both* had to make it out.

Ahead, past the irregularly shaped tiles that surrounded them, was one that was large and extensive. A solid finish line that wasn't included in Nick's mental map. He considered it safe on instinct and took a final step forward. No need to jump, after all, it was right there. His right foot mirrored his left and he planted himself in an attentive stance. He was still. Hands gripped, he counted. *One. Two. Three.*

It was safe.

Raspberry followed suit after Nick turned his head and produced a nod. One more miserable jump and they were reunited. Hole in a foot, gouge in his shin, Raspberry still made it to the door, owing everything to Nick.

The door. The end. The exit.

What if it's locked?

The thought hadn't crossed Nick's mind. So focused on moving and analyzing, he failed to question simple things.

Had I not walked in, maybe I could've been safe. It's dark, sure. But maybe there was another way. What if it's been locked this whole time.

This one doubt set off a chain reaction in his mind.

What about the spikes? The bodies? It happened after they made it to the end. Did they lock the door? Maybe they were running from something? Then who set the hallway? Focus. Focus. Move forward.

He reassured himself. He couldn't afford to query everything. They were so close. There was a new door. A way out.

"Nick!" Raspberry shouted. "Look!"

Nick quickly rocked his head, snapping out of his reasoning. His eyes rolled up to the locked door. *Wait…*

"It's open," Raspberry added.

Nick was in disbelief.

Raspberry limped toward the entryway, still holding his wounded foot, he moved quickly enough. His eyes were wide with relief, the intense pain in his voice now replaced with something resembling hope.

"Thank God," Raspberry gasped, breathing heavily.

Nick stepped aside to let him pass. The room on the other end was starkly different from the hallway they'd just left. It was brighter, though the harsh lighting made the walls seem sterile and lifeless. The floor was smooth, almost too perfect, devoid of the grime and blood that coated the tiles they'd just crossed.

They both stepped inside, and the door clicked shut behind them. Locked.
Nick took a moment to scan the room. It was small, maybe just a four-foot-wide space, and the walls, ceiling, and floor were all one large tile, unbroken and seamless. A cube. There were no buttons, no switches—nothing that would give away the purpose of the space.

"There's no buttons," Raspberry said with concern in his voice.

"Buttons?" Nick was still hazy from breaking out of his contemplation. "We shouldn't have walked this way Rasp."

Lines formed between Raspberry's eyebrows. After all that, now he had a nickname. He paused and swayed.

"What if someone wants us to be in here?" Now, of all times, Nick had concerns.

"After all that. I-I wouldn't t-take you as the paranoid type," Raspberry said, twitching in pain.

"Think about it for a sec." That affirmative mild tone continued.

"After almost d-drowin… AH!" he shrieked as pain shot up his leg, knocking him off his knees. "I think someone wanted us dead an hour ago b-bud."

Nick gave him a moment and also took one for himself.

Why am I here? Is this trial through death? Was I kidnapped? What was I doing before?

No matter what he thought about, it always drew a blank. He couldn't remember anything.

I have a name that might not be my own.

Suddenly, the floor started to tremble. A faint ring screeched into Nick's ears like steel scraping against steel. A loud sound started low, then climbed high. Like a dog whistle reminding him to settle down, Nick obeyed and fell over his knees. Both men lay there, covered in blood, wiggling on the floor like fresh worms. They were simple bait, helpless and controlled.

A perpetual scream persisted. The noise reverberated around the cube, growing intense. As they squirmed—convulsing, shoving their fingers deep into their ears—veins began to protrude. The surging blood was black and wrapped itself around their skin. Worse than a spike through the foot, Raspberry's eyes began to bleed. Their veins wanted to break through their flesh. However, the webs of black lost their chance when the noise abruptly stopped.

In a moment that could never be explained, their vessels recovered instantly.

"What was that?!" Nick shouted, hands still over his ears.

"What's happening?" Raspberry reached for air.

"That sound! I felt like I was dying," Nick said, pulling himself up.

"Is everything trying to kill us?" Raspberry, sprawled out on the floor, clutched his head.

Then the walls began to shake.

"Now what?"

"I think we're moving," Nick said, feeling the walls, "Is this… an elevator?"

"A coffin more likely." Raspberry wasn't having it.

Whatever it was, it moved slowly and quietly. They couldn't tell up from down, only that the hell they'd escaped was no longer behind them. For now, it was safe. But Nick—never one to mistake silence for peace—knew better. Safety in this place was just the eye of the storm.

[CH.08]

C R O S S F I R E

"How do you know Russian?" The brute, who had been looking over at Dunn, finally decided now was the time for answers.

However, Dunn had been immersed in the blood and guts spread around him. He was too busy for the cop's questions. For some reason, he had no problem showing his interest in the nonliving. He took a knee and inspected the detached hand that had been severed off the only corpse in the room. The others could only watch Dunn's shaking back, his elbows wagging at his sides.

Even though the small square room was lit and the brute had no need for his torch, it was still dismally dark. A visible paradox. The blood that had been spread across the walls created a vibrant red hue—like a darkroom for a photographer.

"Ever wonder how someone could lose so much blood? Like, how much ya think someone can hold?" Dunn asked out loud.

The brute felt that Dunn's accent was stronger in the presence of a Russian. "Dunn!" The cop's tone remained inimical, reflecting his posture.

The loon pulled back from his investigation of the severed hand and turned his head to the brute. "Yah?" Dunn's smirk flared inside the red hue. His awkward long head and his buzz cut made him look villainous, just standing there, grinning in the red mist.

"I said, how do you know Russian?" Like a walking skyscraper, the brute advanced and towered over Dunn. He demanded an answer.

"I-I don't know. I mean, how would I know?"

"Он не знал бы!" the Russian interjected.

"WHAT!?" The cop spun and aimed his shotgun at the blood-ridden man.

The Russian had stayed on his knees with his hands on his head, remaining defenseless after Dunn had taken his pistol. Since then, the empty pistol had found a new home, tucked in Dunn's pants. He hadn't heard the brute argue against the weapon's immigration, so he neatly folded his shirt over the handle protruding from his trousers.

"I said, he wouldn't know," he said, accent thick and nasal. "Nikolai. It's all I remember."

"So, he does speak the same language? Can we keep him?" Dunn hopped to his feet, bored with the severed hand. Their hostage now had his full attention.

"Where'd you come from?" The cop advanced on the Russian.

It was near impossible to see anything in fine detail within the room, but as the brute came face to face with Nikolai, he noticed something odd. With tensions eased, or rather much less so than when they first met, the cop unclipped his flashlight and beamed it onto Nikolai's clothes. They were brown or maybe they were a shade of dark green. He had on rugged trousers with cargo pockets and a jacket; red epaulettes on his shoulders. His belt was taut and black just like his leather boots. On the top of his left jacket sleeve was a red badge; stitched inside some gold trim was a hammer and sickle. On the jacket collar, there was a red star pin with the same hammer and sickle.

"Wait…" The brute took a step back and contemplated.

As thoughts filled the officer's head, he had an epiphany. He could summon no memory of himself. Not of where he came from, nothing of his past, not even his intentions prior to waking up in a cage. He absolutely failed to recollect any detail of himself. And yet, for some reason, he could acknowledge things that did not pertain to him specifically. The Red Star. It was such an odd feeling, one that hurt under contemplation. He could not remember a time where he had seen it himself, but he knew what it was.

"You're a soldier." He lowered his shotgun. "You're military."

"я не знаю."

"ENGLISH!" He returned the shotgun to the hostage's forehead.

"I do not know," the Russian replied calmly.

Dunn enjoyed watching the cop dig for answers as he yelled at the surely clueless man. He knew Nikolai had no recollection of past events. After all, they woke up in the same shit—dark rooms and white tiled halls. It was all the same. But this didn't stop his enjoyment of coarseness.

There in that grisly room, Dunn was in heaven. His own heaven. One filled with gore and vanity. As he rolled his shoulders against the wall behind him, his beige jacket turned red. Dunn was crimson, brewing diabolical thoughts. What if he could reload the pistol? Why would he ever hand it over to anyone else, when he was the one that wanted it.

"I DO NOT KNOW!" The soldier's heavy tone came with force this time, growing impatient with the officer's questions.

Nikolai had been on his knees for almost thirty minutes now; clinging to his short brown hair, his arms began to tremble. However, he kept to himself, for he did not want any retaliation from the cop. In between responding to ignorant interrogations, he considered his options at getting control of the situation. Maybe there was a weapon hidden somewhere on his person, or even in the room. Or he could just get his gun back, right?

"How did you get in this room?" The brute could no longer stand reserved. He paced between the walls. "Nikolai, the room?"

"Я проснулся здесь!"

"DUNN!" The brute turned, his piercing stare demanded attention. The loon understood his place as the man's tool and continued to prove himself an asset. The cop brought himself back in front of Nikolai, shotgun ready.

"Ya can't stand this Russian gibberish, can ya?" Dunn grinned as he regrouped with the other two in the center of the room. "He said he woke up here. I think he's telling the truth."

After a deep exhale, the cop lowered his gun and collected his thoughts once more. Had it not been for this need of control, his mind may not have been stricken with anger. Reflection was beyond him though. Dunn, who had been a bystander the entire time, felt he had more control here. The blood; the sight and smell. It gave him the power of enjoyment, giving him a window into these two men before him. He knew the brute, much more than the cop knew himself right now. He could smell an underlying flavor of enmity emanating off the man. Dunn had felt it since he released him from those gurney straps. It was in his veins, pumping into his heart and mind. It's what fueled his thoughts and intentions. And kneeling in front of the inimical man was Nikolai.

Nikolai was a man of patience and intent. Dunn inhaled deeply through his nose. Yes, Nikolai was a soldier; he was controlled. Amnesic but aware. Dunn pondered what the Russian might be scheming. Even if the guy couldn't remember anything, would his skill set still be intact? It clearly was for the brute, so why not him? It occurred to Dunn that Nikolai had maintained his finesse. The corners of his mouth curled upward.

"What's ya name?" Dunn turned to the brute.

The cop in return tried his piercing stare once more on Dunn. "What did you say?"

"I said, what's ya name?" Dunn's grin grew more malicious.

The brute's stare persisted. Dunn took his silence as a stage setter.

"Ya know, officer, this whole time we've never got to know your name. You'd be the one to respond to something like this anyways, right?" Dunn began to stroll in circles around the two.

"Ya know who I am, says it right here!" Dunn pointed to his name in print on his Creedmoor Asylum jacket. "And we know this fella is Nikolai," he said pointing to the man on his knees.

Nikolai smirked and gave him a nod. Dunn kept his eyes fixated on the brute.

"But we have no clue who you are, now do we?"

The cop's stern face never changed. His bushy black eyebrows were parallel with his round face. These details were some Dunn never picked up on in the few hours they had been together. Always facing his back, now he was in the front. The red light shimmered across the brute's bald head. He truly was a broad, inimical man, and Dunn was getting the picture. If only he was aware of the cop's intentions or, as fate would have it, he found that his assumptions of the man could be true after all.

"Ya see… I know who you are. Let's say I've felt the type. Tall. Cold blooded."

The shotgun swung up. Dunn, in return, crossed his hands in front of the 9mm tucked in his trousers. Little did they know while Dunn was toying with the severed hand, he found a small metal rectangle that fit perfectly in the bottom of that pistol.

"Doesn't surprise me, a man like you don't like to be questioned."

"Say it Dunn!" The brute had enough.

In the middle of Dunn's rebellion, Nikolai had released his arms. With the attention off him, there was a moment of opportunity. If they didn't notice he dropped his arms, maybe they wouldn't see him check his pockets. Or maybe his jacket. No? Would they see him check the knife tucked into his left boot? There wasn't much time. What if they caught him reaching?

"The truth is sir… is that you're a liar."

The brute scoffed.

"I'm telling ya, I know the type."

The shotgun cocked and rose to Dunn's nose.

"Tell me this Dunn, am I the type that'll blow your face off?"

Dunn's smile mocked the brute's cold stare. In another life, these men could have been brothers. Dunn gripped the 9mm under his jacket. The cop, in unison, tightened his grip under the barrel of the shotgun as he readjusted the stock against his shoulder.

"Ha, ya most certainly are. The thing is-"

Nikolai's fingers stretched into his boot while his arms hung by his sides.

"-I'm the type that don't care."

As if every god ever conceived clapped hands together and made thunder, all three men in the room struck like lightning. The brute's index finger jerked back over the shotgun trigger while Dunn dove to the left. Dunn in return drove the 9mm barrel towards the cop and readied his aim. Nikolai quickly lurched into the brute holding a five-inch blade in his hand.

The shell exploded and pellets dispersed into the air. Faster than the muzzle flash itself, Dunn dropped to the tiled floor on his side, clutching the 9mm, holding back the shot. Nikolai had caught the cop before he could reload another shell and positioned himself in an authoritative stance. He wrapped his right hand around the barrel of the shotgun and threw it to the ground. His left hand, wielding the knife, dug into the cop's throat.

Dunn rose to his feet while Nikolai seized the officer's right hand. As he detained the man, Nikolai leaned in close, his head near the cop's ear, and whispered something—more cryptic nonsense. The cop would never know its meaning, nor would he care to remember it, but Dunn heard it: *A man is only as good as he treats another.*

The loon broke out in laughter. He lowered his pistol and hugged himself, still laughing. "HAHAHA!"

Nikolai took him for what he was, crazy, and kept his dagger dug into the brute's throat. The cop grasped Nikolai's left arm to hold the blade at bay. As a pellet of blood rolled down his throat, the room started to shake.

Like an earthquake, it convulsed the small square enclosure. Every tile that was bursting with light now flickered. The vibrations grew heavy. The brute's eyes rolled in unison with Nikolai's as they tried to trace the source. Dunn just kept laughing.

"What is happening?" the Russian demanded.

The walls were quivering so forcefully from the vibration, blood rolled off and onto the floor. The ceiling dripped and the ground pooled. Ignoring Dunn's riotous laughter, Nikolai tried the cop, "WHAT IS THIS!?"

The square room continued to rattle with a consistent motion as the subdued endured the knife in his throat. Nikolai wasn't going to let up and Dunn wasn't going to stop. Everything and everyone shook with intensity. Amidst all the clamor, the brute bargained with his pride and entertained some possibilities.

"We're moving," the cop said under his breath.

[CH.09]

I N T O
T H E
V O I D

"What time is it?" James had been pacing by the bar while Sean was digging his fingers into a squishy bag labeled 'beef'. The group had agreed they might not come across something edible for a while, so they gnawed on some of the chilled, raw meat from the fridge. They'd take a pinch and drop it into their mouths like hatchlings being fed.

James could only handle one scoop. After which, he resorted to frantically pacing around the room. Rubbing his stomach, he wondered if it was human flesh. Ashley beat him by one pinch and sat, sick and rather unsatisfied.

The group remained holed up since the gunfire ceased. They decided to leave the fridge open to shed some light in the black room. Blue light bled from the fridge's interior trim. It gave off a soft ocean blue hue, one that reached hardly five feet away. Sean was on the floor, legs stretched, his back against the oven. James would trot in and out of the light, disappearing and reappearing every couple seconds.

"Says here, it's 2 p.m." Ashley had checked her Garmin wristwatch. While the trio waited in hiding, she had time to tinker with the clock, only to find she had a global positioning system and an altimeter that didn't work.

"Four hours? It feels like we've been here forever," James muttered, his hand clutching his stomach. His frustration wasn't just about time—it was about the crushing ambiguity of it all. "We're stuck in a damn loop."

"Shh," Ashley and Sean simultaneously uttered to James.

Sean flung a chunk of beef in James' direction as he insisted on quiet. He apparently had no issue with foreign food from a strange refrigerator. In fact, by now, he had managed to eat ten pinches of raw meat. This was gross enough for Ashley to sit at one of the tables across the room. She was back in complete darkness. James continued pacing between the soft blue light and the dark side of the room. Sean endured eating a few more bites.

"Guys we've got to get out of here." James paused and threw his hands up. "Sean, quit eating that stuff!"

Sean was on his fifteenth pinch. "Keep it down. That guy could be close."

"Sean, are you seriously still eating that?" Ashley's voice cracked with frustration. She watched him consume another pinch, the raw meat clinging to his fingers like an addiction. "We have no idea what's in this, and you just keep going."

"I'm hungry," Sean said, licking his fingers. "We might not get to eat again for a while."

"We also might never see a hospital." James scrunched his nose as he watched Sean take one last pinch before putting the rest of the bag in the fridge. "If you get food poisoning."

"Shut up," Sean snapped, his irritation building.

James kept his distance, wrapped up in his own thoughts. He wasn't ready to face the reality of the situation.

Ashley crossed her arms, extremely curious despite knowing it was a pointless question. "Where are you from?"

"How the hell would I know? I don't remember shit," Sean said, his voice raw with frustration. He spread his arms out and mimicked Ashley's expression, but the tremor in his voice betrayed him. It was all he had left— anger. He didn't want to look scared.

Ashley flicked the flashlight switch, her eyes tracing the edges of the room before landing on James. She trusted him more than she wanted to admit but concerns still lingered.

Sean stood up, holding a forearm in front of his face. The light was so damn bright. He could feel Ashley's presence bearing down on him with authority, even though she was ten feet away.

Ashley took note of his brown leather jacket and plain blue jeans and saw him differently than before. Slick hair and casual clothes. She felt he was different from her and James, not necessarily because of his clothes but his character, his energy. He seemed out of place, although she couldn't think of why. It was always so hard to think. Making any consideration outside of their present experience was unthinkable. It just plain hurt. Most or all of their actions and thoughts were based on feel. And right now, she felt he was out of place more than they were. She called it intuition.

"Do you guys think we can leave now?" James asked, his words lighter than he felt.

There was a moment of silence.

Sean straightened his jacket as he rolled his shoulders back. Ignoring Ashley's interest, he walked over to the door and put his ear up against the steel entryway. "You ask a lot of questions James."

"Call it—I want to get the fuck out of here." James stepped behind Sean, mirroring his every movement.

Sean kept his ear to the door, pulse quickening. "I don't hear anything."

"It's probably best to be sure." Ashley kept the light trained on him as she closed in.

Sean didn't enjoy the light burning at his eyes, nor did he enjoy James breathing down his neck. Unlike the other two, who were eager to trust one another for safety, Sean looked to himself. Only himself. This notion had remained with him and as far as he knew it, it would stay there.

Maybe they did save his life, but that didn't change the fact that he couldn't afford to rely on anyone in here. Not again. Not after that cage. Sean looked over to James as he pondered who could be the deviant that locked him in that tiny steel prison.

"Sean?" James noticed he had been a bit too still.

Sean's head tilted, his ears straining. Every creak of the floor seemed amplified. For a long moment, the silence was suffocating.

"Well?" Ashley asked, her voice a low whisper.

Sean slowly pulled his ear from the door, looking back at them with quiet resolve. "I think we're okay. Let's roll."

James and Ashley followed close behind with Sean leading them down the hallway. Their line maintained straight, despite the pitch-blackness. Footsteps padded as they kept their noise light. James had felt their adaptability was one thing they all had in common. After being in this midnight facility for so long, they became too familiar with it, more than any of them wanted to. He considered asking Sean to check a few more rooms but his speed was so quick, he didn't bother.

"Sean?" Ashley breathed, the name slipping out on an exhale.

"What is it?" His steps slowed.

"Any idea where you're trying to go?" Ashley asked, her tone tinged with concern; she thought Sean was rash.

"Let's just get some distance, alright?" Sean quickened his gait, eager to move forward.

"Distance from what?" James asked. "Why don't we check a couple more rooms? Maybe we can find something that will help, like a phone or-"

"—Or a map?" Ashley interjected, flicking her torch back on.

"Yeah, or a map." James glanced at her, his gaze lingering on her hazel eyes for a moment longer than necessary.

Remarkable.

"Sean, seriously, let's check some of these rooms."

"I just want to find some light. Look under the doors. Maybe look around. We have to find an exit, not another place to hide," Sean said.

"But there might be something that could help us?" Ashley was insistent on getting answers.

"Sean, man take a break." James raised his hand, trying to calm the situation.

"Get away from me!" Sean slapped James' hand away and shoved him back, his voice edged with anger.

James felt the force shiver down to his feet. This made him agitated. There was no need for more violent reaction. He didn't like Sean pushing him around, but he thought about Ashley.

I've got to keep calm around her. She's the one who keeps it together, and I need her trust. If I lose my temper, I could lose her. And right now, I can't afford that.

James considered his options. Whatever he chose would be in her favor. He just hoped she would feel the same.

"Cool it, Sean!" Ashley demanded.

Sean trudged over to a random steel door.

Like the others, this door stood across from another, a steel barrier facing its twin. Everything was symmetrical. James caught glimpses of the facility's fractal design, the repeating patterns that seemed almost unnervingly perfect. It was as though the whole place shouldn't exist—an elaborate maze built to deceive.

"Do you think it ever ends?" James looked over to Ashley.

"Everything has an end, James," Ashley said, glancing at him through the darkness. He could feel her light smirk.

"Guys, come here." Sean cut between them and motioned them over. They could see his silhouette crouching outside a room three doors down. After a couple of clicks, he had the door open before they reconvened.

Is this guy good at lock picking or what? James thought, his eyes narrowing in disbelief. *How had Sean managed that so easily? What else does he know?*

James walked through the doorway with Ashley behind him. He wondered what it'd be like if he could lock pick, would he be able to impress Ashley?

Focus. We just have to find something to get us out of here.

James stumbled, a wave of frustration coursing through him. The room was just like the others—sterile, perfect, and utterly meaningless. He looked around, feeling the walls closing in.

"Check this out." Sean beckoned from a dark corner.

His hand moved in a sweeping motion across the glass, wiping it clean of invisible dust. Ashley's flashlight followed, catching the gleam of metal hinges securing the frame to the wall. They all felt the shift in the air—this was something important. Something they couldn't ignore. The hinges were obscure and varied with color, like burnt steel. The glass was clean and thick. When the flashlight panned across its surface, the room sparked—but only for an instant.

"What do you think this is?" Sean's voice carried a hint of curiosity.

James hurried over, eager to examine the tech. He noticed some wires protruding underneath the glass. "Looks like a monitor. Maybe it catches a projection?" James traced his finger around the metal hinges. "This stuff looks pretty advanced."

"What do you think this room is?" Ashley's light broke away from James and traced the outbound walls. Like the room before, curvy

102

chairs and steel tables were scattered and paired, though there was no bar this time.

"Look, there's a desk across the room," he said, pointing.

James scanned the desk, his hands sifting through drawers and papers, before something caught his eye. The sheet he held was old, brittle, and heavy with implication. His fingers tightened around it as he pulled it free. He laid it on the table; his breath caught in his chest.

"Why are we doing this again?" Sean asked, watching James scavenge.

"Don't you want to know what's going on?" While Ashley kept her light anchored to James, she directed her full attention to Sean. "Or are you just that scared?" she taunted.

Sean chuckled and straightened his jacket. He raked his fingers through his slick black hair before flopping back into a chair. "I just want to get out of here, bitch," he whined, as if the words might somehow make the situation feel less real.

Ashley's patience was running thin. The tension between them simmered, but she wasn't about to back down. "Don't you think figuring out what's going on is more important? Seeing as how we saved your fucking life and all. You owe us, so shut the hell up!"

Her eyes burned through Sean as he leaned back, his insolence hanging in the air. The space between them crackled with tension. She refused to back down with her light focused on him like a spotlight. The silence stretched until Sean scoffed.

"Whatever," he muttered, slumping further into his seat.

"Hey, Ashley! I think I found something." James perked up, holding a single sheet of paper in his hand. He waved it above, motioning her to the desk, "Hurry! I need the light."

Ashley casually crept forward, glancing back at Sean every few steps. She thought about his stupid grin and hair. She thought about ditching him and telling James, hoping he'd agree. She cast the beam higher in the air and provided the light James had requested. There was new evidence ready on the tabletop.

James positioned the sheet at the center, his palms gripping the edges of the table with white-knuckled intensity. The muscles in his arms tensed like coiled springs. His head hung low, eyes wide and straining, as if they might burst from their sockets at any moment. Sweat beaded on his forehead, tracing a slow path down the side of his face. The atmosphere felt suffocating, pressing against his skin, his breath shallow and rapid. The silence around him was deafening, broken only by the pounding of his heartbeat in his ears. Every instinct told him to pull away, but something deeper, darker, kept him locked in place—compelled to stare, to wait, to understand.

The top page read:

ANALYSIS OF SMART ARCHITECTURE OPERATIONS FOR BEHAVIORAL ANALYSIS STUDIES

Abstract: Recent advancements in artificially intelligent architecture have provided opportunities for controlled studies. With AI's ability to be programmed in conjunction to a control, studies have found increased accuracy in test results. Gregorian's buachaille (herd) study found significant veracity in data collected by the AI utilized in the architectural base. Subjects remained incognizant to such use despite constant setting modification. We predict promising and accurate data collection if Smart Architecture is approved for behavioral studies. Furthermore, the works of the Miter experiments, Sepharim's analysis "Architecture and AI: Futures Building Futures," and Rebo's port experiments have been supplemented in this analysis.

"Smart Architecture?" Ashley was still, one brow arched.

The words hit James like a punch to the gut. He skimmed the rest of the page, his mind racing. "Port experiments? What the hell is this?"

He paused and stopped reading. Pondering made his head ache, so he walked over to a dark corner. More thoughts spiraled, but he pushed them away, leaving Ashley and Sean to themselves. With more unanswered questions, his thoughts scrambled, then settled on the one possibility he accepted as truth. Whatever was going on had something to do with where they were. And where they were had something to do with what was going on. It was a paradox that crushed his contemplation.

No matter how many papers they found in each room, none were keys to his padlocked problems.

With his mind clouded, it was hard to get a sense of who he was. Perhaps it didn't matter. Or maybe it mattered most.

"You two can keep asking yourselves what's going on. It ain't going to help you get out of here. It ain't going to do shit!" Sean rocked forward in his chair and smiled. He planted his elbows on his knees, fingers rolling through his slick black hair.

"I don't see you doing anything!" Ashley was almost at her tipping point. At least she thought so.

Despite Sean's attempts to get under their skin, he was secretly intimidated by Ashley. Being an asshole might have been his way of countering the feeling. Regardless, his attitude wasn't helping. Sean laughed to himself before standing up. "You know what, how about the both of you stay here and keep looking for whatever it is you think might help. I'm going to go ahead and see if I can actually find a way out of here."

Before Ashley or James could say anything, Sean walked out of the room and made his way further down the hall. Hearing the pat of his footsteps grow soft, Ashley seized the opportunity to speak without judgment.

"James," she kept her voice low, "I don't know if we can trust this guy."
"He's a bit of a dick, yeah, but the lock picking? He's useful."

"He called me a bitch, James!"

"I know, I saw you about to kick his ass."

"I probably could," Ashley said proudly.

"We are getting out of here, Ash, don't worry. The second we don't need him anymore, we can leave, just us. We just have to secure a way out of here."

Ashley's frustration was mounting, but she kept it buried beneath a surface of cool control. Trust wasn't easy for her, and Sean wasn't making it any better. Still, he'd opened doors they couldn't, and as much as she wanted to push him away, she knew he had something she needed.

She sighed and peered out from the door. Her ears tuned into the faint pat of Sean's steps. He hadn't gone far. "Okay James, I'll hold out, but the next time he calls me a bitch…"

James stuck his arms up. "I get it! Hit him, go for it."

"As long as we agree."

Ashley walked out into the hall with James following this time. She assumed it was safe to use the flashlight again, having not heard screams or gunshots for a while. Sean's volume increased as the two hastily jogged to his position. The flashlight pierced through the dark to reveal Sean kneeling in an intersection. Randomly placed in the center of the floor was a square trapdoor. An anomaly. Out of place in a symmetric maze of halls.

"Sean, what are you doing?" James asked as he jumped ahead of Ashley.

"What does it look like?"

"We don't need to be going down Sean," Ashley said.

"Sometimes down is up," Sean said.

Ashley raised her torch. "What did you s-"

"No wait, Ashley." James held her back. "He has a point."

"James, don't."

"Remember the cave? How we fell in the hall. Remember! After you freed me from the rope, we ended up in this facility."

Ashley's eyes peered down as she gave the situation some serious thought.

"Yeah, listen to James."

Ashley broke her trance and flipped the flashlight around, readying it over Sean's skull.

"Shut the fuck up, Sean. Enough." James' shoulders spread, his chin was up.

Both Ashley and Sean backed down.

"We're never going to make it out of here if you guys don't stop. Just stop." The intersection was silent. James basked in his authority, circulating one thought.

I need to give her a reason to trust me.

This was the foundation of his impetus. Perhaps it was the only reason that made him continue. What would've happened had he not found her? He could still be stuck in a net or dead for all he knew. Maybe Sean would be dead too.

All of their actions in combination led them to where they were now. James knew something was at play. Perhaps fate. Cursed with amnesia, basking in blackness, James felt they were where they needed to be.

CREAK!

Sean hesitated before he pulled the trapdoor open. He spat into the darkness, listening for it to land. The hollow thud echoed up from the depths. A deep, endless void. He leaned back and turned to them, his voice flat. "I'm not going down there first. Someone's gotta take the leap."

"You're disgusting," Ashley said, turning to reveal Sean's face with her light. "You sure about this, James?" she asked over her shoulder.

"I don't want to waste time finding out." James took a step into the hole. There was a ladder bound inside the downward tunnel. Crouching into the gap, he climbed down first.

"Here, take this." Ashley handed him the light and then waited for Sean to go second.

Ashley stood alone, her breath shallow in the void. The silence wrapped around her, and in that stillness, time seemed to stretch endlessly. The absence of light, of sound, of everything, made her feel small and insignificant. It was as if she were both everywhere and nowhere simultaneously.

"Ashley, you coming?" James called from below.

She snapped back to reality and hurried into the opening. Once she climbed down a few feet, the trapdoor closed itself. She looked up. "No turning back now."

[CH.10]

B R E A K I N G

P O I N T

The journey down the ladder was cramped and suffocating. The confined space pressed in on them with every movement. They all just wanted to get down. After a near thirty-foot descent, the three regrouped at the base of the ladder. James returned the flashlight to Ashley. He felt it was safer in her hands. Ashley in return took the liberty of sweeping the light in circles around the room. It didn't take them long to realize their mistake.

The ladder, standing upright in the center of the room, was crowded by five walls only four feet away. Legs would have to be broken for anyone to be able to sit down. As cramped as the descent itself, the three struggled to create space, huddling together in the tight, pentagon-shaped room. Their own breath, gripping the others' throats.

"James, you seeing this?" Ashley's light continued to dance around the oddly tight closet.

"So this wasn't the right way." Sean kept his criticism to himself. He knew he was the one they would blame. After all, he was trying to escape through the trapdoor before they made their way back to him, but he wasn't going to let anyone know that.

Like everywhere else, the room was tiled floor to ceiling, though here the tiles lay cloaked in shadow. No doors, no exits, no hidden gaps to squeeze through. Only the oppressive gloom of yet another room, silent and stark. Another dead end.

"I guess we should go back up." Sean grasped the ladder with one hand.

"No point, the door shut itself." Ashley reminded him of what she saw on her descent.

"A door doesn't shut itself. Did you lock us in here?" Sean's frustration boiled over, his face reddening as he clenched his fists.

"Need I remind you of where we found you."

Before Sean could reply, James interjected. "She's right. There's no way back."

"Great! I can hardly move in here." Feeling claustrophobic, Sean decided to lean on the ladder and mumble to himself. The others didn't say anything about it.

He should stay with what he knows best, lock picking. That's it!

"This is right," James declared.

"How do you know that?" Ashley asked.

"It's hard to explain." James felt the walls. His hands brushed each tile vertically, then horizontally. "Remember that paper?"

"You mean the abstract we found? Yeah." Ashley followed James with her light.

His hands studied every tile, first with a gentle brush, then with a few taps from his fist. "It said Smart Architecture."

"Yeah and?" Ashley kept up with the spotlight as James reached the third wall.

"Well, what if it's like a computer."

"Computer?" Sean was lost.

"What rock did you crawl out of?" Ashley glanced at his jacket.

"How would I know!" Sean barked.

"Enough!" James didn't want any bickering. "Maybe that explains where we are. Ever since we've been here, everything keeps changing." James had everyone's full attention. "I mean think about it. Where we started and where we ended up. Even if we don't remember anything, we can all agree we've never seen a place like this."

"Okay, your point?" Sean scoffed.

"What if it changes for us. Like we have something to do with it," James concluded.

"You mean the building? That's crazy James. We didn't change anything." Ashley tried reasoning with him.

"But what if we can change it?" James hammered his fist around the fourth wall, then they heard it.

Click!

Sean hopped to his feet and huddled behind Ashley, while her light illuminated the switch

James had just discovered. One of the large tiles receded into the wall and an exit revealed itself.

"How did you know about that?" Sean became agitated. Perhaps James was hiding something from him. However, being uncertain he decided to bottle his angst for now.

"I didn't. I guess I felt it." James gave no more thought to it and ventured into the adjoining abyss. Sean trailed in second and Ashley, who did nothing but smile, filed in third.

As the three stepped into the new room, the wall behind them briskly shut. Ashley quickly directed her light toward the magic wall, but by the time she turned, the area was engulfed in blinding light. They dropped to their knees, shielding their eyes. It was as if they had been hit by a flashbang, their senses overwhelmed as they collapsed to the floor. All they wanted was to see, but each time, the privilege came at a painful price. James clenched his jaw; his eyes were forced shut as the pain rushed through him.

Can the light just make up its mind?

It had taken James a solid ten minutes for his pupils to adjust. The room was large and spacious. It was also five-sided. Every large white tile roared with energy and strewn across each one was dark red blood. No bodies or remnants—just light, blood, and a vile, festering stench.

"Jesus Christ!" James blared.

"What the fuck happened here?" Sean cornered James. "I want to get out. I've had it. This is bullshit!"

"Calm down, Sean." Ashley tried towering over him again, but that wouldn't work here. There was light and he could tell he had a few inches over her.

"Back off!" James was stiff. "This isn't helping."

"How did you really know about the switch?" Sean pushed his face into James. It was clear he was breaking.

"I didn't."

"Bullshit!"

"Sean, we have to get out of here. This isn't going to lead us anywhere." Ashley got between them, pushing them both back. Her hands held high, demanding they separate. Both acknowledged the gesture and walked away from one another. Sean ranted to himself under his breath in a corner while James tried more tiles.

No amount of time would ever be enough to help them understand anything here. It hurt to try and do so. The more colorful the room, the more riddles would go unanswered. It was useless. So without thinking much about it, Ashley turned off her light to conserve the dying battery, while James used the same technique he did in the adjacent room. Sean chose to stride around avoiding the walls; his jacket was too expensive to be stained.

Contrarily, James' hands were painted with blood as he inspected each tile. No one even bothered to ask, they just covered their face with their shirt and let James get to work. By the time he had reached the fourth wall, Ashley, although calm, felt unconvinced.

"James!"

"I know, I'm trying to hurry Ash."

"No. It's not that it's… I have a bad feeling."

On the fifth wall, James stopped his inspection and turned to Ashley. Looking into her eyes, he didn't need to say anything. He felt it too.

Sean noticed their stare and cut between them. "What? What are you guys talking about?"

During this awkward exchange, the sound of shuffling resonated above them beyond the ceiling tiles.

Sch. Sch. Sch.

"What is that?" Sean took a step back and positioned himself between Ashley and James. All three were still, jaw dropped gazing into the ceiling above. What was that sound? A gaping space revealed itself above their heads. Only a second passed before a blur hit the floor.

SLAM!

Soon after, the hole above them closed and the room returned to its blood-spilled state. Everyone took a step back from a figure curled up on the floor. James, white-knuckled, was resolute while Sean took another step back. Ashley kept her place, watching the figure roll open to reveal itself as an injured man. His clothes matched the walls and were tainted with gore. He shook violently as he climbed to his feet. Without the assistance of his knee, it was unclear if he would've made it.

Upright, the man exposed his wounded body and dyed clothes. His shirt was torn, and his pants were drenched. He was missing one shoe and had three slashes on his neck. This was all James could make out between his blood-covered skin, hair, and face. It was hard to tell where else he may have been injured.

He groaned, his body aching as he struggled to rise in front of them. James stood in awe still gripping his fists. More thoughts raced through his mind.

How did HE get here? That can't all be his blood. If it was, would he be able to stand?

The man's body was a truly grotesque mess, blood-soaked, bruised, and barely holding itself together. His clothes clung to his form. When he rose, his movements were drawn-out and forced, as if the weight of his injuries was a burden too great to bear. The room went utterly still as the man's hair parted, revealing the chilling message carved into his forehead: 'KILL ME'.

James felt the gravity. He had no answers. Only more questions.

He immediately drew his attention to Ashley for reassurance. Her head turned toward him in unison; her eyes wide. Sean conversely stepped towards the man as he unveiled himself.

Right when the man's eyes discovered his audience, another sound knocked in the ceiling. Seconds later, a loud clang rattled inside the larger pentagon room. No one knew where it came from. As everyone anxiously twisted their necks, Sean had already taken another step forward. The man mirrored Sean's movement. Taking each step casually with precision. Roughly six feet apart, their eyes remained fixed onto one another. James and Ashley just watched as this peculiar lull took over.

Hearing his own heartbeat, James took a deep breath and traced Sean's path. Between the two men lay a steel bat. Clean and solid like the facility. Except for the blood. Then it dawned on James. Before he could lunge between them, it was too late. Sean and the man both dove headfirst into the bat.

Sean managed to seize the handle at the same time that the stranger clutched the barrel. Together they rolled left in the direction of James and Ashley. James braced himself into a fighter's stance ready to break up the altercation when he looked over to Ashley. Piercing him with hazel eyes, she shook her head no. Grinding his teeth, James felt an imaginary leash pull him back. He desperately wanted to intervene but rationalized with Ashley's decision making. He knew she was right, though at what cost would he risk it?

Sean and the man continued to brawl on the floor as their grunts shattered the room's silence. James' heartbeat played its rhythm in his ears as the two exchanged fists. Blood dripped from Sean's mouth as he pried the bat free from the stranger. He retreated to catch his breath while the man climbed back to his feet.

"I've had it!" Sean cleaned off his bottom lip leaving a streak of blood across his hand.

"This guy is going to tell us where we are." He held his arms up with the bat in his right hand. He circled around the man who was struggling to keep himself up. Sean embraced the adrenaline. He felt awake and aware. He was alive.

"SEAN!" James blurted.

"James no," Ashley insisted under her breath.

Sean ignored them both, he was in his own world. Approaching the man, he extended the metal bat under his chin. "You're going to tell me what I want to know." The man fell to his knees and dropped his head. Blood rained onto the floor when he started to sob.

"Come on man, just answer the question."

A foot met the man's skull and pushed him back onto the floor. With his limbs stretched out, the stranger's cry turned into a laugh. James looked away.

"What's so funny?" Sean rallied to the guy's side and the barrel of the bat rose into the air. "LAST TIME!"

In addition to the lone man's gurgling laugh were spurts of blood. The droplets grew larger as his mouth expanded. When Sean peered down on the ill figure, bat overhead, he saw inside his mouth that he had no tongue. His nose wrinkled in disgust. In the midst of his laughing, Sean felt the faintest ball of blood land on his cheek. Then the bat came down. Ashley now understood what they were dealing with, something James had figured out hours ago.

Without warning or notice, Sean swung the pristine metal bat, repeatedly smashing the

118

man's face. Blood splattered into the air with each upward motion. Ashley clenched her eyes shut while James kept his averted.

James wanted to stop him. Every part of him screamed to jump in and end this madness, but he held back, staring at Ashley. Her gaze met his, and without a word, he knew she didn't want him to intervene. The silence between them spoke volumes. Sean was beyond reason, but they needed him—for now.

Hearing cracks and gargling, Sean persisted. Every hard hit left behind a gushing whine. James counted them all, every swing. All *sixteen* of them. And when Sean finally stopped, the room became placid and deathly quiet. Sean released the bat and gasped for air. He was so winded, he fell to his knees and fought off hyperventilation.

Neither of the other two bothered to help him. James finally built up the nerve to see what was left. The man who had randomly fallen into the room only moments ago, lay spread out, headless. His skull was nonexistent. His face looked like a crushed berry turned to jam.

No one spoke in the pentagonal chamber after that. Fear thinned the tension leaving something heavier behind—suspicion, sharp and lingering. It would remind them this wasn't over. Not even close.

They stood in silence, each wrestling with thoughts that wouldn't settle, when the floor gave a subtle quiver.

None of them questioned how they'd gotten here. Hypnotized by the assault, their transition had become routine. A horror so common it hardly registered anymore. Instead, they stood in place, brushing dust and grime from their clothes, and waited.

The vibration deepened, a low tremor crawling up through the soles of their boots. The five walls began to slide inward, grinding with a metallic groan that coiled through their bones. The pentagon shrank, forcing the trio into a huddle, shoulder to shoulder at the center.

This time, it wasn't just vibration. James felt the floor tilt—no, descend—as if the entire chamber were being lowered on unseen rails. He kept running the thought through his head: *activation*. Some hidden mechanism had triggered this, and now they were part of it. He wanted Ashley's take, he needed it, but Sean's looming presence nailed the words inside his throat.

[CH.11]

THE
SANCTUARY

Their experience inside the cramped pentagon came to an end fairly fast. The vibration was subtle and thankfully the room was modestly lit, a trend they all hoped would continue to repeat itself. Although, beyond the white tiles, nothing about this place seemed like it would ever repeat itself. That expectation was immediately confirmed when the tiny chamber came to a halt, and an entire wall receded.

Through the open wall, a sight both familiar and surreal greeted them. Before their feet could fully lift from the floor, the sharp rush of wind and the melodic calls of birds wrapped around them. Beyond the threshold, endless pines soared into the sky, their dark green needles swaying in the breeze, while the tall grass swayed like an emerald sea. James darted into the newfound wilderness, inhaling the crisp air as if it were his first breath.

It was fresh. A place unlike anything he'd felt in so long. Shouts of glee accompanied the troupe while they rushed further into a thick crowd of trees. How nice it was to be free of that haunting facility, to feel the warm wind and breathe the clean air. If they could ever remember a home, this would be the closest thing to it. Ashley jogged further into the forest with Sean while James lagged behind. His enjoyment inevitably dissipated. He knew this miracle came at a cost and to him it was sixteen swings. The bass of battered brains lingered in his eardrums. It was a hard melody he had yet to shake. The ethereal chirps of birds would never drown it out. Birds James couldn't even see.

Wait…

James reviewed his surroundings again. Then he noticed they had made another grave mistake. At first the wilderness was so properly distinguishable, it was as if they'd made it mid-day for a picnic. The sun was perfect, the temperature under control. But something was off.

James stared into the sky and adjusted his eyes beyond the light. There, up on the ceiling, the same white tiles. This wasn't outside.

Is this even real?

James stood still for a moment, staring at the trees around him. His fingers lurched forward as he drove his arm down, brushing the bark with his fingertips. It was rough and rugged.

How could this be? How could there be trees?

He took a knee and caressed the grass before gripping a handful of blades. Ripping them from their roots, he discovered the soil. Real dirt. Real plants.

Perplexed, his deliberations ceased once he realized Ashley and Sean broke his line of sight. *Ashley?* Jumping into action, James dashed in the direction they had last traveled.

I hope Sean didn't try anything. I need to catch up to them. I can't be left behind. Not now.

To his relief, they weren't too far ahead. They waited over a hill, amid more pine trees. Ashley was leaning over Sean, who was crouched beside a stream.

"Look at this James!" Ashley shouted, "There's actual water!"

Sean dove into the stream, gulping down the water greedily as if it could wash away his sin. Ashley followed suit, drinking deeply. The water was delicious. Yet James couldn't shake the nagging feeling that this place—this water—was too perfect, too convenient.

"James drink! You need to hydrate." She took out her bottle and filled it up.

Having exhausted their supply while evading the shooter, Ashley knew they'd have to ration what little remained. With a thoughtful glance, she opened her backpack and carefully tucked it into the bottom, conserving every drop. Beside her, James perched at the edge of the stream, cautiously dipping his hands into the crisp water. He took a long, measured drink from the liquid he'd once thought was impossible.

"I haven't even thought about water." Sean caught his breath, taking a break from his usual gorging. Leaning back, his finger rolled through his hair.

James took note of the bloodstains on Sean's knees. Although he managed to keep his leather jacket immaculate, he would never be able to absolve the stains on his skin. James found him haunting, like a ghost who roamed this place long before he arrived.

This place is a curse, surreal and impossible. I'm past the point of trying to remember. This guy could kill us. I mean what would he do to Ashley?

James continued to drink from the stream, his mind racing. The water tasted pure, as though it had been brought from some distant, untouched place. He still couldn't shake his thoughts.

Do I tell them this isn't real? Should I just tell Ashley we should get away from Sean; I need to talk to her. When there's an opportunity, we will make a plan; but first, this place—they should know.

James was too late to utter his discovery. Sean had advanced further on the hill and encountered something. He called out, "James. Ashley. I think you should come see this."

Ashley swung her body, ready to jog up the hill, until something snagged her back.

"Ashley, wait," James whispered urgently, grabbing her shoulder. He didn't want Sean to overhear. "We need to talk about him. About

Sean," he pointed. "Something's not right with him. I don't trust him."

Ashley froze, watching Sean's back disappear as he pushed ahead widening the gap. Then her eyes locked on James—and in them, she caught the truth. Fear. Not of this place. Of Sean. And she couldn't ignore the reality gnawing at her: that he was more dangerous.

"I don't think this is a good time," Ashley said peeking up the incline.

"You saw what he did!"

"Shh! I know. Don't think about it. Come on, let's go." Ashley grabbed James' shirt and towed him up the hill.

Did she really just say, don't worry about it? He killed a guy!

"Look! Out there!" Sean was pointing out beyond the hill. The land was flat and the pine trees became sparse. Now they had an explanation for where they were. They could see the landscape met with white tiles, which at first looked like a blue sky. They could see that this wild land spanned for miles. It was inconceivable. The enclosure was massive and biblical. The terrain changed just like Earth's precious surface. They seemed to be in the thick of it.

"How could anyone build this?" Ashley was the most impressed.

Her climbing gear didn't fully convey her adoration for nature. Her face expressed it all. Her eyes were like a full moon, covering every inch of the soil she stood on. "This is incredible! I mean there's a stream of water back there. How are they able to sustain this environment?"

Sean turned his head, eyebrows pulled down. "Did you just say they?"

"Yeah, obviously, this was built by someone. Thought you'd figured that out already," Ashley said, her tone full of exasperation.

James felt Sean's presence radiate, dominating the space. Everything seemed to intimidate him, and it was chilling. *What will he do next?* James expected Sean to fly off the handle at any moment and he didn't want to be around to witness it.

James showed no weakness and ventured the conversation elsewhere. "The water at that stream was moving, maybe we can follow it to a source. That's a solid path to follow."

"And if there is no source?" Sean hissed.

James' plan to sidetrack the conversation led to Sean emanating contempt. He was okay with this. "We can get an idea of how big this place is at least. If there's water, maybe there's food too."

Ashley admired James' attempt at optimism and humored him. "Okay if we find food, I'm going to be the one to cook."

James chuckled. "I'd probably burn it anyway. Is it dinner time already? Maybe we should try fishing."

Concurrently, Ashley checked her watch and noted the time. "Well James, it is almost 4:30."

"4:30! That can't be right. We left the room-"

"Around two hours ago." Sean interjected.

Naturally, James burst. "We've been in this hell hole for six hours?"

A silence took over the group and their cheery attitude came to an end. It was these moments where James always felt weakest. Emotions were like waves, rolling in high before crashing. It was possessive, sometimes feeling forced. In these moments where they would be brought back to reality, they were alone. James would be broken down to paranoia while he pondered what was going through Ashley's mind. His reach would stay there as he feared treading into Sean's psyche. It was all dangerous territory, the facility and their conscience.

The group's forethought evaporated under the light of a star, one of which materialized from oblivion. This star levitated far out beyond the hill and pulsated like a beacon. A beacon whose sole purpose was to hypnotize those that peered into its gleam. Captivated by the light, all three marched down the hill. James was temporarily dismissed from his emotional roller coaster and led the way as Ashley and Sean kept up from behind.

The beacon's glow drew them deeper into the forest, beyond the sparse trees and tall grass, until a wide meadow opened up before them. Here the grass was low and sage. The cushioned turf was left stamped with footprints. Their path was now concrete.

Sean, Ashley, and James spread out, an arm's length apart, before the intoxicating trance broke. James thrashed his head hard, making sure he was truly back.

Fifty feet ahead, at the very heart of this meadow, stood a metal monolith. Its exterior was smooth and gleaming, reflecting the sterile glow of the white tiles above. From its crown fanned a torrent of light, streaming skyward in a glistening surge. Then, as the streaks bled away, the ground underneath the beacon came into view.

Around the obelisk, circled a number of shadows revealed by the beacon. Much like James, these other people had been drawn here compelled by the same strange force. Each one appeared downtrodden and fatigued. James traced the circle. There was Ashley, the experienced climber and Sean the arrogant asshole.

Who are these other people?

There was someone in scrubs like a doctor or nurse. Beside him was a woman, bleeding from her shoulder. She was in a red dress holding a pair of high heels in her hand. Next to her was a beaten man, he held his head low and nervously swayed side to side. Adjacent from him was someone James had almost forgotten. An inimical figure whose presence made Sean's fury seem like an adolescent's. The cop. However, he was between two men James hadn't had the pleasure of meeting, a mildly tall, rugged man in a Russian uniform, and a short lunatic whose grin wound around his face.

Beside the madman stood a mismatched duo, soaked to the bone, bound by silence—one dripping rain, the other, blood. It was a bizarre mix; the kind of combination you couldn't quite make sense of. The oddities didn't stop there. Scattered between the groups were more stragglers, drifting aimlessly, as if they didn't quite belong either.

Had they made it this far on their own?

James estimated that ten to twenty people had gathered around this column. This was much bigger than he had originally anticipated.

As the beacon pulsed, the crowd swelled— waking, gathering, saying nothing. Not one left the meadow. A ring a hundred feet wide hemmed them in, enough for James to glimpse a few details. Meaningless details.

What is this place? The sewer, the tunnels, the cages, the halls… are we all survivors of something?

James would wrestle with fate indefinitely. A heavy headache ensued and yet it could never stop his chain of questioning. It would remain a tug of war up until he recovered his memories. Memories James considered vital to his survival and understanding of the facility.

That pursued understanding was trivial when weighed against what James would never know. That of the actions that took place moments ago by each individual in this circle. The relationships their groups possessed.

What if they team up on us? What if we're not alone in this?

Naturally, James picked up on his tendency to end his predicted encounters in violence. Not that it was his choice though. From the moment he woke up, there remained the aura of aggression. Except from Ashley. Whether this energy was brought by this place or their innate humanity, James didn't know. Despite this, he realized a murderous atmosphere was advancing on the front.

A somber dawn choked the meadow as the beacon sank, and the white tiles faded. When its glow finally died, James saw the illusion—specks of light seeping from above, a counterfeit constellation sprawling overhead.

Amber light bled into blue as the energy rippled from the column. Streaks fused into a single torrent, growing, hardening, shaping. The beam contorted into a figure—an old man's head wrought in luminous threads. James reeled, crushed by the enormity of what had appeared.

The projection would flicker occasionally akin to glitching. Nonetheless, this fault would be overlooked as the large blue head made an announcement.

"Welcome! Welcome! We have been eagerly awaiting your arrival. Do forgive our technicians—modesty aside, there have been—complications in recent porting procedures. Still, by His grace, most of you have arrived wonderfully intact. Others, well—less so. But that is no longer your concern."

Sweat crept to the tip of James' nose, his hands clammy as he clenched his fists.

Who the fuck is this guy? His chest tightened.

The man spoke in a flamboyant tone; his cadence was mechanical, almost rhythmic. To James, it was deeply unnerving.

Is this one of the scientists?

"Now, you may find yourselves disoriented. Confused. Perhaps even afraid. We understand. The trials you've encountered en route to the

Sanctuary are part of the process—unpleasant, but necessary. You see, each of you has been chosen for something greater. You are here not by accident, but by divine selection. His grace has called you to serve a higher purpose. We— The Collective—are your observers. Your shepherds. Your mirror. And you… you are the measure of all things still human."

James glanced at Ashley. She stood motionless, eyes wide, body statuesque. Her pupils were blown, locked on nothing, as if the voice had swallowed her whole.

"You are disciples leading us to a better future. For humanity. For all life. We have watched you from the moment of your arrival, and we will continue to watch until the very end."

"Ashley! What the fuck is this?" James shouted, his voice cracking. His pulse hammered in his throat. The terror in his chest grew with every passing second.

She didn't move.

"Ah… Subject 333. We've been watching you closely."

The projection's smile stretched wide. James was suddenly cold. That number—it felt like a curse. It continued.

"In time, you will learn what must be learned. For now, heed this, the SmartArk is an experiment. And like all experiments, it must remain pure. You were brought here to be studied in your natural state. That is why we have taken your memories. To observe you—not as who you were—but as who you are, veiled by the shroud of identity and illusion.

We urge you: act on instinct. Be true to your core. His grace requires you to regress. To fracture. To fail. Only then can we prove the flaw in His design.

Should your memories return prematurely, you will be reprocessed. We, The Collective, welcome you."

A vibration swelled beneath their feet. That high-pitched scream again—rising, splitting—and then devouring. It tore through the group like shrapnel. James collapsed, clutching his head as black veins surfaced across his skin. Eyes bled. Ears ruptured. The entire circle of captives writhed.

And then—silence.

The projection continued, untouched by their pain.

"Yes. We know this is much to absorb but please do keep up. You are among the many to experience the SmartArk, an AI-structured facility approved by the Federation for full-spectrum psychological observation. Its architecture shifts in tandem with cognitive behavior, so what appears anomalous… is merely adaptive. In time, you will understand."

James stood shaking, heart pounding against his ribs. His thoughts raged louder than the silence.

If there is a God, please get me out of this. Wake up! Please wake up!

"Now, *to* the matter of judgment. Humanity has reached a crossroads. Evolution has stagnated, conscience corrupted. After centuries of unchecked indulgence, crime has replaced order. By His grace, The Collective have been given purpose: to test the merit of mankind's survival.

Your task is simple. Survive.

Strip away the illusion of civility. Return to your primal roots. Kill, if you must. Kill until we find one of you still worthy to carry the flame forward. Only through regression can we reveal the design flaw… or the possibility of change.

Throughout the Sanctuary, you will find caches of aid. Use them as you see fit. There is no time limit. There are no rules. Only observation. May His grace guide you through your purification."

The hologram glitched once, then again, and finally imploded—folding inward until the face dissolved into the flickering pillar. James could still hear the words—*strip away the illusion, return to your roots*—as the meadow dimmed under artificial stars.

A frigid mist swept in over the hills, clinging to his face like breath. No one spoke. All around him, people trembled, buckled, and fixed their eyes on the sky as if expecting salvation. But there was none—only the echo of that voice.

Almost every single person who managed to stand in that circle fell into panic, laden with responsibility they could not discern was legitimate. James' mind folded into trepidation.

This can't be real. How could… after all that… why?

POP! POP! POP!

Through the fog, two rounds from a pistol discharged sending the assembly into chaos. James couldn't locate the shooter. He spun, eyes strafing. There had to be a safe escape route, but everyone was running in different directions; it was too hard to tell. Among the havoc, James was the only one who remained in place, anchored by fear. More cries ripped through the woods, piercing the stillness with a haunting urgency.

"ASHLEY!" James shouted, cupping his hands around his mouth.

POP!

Another round! Who could be shooting? WHERE IS SHE!?

A shadow tackled James and he fumbled. Recovering, he felt a hand grab the back of his shirt. He ducked and caught the enforcer in the corner of his eye. *Ashley!* Her hand extended and grabbed James by his collar. His shirt constricted around his throat, cutting off his breath for a second as he struggled to keep up.

BANG!

That shot sounded different!

A few feet from cover, Ashley shoved James behind a tree, her movements quick and practiced. Without a word, she raised her hand in a deliberate, silent gesture—*shut up*. James reactively followed, crawling deeper into the forest's dense underbrush. They slithered through the thick foliage, bodies low and heads braced, every sound magnified in the stillness. Ashley, ever the strategist, started piecing together an escape plan on the fly.

At the edge of the thicket, Ashley stole a look through the leaves, her breath shallow. The meadow was like a never-ending soccer field, with a haunting column in the middle. Ashley climbed a tree and mapped the Sanctuary's rectangular perimeter, giving herself a unique sense of the area.

Even if she didn't know where true north was, she could always make it up. By her own logic, she was on the North end, or a short side. The East and West sides seemed endless, and the South side was too far to see. Taking into account they were still underground, it was safe to say outside the forest must be four walls, one of which presumably, has an exit.

"We need to pick a direction and go," Ashley commanded with such confidence while she shimmied back down the tree.

"What are you talking about?" James shuffled against her, trying to see out through a low bush.

"Follow the tree line. The Sanctuary, this meadow, it looks like a big rectangle. I'd say we're on the North end, and we can pretend the left side over there," Ashley explained, pointing her finger under cover, "and the right side over there are East and West."

James was quick. "How do you kn—"

"I don't, but for the sake of having some sort of idea where the fuck we are, it's better than nothing." Ashley's words struck him with unyielding force; the sheer magnitude of it all hit him hard. He knew he needed her more than ever.

James obediently nodded and laid still beside her. The two remained calm while their ears focused on the *POP* of each gun blast.

I wonder who could be at the end of those weapons? Why would they just start shooting? What kind of person does that?

His contemplation never ceased. After a while, the gunshots grew sparse—each shot more distant, hollower—until they dissolved into nothing.

Ashley rested in a prone state, staring intently out into the meadow. All of her actions were concealed with purpose and presence. James too was intent, but on her. Sweat trickled down his forehead as he watched Ashley, her face still focused—unwavering.

If anyone can get through this, she can.

She never flinched, and amid all the chaos she found consummate cover, seamlessly blending into the shadows. However lucky they were though, James knew others were suffering far worse. That idea remained while Ashley quickly peeked her head out of the bush.

Outside in the meadow, through low gloomy clouds, silhouettes of bodies sprinkled the damp grass; clothes stained, limbs still. After a fast pan side to side, Ashley motioned James out of cover and further into the tree line. As they left the arena behind, James peered back in time to see it—so many strange corpses.

The few bodies he saw vanished as the trees behind them grew dense. It would be a reminder of what's out there, of what could be around them now. In the heavy forest, it was hard to see more than just a few feet ahead. Someone could be there right now. Were they right around the corner?

James picked up the pace as Ashley's legs stretched into a full sprint. She seemed convinced distance from the meadow was their best option. Then again, there were the caches.

Would a gun be sufficient enough to hold off an attacker? What if there was more than one? What if they don't even have weapons? An exit has to be the best option, right? If the scientist guy was here, then there has to be a way out!

James couldn't quite decipher what Ashley was searching for, but he knew one thing for sure—she was an invaluable asset. The kind that kept him alive, even if it was a struggle to keep up.

He wrestled for air, battling to match Ashley's tempo as she sprinted ahead, weaving effortlessly through the thickening forest. His legs ached with each step, but he couldn't afford to let her slip from his sight.

"Ashley! W-Where are we going?"

She was mute. Her legs slowed from strides to steps. James watched her drift through the trees and down a small hill. Feeling the wet atmosphere, he held his ground as a blue fog crept deeper into the forest. The milky mist slid between the trunks and coiled through the brush; its low reach thickening the night. Then —a sharp crack. A branch snapped, jerking James upright. His head whipped left to find Ashley climbing a tree again.

"How do you know where we're at?" James watched at the base of the evergreen.

"Shh!" Ashley's interjection was all that was needed to remind James of the situation.

He waited below, prying bark from the tree's trunk with his fingertips, like a bored child.

Right there, in the thick of a synthetic forest, James stood as an easy target. It wouldn't take much to strike him down—an innocent man adrift in the storm. How long could he last unfocused? He could have only seconds left. James didn't care to consider these probabilities, he was too curious about Ashley up above, peering atop a tree.

Man, she's good at climbing.

Before he could even finish another thought, Ashley was already halfway back down the tree.

"What'd you find?"

"This way." Ashley dropped from a branch and pulled James away.

"Where are we going?" James tripped behind her.

"Keep up okay!" Ashley picked up her speed once again, leading the two into concentrated forest. Soon the grass grew high and vines stitched themselves around trunks. The shrubbery had grown so dense it closed in around them, waist-deep in a pale tide of green.

"Are you sure this is the right way?" Jagged thorns ripped through the skin of James' shoulders as he wiggled his way through, trying to keep a meter's distance away.

If she gets any further ahead, I might lose sight of her.

"Shut up and keep moving!"

The darkness devoured them as they ran. Each step drew the void closer, winding like a noose around their ribs. The air thickened, clawing at their lungs, dragging them toward an infinite nothing.

In a panic, James leapt forward stretching his arms out, palms open. Ahead of crashing, his hands clenched, and his eyes squeezed shut.

"Are you serious?"

When James opened his eyes, only half his body had escaped into the clearing. Ashley hovered over him, smiling, her head swaying side to side. He glanced back. His feet were gone, consumed by the trees.

"At least half of you made it out," she said, laughing.

She leaned against a white-tiled wall and crossed her arms. James figured they had hit the outside perimeter. Despite the fresh air and cool breeze, the living plants and flowing water, the Sanctuary was just another part of the hell that was this facility. A green oasis of death imprisoned by the same walls that refused to let James go.

Do these walls really go all the way around?

James lowered his eyebrows as he stared back into the forest. Ashley watched him for a moment before breaking his silence.

"There's no way out, James."

He turned around, eyes wide.

"I mean there's no way out, at least from here," Ashley turned her back to him. "So, I guess we better get moving."

"Should we leave the others? I mean all those people?"

"That's not our responsibility James. Plus, how do you know you can trust any of them? You don't know what any of those people are capable of." Ashley took one step forward. "Come on, we don't have time for this. It looks like there's a way out up ahead."

Ashley advanced following the sidewall, leaving James seated on the ground. He pulled his legs out of the thick and sprang upright. Ashley had already picked up speed. James was left with a choice—stay behind, or push forward? The weight of the decision pressed down on him as the sounds of chaos roared behind them.

Brushing himself off, he watched as Ashley grew smaller, her figure fading into the distance. He tuned into the sounds around him, the sharp, distant *cracks* of gunfire still piercing the air. For a moment, he wondered if it was a haunting echo from his own mind, a tragic memory that would forever linger in the recesses of his thoughts. His right foot shuffled forward. He lunged.

"Ash, wait up!"

[CH.12]

SHELTER FROM THE STORM

Nick stared ahead and watched Raspberry fall into a ditch. The wounded man in a suit had waddled through an open field with haste. Amid all the violence, Nick found it funny watching blood-soaked Rasp hop with such enthusiasm.

If only he had been that adamant earlier.

BANG!

Nick jolted forward, sprinting across the open field, his body low and tense. Sweat soaked his skin as his eyes squeezed shut, desperate for a moment to catch his breath.

When he opened them again, he quickly wiped the back of his hand across his burning eyelids. He needed his glasses. *Now wasn't the time to think*! Bullets zipped by overhead, brushing the split ends of his hair. He held his momentum until the last possible moment, diving headfirst into the ditch.

"Nick! Where are you?" Raspberry shouted from the ground, clutching his bleeding foot.

Nick snapped back to awareness, realizing that he hadn't bothered to duck. His head was exposed. A perfect target. About thirty feet down, Raspberry was huddled low in the dirt, blending into the earth like a shadow. Nick, staying low and moving cautiously, shuffled his way toward him, keeping his head down and every sense alert.

He rolled back and lay beside Raspberry. It didn't take long for him to notice they weren't the only ones hiding here. There was a man in scrubs tending to another man in ragged clothes. He had a ripped yellow shirt and stained blue jeans. Not with blood, but with age. His shoes were beaten and torn, with the logo on the sides fading away. He had a white beard and curly white hair; wrinkles covered his exposed skin.

Has this man been here for years?

Regardless of Nick's consideration, he heard the man mumbling something to himself. The other man in scrubs patted down the beaten individual.

"Hey!" Nick tried to stay quiet. "I said HEY!" He motioned to the acting medic.

The other man simply glanced back.

"What are you doing?" Nick crawled forward.

"I'm a doctor. I was checking this man," the stranger explained in a rush.

Nick felt unsure about him.

"What's your name then, doc?"

"Luke. I think."

"I'm Nick," he said, turning his head to the left, "and this guy?"

"I don't know, he kept mentioning Elias in all his rambling, but that could be anybody."

"I think that's him." Nick motioned the doctor away and grabbed Elias' shoulders. He squeezed his eyes shut, then stared into the man's brittle gaze.

"How do you know that?" Luke interrupted.

"Have you not been paying attention to what's going on? When did you get down here?" Nick was stern. Before Luke could respond, Nick whispered harshly to Elias. "How did you get in here old man? Can you hear me? Nod if you can hear me?"

"I've tried this." The doctor knew it wouldn't work.

"SHUT THE HELL UP!" Nick's voice cut through the air, sharp and unforgiving. He glared at Luke with contempt before turning to the ragged figure. "Old man, is your name Elias?"

His mumbling stopped. Then he made a solid sound, still unintelligible.

"Come on, speak up," Nick persisted.

"Y-y… yes." Elias stared into Nick's brown eyes. "You came from the light… I came from the dark."

The doctor fell back; his eyes widened. "What does that mean?" Luke asked out loud.

Elias had said enough. Nick gave him space and turned back to Luke. "Alright, what's your story?"

"I told you already, my name is Luke. That's all I know."

"And you're a doctor?"

"I mean, I can't remember my profession exactly, but I would like to think so. I know what I can do. I—it's hard to explain. Why would I wake up in scrubs with a stethoscope around my neck?"

"And after everything that's happened in here, you didn't lose it?"

Luke didn't respond.

Nick kept on. "Where did you wake up?"

"I SAID WHERE DID YOU WAKE UP!" Nick shouted with force, not afraid to give their position away anymore.

"SHH! Okay, we woke up in some halls! Keep it down!"

"We?" Nick wanted to know everything.

"Elias and I. There were two others with us. Th-they didn't make it."

"And why's that?"

"They ran off as soon as we made it in here." Luke's head turned, scanning the area. "This sanctuary or whatever the guy called it."

Nick paused for a moment and considered Luke's story. His eyes traced to Raspberry, followed by a sharp exhale. "Think you can take a look at him?" Nick pointed over his shoulder at Raspberry, who was clutching his foot, moaning in agony.

Luke nodded and crawled over to Rasp and started his checkup. Nick guided Elias to the bottom of the ditch and laid him down. "What the hell are you doing here old man?"

He sat back and scoped his surroundings this time. The ditch ran parallel with the meadow. There was a good five feet of decline before it leveled out, giving them excellent cover as long as they kept their heads down. At the bottom, the trees grew thick, the edge of a mysterious forest. Nick was so caught up in counting heads, the sound of whizzing brass escaped him.

Fortunately, the shooting had ceased, at least for now. How much time did they have until a shooter paraded down the ditch? Before their cover was blown? Nick couldn't think about that. He needed numbers. How far were they from the column? How large was the Sanctuary? As these problems circulated Nick's mind, he envisioned a map. Something he could go by, something that could help him see.

"Okay, I think I have a plan," Nick called out to everyone. "This place has to have an exit. Me and Raspberry came from that way beyond the meadow." Nick knelt and instructed with his hand. "We know what's over the ditch, so that gives us two directions. We're definitely inside, so we just have to figure out the shape of the room. Either way, we will inevitably end up at a wall, right? But which way is faster? That I don't know."

"We came from that way." Luke pointed in the opposite direction of where Nick and Raspberry came from.

"Well, that narrows it down," Nick said.

"I say we go for it. AHH!" Raspberry jerked as Luke cinched a tourniquet around his foot.

"Anything to get out of here." Luke helped Rasp to his feet.

"Can you walk old man?" Nick lowered his arm to Elias who was lying on his back.

"I-I suppose."

Nick helped Elias up and the four of them formed a line. He led them in their agreed upon direction and stayed low. The group remained tight, disappearing into the thick of trees. Nick was sure to keep a good pace, well enough that they'd all be able to keep up. It dawned on him briefly, why bother with a politician who couldn't walk and an old man that could hardly talk.

They could be useful! Nick told himself, breaking his thoughts. "Come on, keep up!"

Elias, second in line, surprisingly kept up behind Nick, despite the occasional push from Luke. Who, unfortunately, was bound to keeping the anchor attached, being sure that Raspberry didn't get too far away. After all the carnage they'd witnessed in their short time together, the four men insisted on staying together—each with their own reasons. Nick was the one leading, and Elias, Luke, and Raspberry knew why.

"I think we're close." Nick's arm moved in circles.

Tree limbs scratched at their faces as they ran low through vines and brush, rushing to break free of the dense sage. Their momentum increased as their shirts were snagged and shredded by briers and broken limbs. The gunfire returned with renewed fury.

BANG! BANG! POP!

COME ON! HURRY NICK! He motivated himself.

They pushed forward with increasing urgency, their steps growing heavier as the thick green foliage gave way to ominous shadows of black. Elias fought to maintain his footing, charging through the dense underbrush, his balance faltering. Desperate, he lunged forward, grabbing at Nick's shirt for support. Luke, reacting out of reflex, reached out for Elias, while Raspberry—lagging behind, too battered to keep up—struggled to stay upright, his injuries dragging him down.

Their convoy crashed as each man toppled over the other in front of them. The surrounding limbs weren't strong enough to hold onto. They rolled for thirty feet, slamming into the ground. Gasping for air, they scrambled in the dirt, subconsciously checking for wounds.

Nick forced himself upright, blinking hard as his eyes opened once more. Against all odds, they made it out. Standing before them all was a familiar white tiled wall, stretching all the way into the fraudulent sky.

"We made it to the end!" Nick shouted, his voice breaking with a mix of relief and disbelief.

BANG! BANG!

Shots sent them all to their stomachs—too close for comfort. Nick glanced around before jumping back up. "Come on, we have to go!" his arm swept forward.

The others climbed to their feet and formed up behind Nick as he took off. They jogged parallel with the wall in a straight line. "I hope you know what you're doing," Luke called out.

"You already know what I'm doing," Nick replied.

"ASHLEY, WHERE ARE YOU GOING?" a voice barked up ahead.

The line halted abruptly, this time without any collision. As Nick's eyes kept straight, two blurry figures came into view, a young man and a woman.

[CH.13]

E D G E

O F

C O N T R O L

The inimical man was the first to stir after the hologram's broadcast flickered out. While the others in the large circle remained disoriented, their minds reeling, the cop took a deliberate step back. With practiced ease, he swung his shotgun from his shoulder into his hands, grip steadying with a deep breath. His eyes narrowed as he braced for whatever was to come. Dunn and Nikolai stood frozen to his left, still caught in a trance, their expressions vacant and distant.

With a stern face, he took two more steps back and embraced the weapon. He looked left, then right. Again, he took steps further away from the crowd. By now the majority were wiping their eyes, unable to grasp the gravity of the situation at hand. However, the brute knew, he was ready. He had been ready from the very beginning, always anticipating the mayhem to come.

By the time Dunn and Nikolai became aware, the cop had made his way into the tree line and concealed himself in the brush. Nikolai impulsively turned to Dunn, who did nothing but grin. The Russian did not hesitate to sprint backwards, caring only to get as far away from the loon as possible.

Dunn, on the other hand, held his tight smile until Nikolai was out of sight. He reveled in what he was about to do, eager for their inevitable reunion—a reunion of chaos. Caring not what the hologram had lectured, but only that of what he wanted to do—which seemed to change at any given moment. Dunn turned his head to the large company of strangers, dropped his smile, and reached for his gun.

POP!

POP!

POP!

He sent three rounds in three directions, following the blare with a laugh. The shots bewitched the crowd into a panic. Sharp cries filled the air as Dunn replied to them all with his horrible chuckle and another round.

"HAHAHAH!"

POP!

Dunn twirled around, laughing maniacally, as people scrambled for safety. Security was a concept unknown to him, none of which he needed. He felt in control of the disarray, his true element. The sensation of the fear he created washed over him. His hands raised to the sky before he rested them on his head to relax with a deep exhale.

"Ya don't know who I am, but now you do!" Dunn's comment to himself rippled in the ocean of cries caused by his wake. Now he was entranced again, by his own doing. "NO ONE CONTROLS ME!"

BANG!

A sudden gust slammed Dunn's back, forcing him to spin around.

"You're not going anywhere, you crazy son of a bitch!"

The officer had unloaded a round from the woods—unfortunately too far away to kill his target. He marched forward through the panicked crowd. "You're finished Dunn!"

His grin returned. "HAH! I'm just getting started."

Dunn quickly sent another round his way.

POP!

The cop hit the ground in a desperate dive, his body slamming against the earth. Before he could even push himself up, the loon vanished into the thickening fog, disappearing like a wisp swallowed by the haze.

The brute squinted, trying to make out a silhouette through the dense mist. His concentration broke when a straggler tackled him. He was sent to the ground again. It was getting annoying.

The cop rolled over his shoulder into a kneeling position and raised his shotgun. The straggler ran away. He steadied his aim and wrapped his finger around the trigger. He had to be quick as the straggler was becoming dim. With his aim exact, the cop grew hesitant and eventually lowered his weapon.

To him, every shot mattered—especially in a place like this, where resources were scarce. He scanned the area and considered his options. Dunn was on his shit list, a list he was determined to settle. Dunn and that kid that took him down in that dark hall. He would not forget about them, no matter how much occupied his mind.

With wails of despair, blood, and violence—no matter how much he didn't remember—these elements felt familiar. He knew this wouldn't end any other way than his own terms.

The cop briefly weighed his limited options. Would it be best to find Dunn and take him down once and for all? Would it be better to be prepared? What if there were others who were armed that he hadn't discovered? Ultimately, he came to the conclusion that the caches might be his best bet. Not only would he be well equipped, he'd also be removing that advantage from someone else who might be a threat. Where would they even be? He had no clue how big the Sanctuary was nor how endless the facility was. It's not like he had anything to lose, though; here there was only gain.

So, without much further thought, the brute picked a direction and went with it. He jogged forward with his weapon ready and reloaded. His trot maintained, while his eyes panned across the meadow. A few bodies lay still in the red-stained grass, as he marched over them, looking down to see nothing but surprised regret. He marched on until he entered another tree line. In the woods it seemed the cries only swelled. Although the gunfire had ceased, panic remained.

Everyone here knew the deal now. They would either be consumed by fear or driven with determination. The cop didn't care about the strangers' stories or struggles. To him, they were just obstacles in the way of his goal.

The trees thickened, and the grass gave way to waist-high brush. Interwoven with the thick sage, spiraled vines and thorns, which grabbed at his legs, demanding he slow down. And yet his jog became a high knee sprint. The inimical man pressed on, caring not about superficial lacerations. Hell, a knife didn't even faze him, despite his fixation on the caches. Ammunition, water, food, more weapons, to him it was becoming a more solid idea by the second. Nonetheless, how would he find one?

The brute slowed his gallop through the brush; it was becoming unmanageable. The boscage was so deep, his vision was limited. His mind went back to the dark halls and empty rooms. Not that it made him uncomfortable, it was just annoying that he couldn't see anything. Nothing around him now was visible, only the sky. The fake stars twinkling above, a false heaven that he saw through from the start. It didn't seem to scare him. Nothing did. Not the shape shifting layout, the occasional involuntary blindness, nor the lack of memories. He contemplated the possibility of finding one of those precious caches. He just needed a clue, just one little hint. After all that trouble, it's not like the floating head of a strange scientist would lie to anyone, right?

Staring up at the sky, the idea suddenly came to him. The shotgun secured itself behind his back. Without delay, he grabbed a hold of a branch and hoisted himself upward. He would repeat this process until the darkness died and stars thrived. Up atop a tall pine, he scanned the area, impulsively mapping out the layout of his surroundings.

There were walls to his left and right, other than that everything else dissolved into darkness. The Sanctuary truly was a remarkable scene. Down below, about a half mile out, was the meadow he had just left. He watched as the remaining ants still scattered about, so consumed with anxiety they just appeared to run in circles, with no plan and no hope. They were weak, unable to grasp their newfound reality. Their thoughts would not save them, only their actions. Not this however, not panic—that would destroy them, and he knew it. He knew there was no hope for them, so why bother considering it anymore.

Parallel to the meadow, further into the wild, was a small opening surrounded by more jungle. An extremely faint haze filled the glade. His eyes widened; a peculiar sight among a forest as dense as the Amazon. It was convincing enough for him to jump down within seconds. He speculated it couldn't have been over a quarter mile away. Using his keen sense of direction, he made his way back through the wall of undergrowth, this time keeping his speed slow.

POP! POP!

Two more rounds tore through the forest, their deafening roar barely fazing the brute. He listened closely, catching the faint echo of the shots. They were similar to Dunn's weapon but carried a distinct, almost foreign tone. The officer paused, the thought creeping in— just how many others were out there, and where were they?

Without a change in the thickness of the woods, he noticed a subtle adjustment to his environment. An infinitesimal blue hue saturated his vision. The fog was thicker here, perhaps he was close to the glade. His tempo quickened until his leg was pulled back. With his right foot wrestling to break free from a vine, he kept his momentum and ignored the thorns puncturing through his tactical pants, deep into his skin.

To anyone else, these woods would be considered sentient, forcing its trespassers into submission. His leg shook vigorously while his hands began to bleed, having decided to grab the vines to relinquish his foot. He would tug and pull, driving every thorn even deeper into his palms. Again he tore, harder and harder with every yank. Shifting his weight forward, he tried once more.

Crack!

The vine snapped in half and his body tumbled ahead. The momentum carried him through the thick and out into an opening.

He made it. The elusive glade. Just like he had imagined. He rolled off his back and onto his feet to scan the area. The cop was amazed to find the small circle enclosed by a literal wall of shrubbery and trees. There was no opening or weak spot in the forest. This was earned. Hastily he ran into the middle, spinning in circles looking every which way for a sign. Any hint or presence of something, of someone. His head turned left once, then twice. Scanning the grass, the tree line, the sky and the shadows, he kept spinning. Then it stopped.

The whirlwind of detection ceased, and he stood high with his eyes narrowing down to one spot. An idiosyncratic formation of rocks, looming over dead grass.

He fell to his knees astonished, casting a shadow over the anomalous site. His eyebrows grew tight, and his shoulders rolled back. Thrusting his fingers into the earth, he troweled. The dog in him threw dirt between his legs, while his body shook from the cold. The temperature was dropping, and his hand grew damp the deeper he clawed. Having reached a depth of about one foot, his nails scratched and scraped something close. After wiping his chin on his shoulder, he dug faster.

Like knives on a plate, his nails scraped something solid below. A shiver ran down his spine, motivating him to stop digging and just pull out the damn thing. He lowered the wooden box on the ground beside its tombstone. It was relatively small, maybe a foot and a half wide. He inspected it further. It was made of wooden planks and rusted nails and, as expected, was protected by a small lock.

The brute stood and raised his knee, hovering over the box.

CRACK!

With a single, decisive motion, the box was free. But would it hold any real value? The idea lingered briefly before he flipped the box over, shaking its contents onto the grass. The objects hit the ground with a hollow clatter. Tossing the empty box aside, he sank to one knee, his eyes scanning the scattered items as he began counting his prizes.

A water bottle, food rations, a paper map, and a keycard were all that was in the allotment. Immediately, he grabbed the water bottle and stretched his throat wide, being sure to down it as quickly as possible. There was no use in carrying extra baggage. He took liberties with the food rations too. Without knowing when, or even if, he would ever get food again, he thought it best to use it all now. As for the keycard, he simply slipped that into his pocket. All that was left was the map. It had been folded and concealed. Had it not been for the word "MAP" written on the corner of a fold, the man might have been surprised for once.

His eyes shrank as he focused, peering at the paper. With his mouth shut, he exhaled deeply through his nose. Then he unfolded the sheet once, then twice. The brute's eyes expanded. Something between excitement and unease crossed his face. This was very unexpected, yet it was a wake-up call for what was to come. Something he was beginning to think of as fate. This violence and desolation were meant to be and would remain. Now the cop knew the scientist wasn't lying. Wherever they were, nobody would be leaving anytime soon, not until they answered their calling.

Gripping the sides of the paper tightly, his knuckles twisted red. He took a deep breath before placing the map on the ground. Everything had to be remembered, every detail, every line. This was his advantage. Tracing over the details with one finger, he went through all the options, circling through each idea in his mind. Thinking of every action and every consequence, he contemplated his options with eagerness.

The map below would begin to paint a picture.

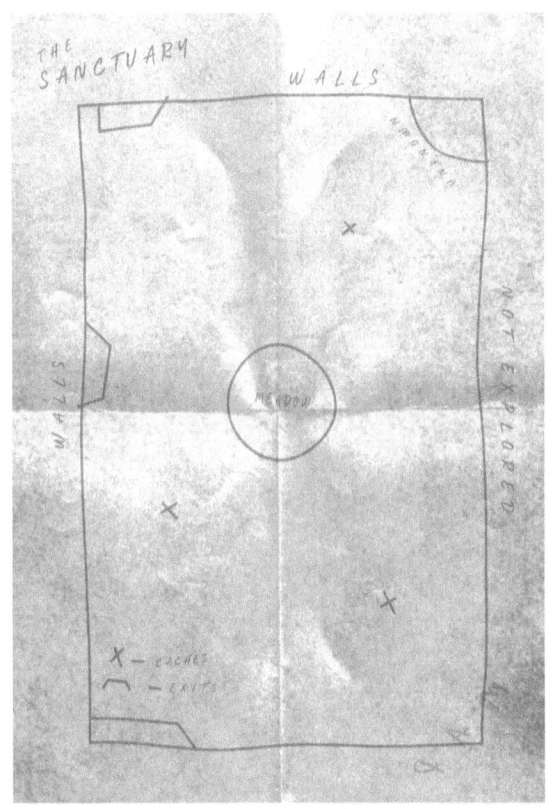

Who wrote this and why? How did it even get in the cache? The detective began to ponder more than he ever had since the beginning. The beaten map listed two more cache locations, but who put those there and for what reason?

Hoping to discover ammo or some tools, he was more grateful for these finds instead. He weighed the options: find the other caches, or push straight for an exit. Would he let his curiosity get the best of him and explore the unexplored or visit the unknown feature located on the map? No, he was too stern for that, there was no space here for curiosity, only survival and punishment.

He thought about Dunn and how hours ago he was strapped to a gurney and detained. Had he not let him loose, could he not have prevented what might have happened anyway? The thought split him—guilt on one side, reason on the other. A duality that seemed to meld all the minds that walked this place.

This *Sanctuary*. The hair on his forearms struck upright thinking about it all. With a soft scoff, the tall man collected the map and stood up. He had an idea of what to do, he just had to figure out which side of the map he was on. With no cardinal direction, it was impossible to tell with minimal details. So going off a gut instinct, the inimical man quickly made his way to the perimeter of the glade and pried his body through the brush wall. His muscles tightened as he braced for more thorns to shred through his clothes.

Upon breaking free of the thick underbrush, he strode forward with confidence. If he could make it to the perimeter, he could get a sense of the space. That could lead him to a door according to the map, or more unexplored territory. He figured there wasn't any more use in considering the alternatives. He had a direction, so he was going with it.

Bobbing and weaving through the low hanging branches and thorns, the brute pressed on with renewed pace he had not shown before. This man was motivated. He knew if he had to kill, he would. And if he were to survive, he would.

The thorns became less oppressive as the tree limbs stretched higher, their branches forming a canopy above. With a swift, almost frantic pace that surpassed any he had held before, he pushed forward. His focus never wavered. His movements were precise as he carved a path back to the edge of the meadow. The fog deepened, smothering the grassland and obscuring the forest's boundary. Through the mist, the brute's eyes caught dark silhouettes, motionless in the distance. It was impossible to gauge their number.

With a deep inhale, he knew this carnage would stay with him. Who were these people? Innocent or guilty, who here bore authority of these grave decisions they would make? Were they their own executioners? Again, his mind would break out of its shell and grasp for reasoning. As always, he exhaled, shook it off, and moved on.

After surveying through the fog once more, he pulled out the map and laid it on the ground. Every five seconds, he would rotate the paper attempting to visualize unrevealed landmarks. If the white tiled walls were to his left, maybe that would be the shortest distance to cover. Or was it straight ahead? It could be to the right.

His eyes scanned the map methodically, darting from one corner to the next before glancing up, left, then sweeping to the right. Over and over, he repeated the motion, weighing his options with the precision of someone seeking the most informed decision. Frustration began to build, and eventually, he shut his eyes, lowering himself to one knee. With a deep, steadying breath, he became still, the world around him fading into silence. For a moment, he did nothing but breathe, allowing the calm to settle into him.

"Hurry up."

Dead ahead, a voice slashed through the thick fog, sharp and unexpected. His eyes snapped open, pupils dilating in an instant. His body lurched upright, every muscle tight with alertness. His hand reflexively hovered over his sidearm, fingers brushing the grip, the chill metal still tucked in its holster, ready to react.

"This way, come on!"

They weren't that far. He had to make a move. The brute braced his pistol in both hands and barreled forward. He kept his head low and his steps light. The voice, louder, mixed with incomprehensible chatter. Without a sound, he eased his pace and veered left. Thinking he could get behind them, he'd rather observe than to draw attention from a group whose number was unknown.

The fog felt like milk as he swam through, crossing over into the tree line. Zig-zagging tree to tree, he moved in closer. He could hear three, maybe four people talking, surprised their loud banter had not gotten them killed already. They compromised their position within minutes after the cop heard them. He couldn't see them, but he knew they were right around the corner. He crouched behind a thick pine and tuned in.

"We're going the wrong way," said the thin one.

"I'm telling you, it's this way," the burly man barked back.

"Both of you need to be quiet," the woman whispered harshly. "Someone will hear us."

"Then hurry up. I'm not waiting for you anymore," said the thick-shouldered leader, brushing past them.

"You don't even know where we're going," the thin man called him out.

That stopped the leader. He turned. "What did you just say?"

"I said we don't know where we're going. You keep changing direction."

"I know what I'm doing," the leader replied, voice low, deliberate. "You want to lead us instead?"

The woman put a hand on the thinner man's arm. "Just drop it."

He stalled. "I'm just saying… maybe we should think things through."

That was enough. The burly man closed the gap fast. He didn't swing—not yet. He got in the other's face, chest heaving.

The cop peeked, shrouded by brush. He saw three people. Two males, one female. He watched the larger one stick his finger out towards the others.

"You think this is a democracy?" he spat. "You want to start a group vote out here? We'll all die while you're thinking."

"Okay, alright—back off," the woman said.

The alpha didn't flinch. He stepped in closer, staring the thin man down.

"You want to take the lead?" he asked again, louder now. "Go on, try. I'll be right behind you. We'll see how long you last."

The thinner man didn't move. His jaw was set, and his feet were rooted.

"That's what I thought." The alpha backed off a step and kept his eyes on him. "Now shut up and follow me. Or don't. I'm not going to babysit anyone."

He turned and started walking again. The forest swallowed the sound of his footsteps.

The woman exhaled and looked at her companion. "We should go," she said, though her voice was weak.

He hesitated. "This doesn't feel right."

"I know. What else are we going to do?"

She took a step after the big one. The slimmer one watched her go, still unsure. Then he followed. Slowly.

Behind a nearby tree, the detective stayed crouched, watching the uneasy alliance stagger forward. His grip on the pistol eased slightly. His suspicion did not.

He was as solid as ice behind the pine. His grip grew tighter, and he pressed into the trunk even more. The stillness was making him uncomfortable, so he made an attempt to readjust. Shifting his leg on the ground caused a twig to crack. Then all was silent.

Far off, the alpha halted. "Did you two hear that?" he asked the girl and defeated man. They remained speechless and looked down to the ground. The alpha quickly spun around and traced the tree line.

"Hey, who's there?"

The cop didn't dare breathe as he heard soft footsteps approaching. Holding his body like steel, he kept his firearm at the ready. The man neared closer to the other side of the concealing tree. The cop's lungs closed.

"Is anyone there?" The stranger called out once more, standing directly beside the detective, completely oblivious to his position.

The alpha's head started to round the tree. The officer held his pistol at a forty-five degree angle upward, ready to pull the trigger. He could see the guy's nose poke past the trunk and then he paused.

"Can we please just go?" The woman broke the silence.

The alpha kept his head at the side of the tree being sure to look left and right, taking his time in doing so. Then he pulled back and turned around.

"Come on you two, let's get moving." As he regrouped with the others, they took formation behind the man and followed him.

The cop held his position until their footsteps faded. A heavy breath slipped from his lungs, dragging like an anchor. He eased the pistol down and leaned just far enough to glimpse their backs disappearing into the brush. His pulse steadied. With a final glance around the trees, he moved—trailing them from a distance, nothing more than a shadow stitched into the forest.

[CH.14]

T E N O U S
B O N D S

Moments ago, deep in the woods of the
Sanctuary, a small group of confused
individuals formed a circle around each other.
Across from them lay a red man in a field,
clutching his wounded leg. His thigh had been
pierced by a stray bullet, and his howls didn't
echo—they remained trapped within his reach.

They stayed within his sight, paralyzed by
their own fear, unable to look away as the
man's cries resonated in the air. His body
shuddered with each tortured breath, rising and
falling, only to repeat the agonizing cycle.
The blood from his wound would soon claim him.
Captive in shared disbelief, they watched this
broken soul—the cries, the moans, even the
twisted laughter—each sound more desperate than

the last. He was beyond saving, slipping further away with each passing moment.

They had been lucky, having managed to break the tree line at the first sign of shooting. The shooter responsible for the initial frenzy among these strangers was an unknown figure, a *loon*. Fortunately, they hadn't met him—or each other—until now.

"What the hell is happening?"

"I'm so scared!"

"I don't remember who shot first!"

"Did you see how many people there were?"

"I wonder how many are left."

"Please help me! I can't do this."

Among the chatter, two men and a woman stood out. The woman, her accent warm and languid, begged for comfort, while the other two wondered if it was something they could provide in a place like this—or worse, should.

Before they had banded together, they'd each been lost in the same circle, listening to the hologram's vague instructions. The tall one was Sam—skinny, brittle, and fatigued. Cora was the shortest of the three, with medium-length purple hair. Ashton was the burly one, shorter than Sam, stocky and physically fit. They introduced themselves, seeking affirmation, reassurance, and answers.

They recounted their stories. Where they woke up. How each got there.

Sam came to in a room full of corpses. He found a crawl space that led to a hallway. The dark hallway led him to the Sanctuary.

Cora had been found in a cage, lying in a room full of rocks, by a man who would later be crushed by a door. Driven by terror, she found a hall that led her here.

Ashton had been in the Sanctuary the entire time. He claimed to have never encountered anyone until the hologram summoned them.

Despite his claim, Sam raised an eyebrow.

"Why don't we remember anything?" asked Cora.

"I think that's the point," muttered Ashton.

"What do you mean?" Cora was curious.

"Well, you heard what the giant hologram said."

Sam interjected, "What if it wasn't for us."

"How could it not be?" Ashton's ears pricked up. He couldn't believe they forgot what happened.

"Can someone please explain what's happening? My head hurts just trying to remember anything." Cora assisted herself with a tree while rubbing her head.

"AHH!" the wounded man hollered. The three bolted to attention, turning to the cry. Being so engaged in their conversation, they had forgotten he was even there.

"Should we help him?" asked Sam.

"And go out there? It's too dangerous." Ashton's eyebrows dropped.

It was ironic that this group banded together willingly and unconsciously. The present moment forced them into an alliance they weren't ready for—the same force driving every soul in this place toward the same uneasy conclusion. Little did this group know of the struggles and intentions of the others. That they were not alone in fear, isolation, and blindness.

"PLEASE!" The victim still required assistance.

"What do we do?" Cora asked as she hid behind a tree.

"I don't know! I'm trying to think," Ashton blared.

Sam stepped forward. "We should probably figure out how to get out."

"How can we do that with a crazy guy out there Sam?" Cora continued to cower.

"I have a feeling he's not the only one." Ashton peeked through the wood line, scanning the field. Kneeling, he observed the area.

"But wh—"

"SHH!" Ashton had his finger in front of his face. "You hear that?"

"Hear what?" Sam lowered beside Ashton.

"That man, he stopped."

All three peered out into the open, watching the lifeless body now stretched out. Motionless.

"Oh my God!" Cora recoiled, beginning to cry.

"Poor guy."

"Not our problem. We have to go." Ashton stood up and began to walk away. Sam and Cora quickly followed.

"Okay, where?" Sam pressed. He didn't take too kindly to Ashton's disregard for the dead man, but he kept this to himself.

"If there was a way in, there has to be a way out." Ashton marched on.

"But we can't leave that man…"

"He's dead Cora!"

Sam and Cora were pushed back by Ashton's voice. They stood in place for a moment. Sam gave Ashton a nod, then turned to Cora, who was now red eyed. He looked her in the eyes and bowed his head. No one could take that kind of pressure. Ashton eased up.

"Cora, we have to go. Try not to think about it." Ashton's voice held a hard edge.

"Kind of hard to do, don't you think?" Sam countered.

Sam was met with a deep stare, but he didn't back down. Ashton continued walking away.

"It's okay Cora. We'll get out of here," Sam reassured her.

Leading them on a straight path, Ashton had made his own bearing without explanation. Sam and Cora maintained some distance behind him, enough to keep him in sight. Compared to them, Ashton appeared to have adjusted well to the situation. For now, he was their only hope.

"Thanks Sam," Cora delivered a smile.

"Don't mention it. None of us know what's going on or why this is happening. I'm scared too but if we are going to make it out of here, we have to keep our heads up."

Sniffling, Cora dampened her shirt with tears.

"I'd tell you about myself, but I don't remember anything," Sam shrugged.

Cora giggled, "Maybe we will find out."

"That's the spirit!"

"Hey, guys up here!" Ashton stood still on top of a hill.

On the other side of where they stood, treetops radiated under the false stars. He had led them to a part where the ground was high enough to get a good view of the forest. Stretched out beyond the trees and brush, stood white tiled walls. The edge. Ashton wasted no time getting them out.

"Beyond those treetops is a wall," Ashton said with his finger pointing out. "If we stay straight, that wall will be our way out."

"How do you know this?" Sam asked, with an eyebrow raised.

"If we came through the wall, then there has to be a way out through it as well, right?"

Sam thought his logic was sound, but knowing what Ashton said earlier, it still raised concern. Sam glanced over to Cora for reassurance. When Ashton took off, Cora followed behind, leaving Sam to watch while he contemplated their actions.

Without much resistance, he caught up to Cora and whispered, "How does he know this if we can't remember?"

"I don't know, it does seem strange. But don't you think he will get us out of here? I don't want to be in danger, do you?" Cora said.

"Don't you think it's strange he said he has always been in the Sanctuary. We went through torture before ending up here." Sam was reluctant.

"I guess he's just lucky," Cora countered, walking away.

Sam let out a breath. It didn't take long for Cora to come to terms. He knew they were better off away from the corpses. The image of that half dead man burned in his mind. He couldn't help but wonder why it happened. What were his final thoughts? Like anyone would know. Poor guy. He died alone in the dark, probably just as confused as everyone else. Had he found someone—anyone—who could've helped, would he have lived?

A thorn tore at Sam's skin as his mind trailed, leaving his body following on autopilot. "Ouch!" He groaned covering his wound.

Cora turned, "Are you alright?"

Sam wiped the blood with his finger. "Yeah, I'm fine."

"Guys this way," Ashton called out ahead.

They moved deeper into the trees. The silence between them deepened. Leaves crackled beneath their feet, loud in the absence of words. Cora clung close to Sam, glancing nervously at Ashton, who led the way with sharp, assertive steps.

"I still think we're going the wrong way," Sam muttered.

"I'm telling you, it's this way," Ashton snapped, not even turning his head.

Cora looked between them. "Can we not argue right now? We don't even know what's out here."

"Then hurry up," Ashton said over his shoulder. "I'm done waiting around."

"You don't even know where we're going," Sam snapped, frustration lacing his voice.

Ashton halted.

He turned on his heel with predatory calm, his eyes cold and unreadable in the dark. "What did you say?"

"I said we don't know where we're going," Sam repeated, standing a little straighter. "You keep changing direction. You're guessing."

"I know what I'm doing." Ashton took a step closer. "You want to lead us instead?"

Cora put a hand on Sam's arm. "Drop it. Please."

Sam didn't back down. "I just think we should be careful. That's all."

Ashton's face twitched, his jaw tightening like a vise. He stepped forward, looming over Sam with hot menace. "You think this is a democracy?" he snarled, voice dripping with contempt. "You think we have the luxury to sit around and play pretend, like this is some Goddamn campfire discussion?"

"No, but—"

"Then shut up and follow me."

Cora stepped between them. "This isn't helping."

Ashton ignored her while his finger jabbed Sam's chest. "We move when I say. Or don't. You want to take your chances alone? Go ahead."

Sam's hands tightened into fists. He didn't say anything.

"That's what I thought." Ashton turned back around, muttering something under his breath.

They walked on again. The only sound the crunch of leaves and the occasional snap of a twig underfoot. Cora looked at Sam. Her voice was barely above a whisper. "You okay?"

He nodded. "I don't like him."

"I know. I don't either."

They didn't have time to say more. A nearby branch cracked—not from them.

All three froze.

"Did you two hear that?" Ashton asked. His hand slid toward his side, eyes darting through the dark tree line.

They stood motionless. The wind stilled. Even the insects went quiet.

Ashton stepped toward the trees. "Hey," he called out. "Who's there?"

No answer.

Cora grabbed Sam's wrist. Her palm was damp. "Sam..."

Ashton kept moving, gingerly now, scanning the brush. "Is anyone there?" His voice spiked, brittle with nerves.

He moved toward a thick pine trunk, narrowing his eyes as if he saw something just out of sight.

"Can we please go?" Cora's words pushed hard against the rising tension; every syllable soaked in dread.

Ashton lingered a second longer, then turned around. "Yeah," he said gruffly. "Let's go."

They moved—falling back into formation behind him, like before. Not because they trusted him. Not even because they believed him. Because they were too scared to be alone.

The trio trekked through the soft grass, eventually reaching a wall. The enclosed perimeter. To their right, a wall of trees, shrubs, and brush. To their left, a wall into heaven made of giant white tiles.

"Come on, keep up," Ashton advised.

Sam looked to Cora; she was sweating. Ashton's navigation abilities were dubious, though it was apparent he had skill. The group drifted to a stop as Ashton paused in the shadow of a corner. Sam and Cora didn't speak.

He turned right and began counting his steps to himself. "One… Two… Three."

"What's he doing?" Cora murmured to Sam.

"I have no idea," Sam whispered back.

"Fifteen… Sixteen… Seventeen."

On his final step, Ashton halted and turned toward the wall. Without constraint, he raised his hand and pressed his palm against a white tile. At once, its outline flared bright, light bleeding around the edges. Sam's eyes widened as the tile sank smoothly into the wall, revealing an opening.

Light spilled through the gap ahead. One by one, they leaned out, greeted by glaring white corridors lined with doors on either side—an all too familiar sight. Sam couldn't forget these halls, the same ones that had delivered him here. Still, he smiled, clinging to the idea that this time they might lead him out.

The trio piled through the exit one at a time. Sam crawled in last after he helped Cora through. Before his feet could touch the ground on the other side, the tile slid back into position.

"I guess there's no going back now," Cora said sternly.

"Let's hope not," replied Sam.

"Hope. Now that's a funny word." Ashton had eavesdropped on their conversation.

"What do you mean by that?" Cora asked.

Ashton scoffed and turned towards the end of the hall. "Are you both coming or not?"

As he trailed off in the distance, Sam looked to Cora. "What's with this guy?"

"I'm starting to wonder the same thing," she said. "This is kind of weird, right?"

"All of this is weird, but him, he definitely stands out as beyond that." Sam pointed down the corridor.

"Do you think he will actually help us?" Cora asked.

"I don't know. He doesn't seem to mind us tagging along… but I keep asking myself why," Sam said.

"Either stay with me or stay away! Your choice!" Ashton hollered from afar.

Sam clenched his jaw. Had he and Cora said too much?

Cora galloped towards Ashton. Sam locked in place, running the scenarios like a man defusing a bomb, analyzing his actions with potential outcomes. Looking back to where the tile had opened, he considered what was on the other side, what they had come from. Was it equal to what lay ahead?

"SAM!" Cora called out.

He turned to the call and followed.

[CH.15]

SHATTERED

PATHS

A tingling sensation crawled down his spine. A feeling James was beginning to become accustomed to and one that wouldn't be his last. He watched Nick and Ashley talk. Those two were the only ones standing out of the large group that had gathered.

Everyone else had taken a seat to rest; some of the group discussing their own plan of action. James laughed to himself. He thought of him and Ash—how from the very start, they were the only two not looking for a fight. Now, through happenstance, what was once just two, had become six. Far more than he cared to imagine, although it was enough to ease his conscience. Except for Sean. He was one too many. Seeing the bat drop again and again, splattering someone's brains, haunted his mind.

If Sean would do such a thing, what was everyone else capable of?

Could it happen again? Who here would be capable of such a horrible thing? Not Ashley, she couldn't. Nick seems smart. He has a voice the others seemed to follow. After all, he led his group to us.

James broke away from his thoughts. There was no use in feeding his paranoia. In this moment, everyone here was in the closest form of comfort they'd felt since awakening. Now, everyone seemed more at ease. Whether it was the group's numbers increasing or simply because no one was actively trying to kill each other, James couldn't say.

Upon arrival, Nick's group had lamented their lack of memories so many times that it made James wish he could forget as well. But it did raise concern. No one knew how Elias had survived this long in his fragile state, whether the doctor was truly a doctor, or if Raspberry was really a politician at all. No one knew if any of it mattered.

The moment anything came close to clarity, something new arrived to obscure it. More people, more space, more questions. Everything here was growing. Would this subside?

"How long have you been here?" Nick asked Ashley.

They were pacing along the wall, while the rest of the group sat with each other, backsides against the white tiled walls. None of them dared to turn away from the woods.

"Well… since I've been timing it all on my watch, approximately seven hours," Ashley explained. "I don't know what time it is, just how long we've been here. Not like it matters though."

"Good use of a watch. I'd do the same," Nick nodded.

"Have the four of you been together this entire time?" Ashley asked.

"No, just me and the bloke in the suit. You don't want to know where we woke up. I found the others once the shooting started."

"Good to know they weren't the ones shooting," James interjected, half smiling. He was met with blank expressions from the group, even from Ashley. "So, you two know how we can get out of here?" he quickly asked.

"I've had some ideas," Nick rubbed his red eyes.

"I'd love to hear them," Ashley said, arms crossed, standing still.

"Are your eyes okay?" James questioned.

"Yeah. It seems I'm someone who needs glasses, unfortunately that doesn't matter right now."

"Right, what matters is getting out of here!" Raspberry exclaimed from the ground. Although the doctor was able to treat his wound, it was only temporary. Blood had soaked through his new bandages.

"I think we can all agree on that," James looked to everyone.

Luke focused intently on Raspberry's wound. His hands were stained with blood, seeping into the grass like ink. Elias, though physically there, seemed miles away, his mind adrift in some distant place, muttering to himself as if the world around him no longer existed.

"Where'd you find him, Nick?" James asked, gesturing to Elias.

"He was with the doctor when we started running from the shots. I don't really know anything else," Nick replied, still focused on the tiled wall behind him.

"Luke, was it? Where did you find him?" Ashley asked, probing for more details.

"When there was shooting, I found him on the other side of a mound in these woods. I started treating him instinctively and then Nick showed up. Shouldn't we be focusing on getting out of here?"

James raised an eyebrow, about to speak, but Nick interjected. "He's right. We really shouldn't waste any more time here."

Ashley uncrossed her arms and tapped her chin thoughtfully. Her eyes rolled upward and a soft 'hmm' escaped her. James admired her tactful thinking, though his thoughts always involuntarily drifted back to her.

"Have any ideas?" Nick broke the silence.

"Well, if we go the way we came in, we could try that." Ashley kept pondering.

"Do you remember which way that was?" Luke turned from his patient.

"I have an idea. I would have to get my bearings here to be sure, otherwise it's just a guess," she said, gripping her backpack straps.

James felt Ashley holding back. Her ability to get them to safe places was not far from flawless. She was either bluffing or did much better under pressure than she let on.

"What if we try breaking through the wall, Ash?"

"How do you expect us to do that, James?" Ashley's skepticism broke the mood.

"I don't know. Just throwing out ideas."

"Well, maybe try a reasonable idea," Raspberry added, his voice laced with sarcasm.

"You know," Nick turned toward the trees, "that might be possible."

Every head turned toward Nick.

"With these trees being high enough and your gear, Ashley, maybe we could generate enough force to break a hole through this wall."

"These walls could be solid steel or made of some material we've never even heard of. This building has been shifting constantly. It led us here," Ashley countered.

"Then maybe it will lead us out?" Nick said, more openly.

James noticed Nick didn't smile much, despite his composure. Perhaps it was simply objectivity.

"I don't think it works like that." Ashley's forehead creased.

"To be fair, Ash, we don't really know how anything works here," James chimed in with a trace of confidence. "Did you forget I opened that tile? When we were with Sean?" His face turned uneasy.

Ashley, genuinely having forgotten much of what had happened recently, felt the weight of it all. The shock from Sean, the bat, the documents—it all came rushing back. Trying to hold onto a memory felt increasingly difficult.

"Did you all forget what the hologram said?" Nick was incredulous. "SmartArk? Memory suppression? Smart AI architecture! This all just happened!"

Everyone paused, processing his words. Other than James, everyone's forehead furrowed. It hadn't really dawned on them, the small details they'd forgotten so soon.

"I'll be honest Nick. We've been together the entire time, and I forgot some of that." Raspberry turned to him with round eyes.

"I can second that," Ashley said, looking away.

Worry carved deep lines into James' expression.

What does she remember?

"It's quite possible that it could be due to this memory suppression Nick mentioned," Luke suggested. "If we are suffering short term memory loss, it could be connected."

"Except it doesn't seem to affect me." Nick raised his hand.

"Me too." James proclaimed, "I remember mostly everything that's happened in here."

"Every procedure has a margin of error," Luke stood up, speaking softly, eyes darting around. "If that's possible, then it could be that some of us remember everything."

"Everything?" James raised an eyebrow.

The sudden shock of sound electrified everyone, sending them sprawling to the dirt. Fingers drove into eardrums to block the high-pitched whine. Black veins returned to the surface of their skin as they all seized, strangled by the resonance. James, hellbent to get answers, cringed with his hands over his ears, letting out a raw scream to fend off the piercing pitch. His head jerked upright and his eyes bulged from their sockets. Trapped in place, his jaw locked and his teeth ground together as the black veins overtook his face. His eyes locked onto Ashley. She buried her nose into the ground, seizing neck down.

Before he could blink, it was over.

Everyone gasped for air as they resurfaced, coughing and choking on what little oxygen they had left. Ashley drew the deepest breath, motioning the rest to follow. James inflated his lungs, and they held still. One drawn out exhale later, he was back to his feet.

"Is everyone okay?" Luke's shadow loomed over them.

James hunched over. "I-I think so. My head… it's throbbing."

"What just happened!?" Raspberry shrieked.

"I—," Nick broke off, coughing twice, voice raw, "I think they don't want us talking." He threw his arms out and sucked in a deep breath.

"What do you mean? What were we just talking about?" Luke bent to help Elias.

"Wait, you don't remember?" James straightened, ears pricking like a startled deer. "Ash, what do you remember from one minute ago?"

She had her arm braced against the wall, too weak to stand. "I don't know, James. Does it matter?"

"Well," Nick said with a humorless grin, "looks like our batch learned something."

Ashley's head snapped toward him. "What are you talking about?"

"You haven't figured it out yet?" James asked, tilting his head at her. "Where did you wake up, Ashley?"

She ran a trembling hand through her hair. "I… can't remember. Everything's still hazy, James."

"Yet you remember his name." Nick crossed his arms.

Luke joined in. "So… we can remember names but forget everything else?"

"Some of us forget everything. Not everyone." James said, standing taller now.

"There's no point in explaining this." Nick's hands swept across the blank white tiles. "We have to stop that thing."

James rubbed his throbbing temple and turned toward the forest beyond the wall—a black maw of trees. He understood what Nick meant now. The hologram's words echoed back: *memory suppression as control.* Back then, he didn't know what it meant. Now, he did.

"I'm getting out of here," Raspberry announced, rising as if his injured foot had never existed.

"I have to agree. We can't afford to waste time," Luke stepped between Elias and Raspberry, steadying them both.

"Fine. Don't." Nick continued exploring the wall.

"Nick, you can't be serious," Raspberry pleaded.

"Go with them, Rasp. I've helped you as much as I can." Nick nodded to the bandaged man in a suit.

"Ashley, what do you think?" James approached her. Only an arm's length away, he wanted to brace her shoulder—a tiny, simple gesture to show he cared. A light touch of the hand to remind her he was there. He held back and kept his hands by his sides instead.

"I want to get out of here. I'm not concerned with anything else," she said.

"What if we can stop the sound? What if we can remember?" His eyes gleamed.

"And what if it does nothing, James? There's no guarantee. When you're in a storm, you push through it. You don't try to stop it. You can't." She tightened her backpack.

"This might help us—"

"Survive? No, I've been helping us do that." Ashley backtracked to the edge of the forest.

"Where are you going?" Nick asked, eyes still transfixed on the wall.

"I'm going to find my way back the way we came."

"You can't be serious! The shooter could still be out there," James said urgently.

"I know what I'm doing." Sternly, she took one step into the woods.

"Let her go, James. We can do it ourselves," Nick said.

Appalled, James stood silent, his hair standing on end. His body shuddered as her bitterness hit him.

She'd be willing to leave just like that? After everything? Why would she save me, why bother helping me escape the shooter? She wouldn't do that… would she? I don't understand.

"Rasp, Luke, Elias, do you think it would be best to join her?" Nick motioned, throwing his head back.

Luke paused, looking at the two injured men and then to Ashley. He wasn't sure she was as willing to help like Nick was. He also didn't want anything to do with whatever it was Nick and James had in mind. They'd all been in this hellhole long enough; he'd rather not go deeper.

"You can come, Luke." Ashley's face lit up as she looked back at the others. "But you have to keep up. My eyes will be up front, not on anyone else."

James noticed a shift in Ashley's demeanor.

Did the last shock of that sound rattle her brain? Did she forget too much or remember just enough?

He found this sudden change to be a burden, not the reminder it was meant to be. The reminder that he didn't know who they were. Who he was. Perhaps he should've listened to the hologram a bit more seriously. His eyelids shut as he recollected the hologram's message.

"Ah… Subject 333. We've been watching you closely."

"In time, James, you will learn what must be learned. For now, heed this: the SmartArk is an experiment."

What study was he referring to? What did James have to do with any of this, and why? It was gradually tearing him apart inside—this inexorable pondering of his own past. The whereabouts of this fucking nightmare. The mere fact the building made no logical sense in its design.

"You are among the many to experience the SmartArk—an AI-structured facility approved by the Federation for full-spectrum psychological observation. Its architecture shifts in tandem with cognitive behavior, so what appears anomalous… is merely adaptive. In time, you will understand."

The words replayed over and over in his ears.

The Federation? AI? Every time I get more information, I just have more questions. I just wanted some help. Ashley's help.

James held his head low and stared at the sage grass. Where he stood, it was the perfect height like that of a fresh-cut lawn. Swaying slightly as a breeze barreled by. Impossibly real. James swallowed. It wasn't real. It was all encased by a massive white tiled cube. A manufactured forest of death.

"We have to go now." Ashley glanced over at James. He was still staring at the grass. "James," Ashley said firmly, "good luck."

He rolled his neck up, locked eyes, and nodded. She responded with the same gesture before marching forward into the tree line. He remained still and hurt.

She looked at me as if she didn't remember a thing. I remember.

James became immobile. He watched as the other four trailed off into the unknown. He witnessed Ashley leave him behind.

"She's gone," Nick said bluntly. "It doesn't matter now mate."

James met his gaze. "What does matter Nick?"

"Remembering James. Remembering."

[CH.16]

T R E A D I N G
T H E
L I N E

Now that Ashley was gone, neither Nick nor James had any sense of time. The fake stars above the Sanctuary stayed locked in place, frozen against the ceiling like a painted sky. With brightness at a minimum, it made no difference to the two men. They'd become accustomed to the dark. Nick had moved on from their original location and followed the wall south. At least that's what direction he told James it was.

Probably makes a compass in his head like Ash.

He smacked a tile here and there, pausing to stare at a spot he found peculiar, only to move on to another. James tagged along and stayed quiet. Nick seemed to not care what James did as long as he didn't get in the way. To him they shared a common goal—which usually makes things easier.

"James," Nick said running his fingers between two tiles. "Why don't you help me out. You mentioned earlier you were able to open a path."

"Oh," James was surprised by his curiosity. "Yeah, before we walked into the Sanctuary, I had moved a tile."

"Elaborate."

"I don't know. I remember going off about how we might be able to change our path or something like that. I was flustered at the time. W—we had found a paper, a few actually. One about fungus. The other one was about the smart architecture."

"The same thing the hologram bloke told us?"

"Yes. I'm beginning to think so. Nick why can we remember? Like, things from earlier."

"I don't know." Nick took a break from analyzing the wall.

"The sound, it doesn't seem to affect us. Well other than the feeling like dying part," James scoffed. "Ashley… she should've remembered. I don't know why she can't."

"No use in thinking about it. She's gone. She didn't mind leaving you in a hurry, I doubt she cares as much."

"Hey! You don't know her." James' eyes sparked with fire.

"And you don't know anyone here. Calm down." Nick was unsympathetic. "It's not a coincidence we aren't suffering short term memory loss. They can hit us all they want with that sound, but there's no such thing as coincidence. We have to stop it."

James' breath was deep. "I think the building adjusts to us. I don't know how to explain it. In that moment when we were with Sean, I just didn't want to be in the room with him. So, I smacked the wall, and it all changed."

Pupils moved left as Nick grabbed his chin. James was glad he didn't ask who Sean was. *He just kept dropping that bloody bat.* Perhaps Nick was rather preoccupied with the task at hand. Contrarily, James thought about the cop who he had almost forgotten. The inimical man, nameless, threatening. Nick was lucky to not have run into him or Sean. James felt like he had it the worst, with Nick completely oblivious to the circumstances he encountered.

Nick hummed to himself, intrigued. Unlike the others, he looked for patterns or what he would call an algorithm. Some order among the chaos. Where the others saw carnage and anarchy, he was able to see patterns.

A humid breeze swept across Nick's face, pulling with it every bit of moisture from his eyes. Squeezing both eyelids shut, he tried to alleviate his red eyes with whatever water was left in his body. Right now, his mind had better vision than his eyes—something he knew would not last long.

James watched as Nick pinched the bridge of his nose. "We should get going. I don't think we will find anything here. These walls have to intersect at some point," he said.

"Alright, let's find an intersection. Good thinking James." Nick led with James behind as they continued South down the wall. This time, not fiddling around, smacking tiles.

It wasn't long before they reached the corner of the Sanctuary. The woods stretched like a National Forest, except enclosed by mile-high walls, seamlessly interconnected in a labyrinth of misery. Weaving in and out of holes, caves, tiles, and cages were a bunch of confused lab rats, and James was done being one of them.

"I think there's something here." James shook his head before placing a finger in the intersecting crease.

"Maintenance?" Nick recovered during their stroll. Well, recovered enough to where he wasn't clawing at his eyes every five seconds.

"Exactly. Even if this place changes like it's random—"

"—it was still built by someone."

Their synchronicity felt almost effortless. James found himself toying with the idea of their friendship. He wasn't sure, but he allowed himself to hope. He clung to the possibility that, when their memories returned, it would all make sense—that they had known each other all along. That Ashley would remember and she would come back.

"I wasn't certain if there was one back with the group. Honestly, I'm still not sure they even exist at all. It just makes sense that they would." Nick stood back and watched James drive his left digits into a tile.

"Yeah, this doesn't look like a place for janitors," James chuckled. "By the way, I'm glad the killing each other part doesn't make sense to you." He caressed a sharp edge of a tile on the wall.

"I might have lost my memory, but I haven't lost my wits."

Well, maybe your sight. James kept that thought to himself.

CLICK!

The wall gripped James' fingers in the deep crease, its surface tightening around him. He fought to pull them free. His muscles strained as a bead of sweat raced down his cheek. Doubt gnawed at him. Had the facility ensnared him? Turned him into a puppet without him even realizing it?

Fuck! What'd I do?

The ground rumbled as a bright light projected from the corner, flooding the thin slit in front of them. The two had front-row seats to the detonation of a nuclear bomb.

"GOD DAMMIT!" James was tired of these relentless night and day antics. He clenched his jaw and turned away. Letting light settle, the duo became concrete. One could mistake their stillness for meditation. James gradually opened his eyelids before staring off into hallway-heaven. He managed to grant himself access to the unknown a second time. Raising his shoulders, he didn't feel the least bit empowered.

"You have no idea how you did that, do you?" Nick asked, back on his feet.

"I can't explain it."

"Don't." Nick strode past James into the hallway. "Just get us to the location of that sound."

James nodded and walked with Nick into the light. Leaving the Sanctuary behind, he reminded himself. *Whatever happens, we can't go back there. We have to shut this thing down and then I'll find Ashley.*

[CH.17]

THE
MACHINE

It had only been a few minutes before Nick grew tired of James' anxious questions. He had grown restless.

"I still don't understand it," James muttered, taking the lead down the white tiled corridor, avoiding the doors he passed. They were scattered down the hall like normal, not significant to him, only to Nick. "She just didn't seem that way."

"Really." Nick stopped sternly with his brows low. "You still haven't figured it out yet, huh?"

James halted and turned his side profile to Nick. "What do you mean?"

Corners creased as Nick's mouth tightened. He fumbled with another doorknob. Locked.

"This isn't the place for thinking about things like that. You don't know these people."

James looked down, his head at a slant. *I don't know anything about this place.* He kept silent and let Nick continue.

"I suggest we crack on and get about our plan so we can leave. Now, start checking these doors, will ya?"

He couldn't argue with Nick. James strode parallel to him, and they continued checking the doors on both sides of the hall. Locked. Locked. Locked. Locked. Could he expect one to be open? James wrestled with his optimism, hoping for a way out. If he found two paths now, why not a door that could open? He thought about motioning to Nick to break one down. It wasn't worth the energy.

This went on for a while—both working cooperatively to find something, anything, that would lead them to their objective. To stop the unknown sound in an unknown place filled with blind hatred and violence. An endeavor to reclaim memories in what seemed like an impossible situation. Though they had their own reasons to find a solution, they worked in harmony. It wasn't perfect, but it worked well enough.

Click!

"Finally!" James shouted. "Nick, come here!"

By the time Nick crossed the hall, the door had already swung open. Inside the room, metal chairs were scattered around rectangular tables, clean and perfect like the rooms James had entered before. To the right of the door, a table slightly larger than the others was placed perpendicular, featuring a single chair and a cup full of writing utensils.

Nick moved to the counter and grabbed a pen or two. He clicked the pen and scribbled on his hand. A tiny black stain was enough, so he pocketed the pen. He then moved on, finding two drawers in the large table. Gripping the handle, he slowly moved to open it.

"More papers?" James asked, peering over Nick's shoulder.

Nick rifled through the mixed sheets, hoping something would catch his eye. Nothing was interesting, so he shut the drawer and tried the other one. Inside, he found some information on Smart Architecture, similar to the documents James had seen with Ashley. Nick continued, but once again found nothing useful.

"It's a bust. Let's go."

"Really? Nothing in there was remotely compelling?"

Nick left without saying anything else and went back to checking doors. This continued for another hour until James broke the silence.

"I think we should try something else."

Nick, shaking one last handle before standing tall, rubbed his tired eyes. "And what would you suggest?"

"I don't know. Find another area. Go another direction."

"We've been walking straight for God knows how long. What direction would we go? Back to where we came?"

It didn't dawn on James that they had been moving in a straight line. Unlike other parts of the structure, there hadn't been any intersections, trap doors, or death traps. It was just a long, narrow hallway. Infinite. No end, no beginning.

Although James had no intention of turning back, he glanced behind him, just to be sure. The light absorbed the depth of the hallway, blurring what was already past.

The two let silence accompany the space between them. They took advantage of it, breathing in a moment of clarity. If only that was possible. Nick thought about continuing and how the odds would inevitably be in their favor. James, however, only had one thought on his mind: *RUN*.

Neither moved. They simply stared at each other, then at the floor, then at a door, then back at each other. Several rounds of glances passed before something stopped them both.

Clank.

Simultaneously, Nick and James looked to the sky. With a snap like lightning, a tile gave way and something blurred past, smashing into the floor.

SPLAT!

The space turned red and black as liquid jettisoned in all directions. James in awe wiped his palm across his eyelids, then looked down. His hand was covered in blood. He gasped.

Nick took a step forward, investigating the pool below. Streaks of blood and gore spewed from under the open ceiling. Before they could look up, the tile locked back into place.

Silent, Nick tiptoed closer. The body was completely decimated. The head was gone, though some brains remained. An arm and a leg had made their way in opposite directions down the hall, and a shoe lay beside where the head probably hit the floor from what Nick assumed.

"That had to be a long drop," Nick murmured.

James refused to get any closer. He watched Nick analyze the bits and pieces. The clothes were the only things intact. Impossibly, there was one more thing that survived the fall: a pair of black glasses beside the wall to Nick's right.

Nick grabbed the glasses, wiped the blood off with his shirt, and put them on. The right lens was cracked and they weren't quite his prescription. James watched Nick smirk as he rose.

Now what are the chances of that?

"Nick, can you see?" James asked.

"I think so. We should get going now."

"Um, yeah. I-I think we should forget about the doors," James stumbled over the puddle on the floor trying to catch up with Nick. "I guess we're not going to question what just happened?"

"Nope. Let's just move a bit faster, yeah?" Nick started to jog.

James trailed behind. He stared up at the ceiling above wondering if it could happen again, remembering how he fell into a trap back in the cave.

That could have been me. It still could be me.

"James," Nick said halting. "Look!"

James tripped and caught himself before he hit the end. There was nothing but a blank wall in front of him. An end cap to the long rectangular corridor. Centered on this block was a single door. Nick confronted the handle with a tight grip and a stern look. He turned to James, greeting him with a single nod, driving his hand in a downward fashion. Calmly, he pushed forward and watched the door open. James was ready to see the other side as if he'd expect anything different. It was like looking into a mirror. It was the same as their current situation. Another straight hall.

"You're kidding me!" James threw his hands up.

"It's something different; this is good." Nick proceeded in.

"How is this any good? It's the exact same thing. We're going nowhere!"

"I have a feeling. Keep going mate." Nick waved.

It wasn't long until James noticed a difference. There were fewer doors, and something sounded like a hum. A low reverb filled the air. He wasn't sure if Nick heard it, but as they continued the reverb grew. He felt something was about to change very soon. Panting, he kept up.

"Slow down, will you?" he barked at Nick.

"You see that, James? I see something." Nick's arms swayed, showing no signs of slowing down.

"You finally hear it too?"

"Now that you mention it, yes. Though that's not what I'm talking about." Nick decelerated. "You see that up ahead?"

James, beside him, tried to make out what Nick was talking about. He had no idea what the hell it could be. "Um no."

"There, to the left."

A good distance away, there was a solitary door. Squinting his eyes, James leaned forward. "The handle's different on that door up there?"

"Exactly!"

Without any further discussion, they made their way to the unusual entryway. With one brief glance at each other, James took the lead and grabbed the handle. Once the door was ajar, there was another moment of silence. The flash of a body exploding on the ground shook James. The moment passed when Nick shoved him through.

Empty and barren, they walked directly into a small rectangular room. Walls so sharp, their corners could cut. No more doors to fiddle with here, other than the one they came through. Once Nick was completely inside, the door closed. Automatically, he reached behind for the handle, not surprised by what he found.

"Let me guess, it's locked?" James felt his stomach drop.

"How about you start guessing a way out of here instead?" Nick searched the blank space.

James crossed his arms and lowered his head, watching Nick as he danced around with his feet and hands, tapping white tiles at random. He knew what Nick was trying to do. He just wasn't interested right now. Something about being trapped really put him down.

I mean, what could possibly help us in this room? We'll probably end up in another hallway. I could use the break. James sat down. *I bet*

Ashley would find a way out. Hell, we probably wouldn't even be in this mess.

The image of a head getting beaten by a bat resurfaced in his mind again, only for a moment. James reevaluated. *Actually, it might be safer here. Maybe I should stay near the wall so I don't fall through the floor. Not too close though—I don't want to fall through the wall, or both!*

James repositioned himself into what he assumed was the safest spot. He continued watching Nick conduct his research. Every now and then, he pushed the broken glasses onto the bridge of his nose, only to have them slide down every time he looked at the floor. Nick was adamant, counting each tile he walked over, then raising his head to count the adjacent tiles that extended into the ceiling and around to the other side.

Each row, column, and square inch would be analyzed thoroughly before Nick found it irrelevant. James saw the pedant he was. Out of all the people he had encountered, he was more comfortable with Nick's obsessive compulsion than the latter violence.

"What do you plan on finding in here? It's a dead end," James said, still sitting with his arms crossed.

"Or maybe it's a way in."

Nick's optimism was impressive. Or maybe it was just perseverance. Whatever the case, if it was helpful, James found no issues with it. Watching Nick investigate provided much needed positivity that had been missing since Ashley walked away. Maybe it would get better.

"Hey, come check this o—"

James was upright before Nick could even finish the sentence. He hustled over to see Nick's hand caressing a small, conspicuous block that, from a distance, was hardly observable. It was about five and a half feet up from the floor on the east wall. About four inches in diameter, it was embedded within one of the larger tiles that made up the side.

Although Nick was eager to seek an anomaly, he hesitated to move any further. His hand hovered in the air.

"What are you waiting for?" James pressured. "Press it!"

"I'm thinking."

"Thinking about what?" Without delay, James slammed a fist into the mini-tile and watched it depress. A loud cranking noise sounded off and the two men stepped back. Their heads rose in unison as the entire wall in front of them levitated.

The analog *CLANK, CLANK, CLANK* echoed as the tiled wall receded into the ceiling. Behind it, the white light of a dying star pierced through. James palmed his eyes and Nick grew eager. Behind the opening was a neo-Victorian contraption that stood as tall as the wall that housed it.

Jutting out from both the top and sides were large steel pipes that circumvented the device. It was held together with large rivets and iron brackets. A warm reverb rumbled and vibrated the floor. On the front of the running engine were both large and small cogs that appeared to be driving something. Arrows were embossed into the metal body showing the rotational direction of each gear. Small decals were scattered around that Nick had already begun reading. They mentioned the names of each auxiliary segment housed in this apparent steam-powered device.

The machine reached so high that Nick concluded there was no use in climbing it just to read a few hundred labels scattered about. Around the gears, spun three belts that rolled off into different areas of the contraption. Two were made of metal, what seemed like chain links, and one in particular was made of rubber.

Nick turned to the floor, his gaze hollow. Without a word, he crushed his glasses with his heel, the lenses splintering into jagged fragments. It was as if the need for clarity had evaporated, that seeing the truth was something beyond clear vision.

[CH.18]

INTO

DARKNESS

"Can you slow down a bit?" Raspberry was failing to follow Ashley's lead.

She moved ahead with purpose, her rate neither too fast nor too slow, but enough to leave the others behind. Luke, understanding that they'd be weaker without her, kept his grip firm on Raspberry, forcing his way through the thickening thorns surrounding them. Surprisingly, Elias trailed behind without issue and without a word.

"There's a storm brewing and I ain't gonna be around for it. So keep it up. You signed on for this," Ashley lectured, like she had repeated it a thousand times.

The group endured and formed a line formation as they pressed on through the dense brush. None of them had a clear direction.

Except Ashley. Her boldness hooked into the others and obediently they followed.

The four of them squeezed out of the thick and into an open field. The stars above shone down, casting a haze over the glade. Ashley scanned the horizon, squinting before turning to the false sky above.

Elias watched her with muted admiration, noting her nature and the way she gathered information. She was a woman of action, and he knew that she wouldn't stop until she had a plan.

Turning to Luke, who was supporting a limping Raspberry, Elias saw a man broken by the burden of circumstance; the telltale signs of infection were already creeping in. The suffering went unnoticed by everyone, even Raspberry, who pressed on courageously, ignoring the pain that gnawed at him.

"Come on, this way," Ashley said, pressing forward. The others followed, though Raspberry's progress slowed.

"Any idea where you're going?" Luke asked, his voice curious.

Ashley kept her eyes forward, but her words were clear, "I have an idea."

Luke smirked, lowering his brow, the indifference in his eyes betraying his lack of concern for her response. All that mattered was keeping up, nothing else. They crossed the glade, the brief respite from the thick brush offering a fleeting sense of relief before they would plunge back into the next round of unforgiving thorns.

To their surprise, the other end of the field was indeed a thick of trees, but not with predatory plants. Ashley was the first to cram herself between two trunks. Elias followed, then Raspberry, and then Luke. Luke would be there to grab Raspberry's suit jacket if he tripped over his decaying leg. When Raspberry was grounded, the rest pushed on.

Ashley reveled in the rare freedom, her feet hitting the soft earth without the constant sting of thorns tearing at her skin. There was a grace to her, a natural ease in the way she moved through the woods. She was in her element now. A stark contrast to the tension they'd left behind. It was as if the forest itself had become her ally.

BANG!

A shot rang out through the trees above. Ashley and Elias hit the ground. Raspberry screamed and fell, clutching his leg while trying to shield his face. Luke took a knee, trying to assess the situation.

"I think it wasn't at us," Luke whispered, trying to stay calm.

Ashley, always vigilant, gave a small nod before rising to her feet. "He's right. Let's keep moving." She picked up the pace allowing Raspberry to lag.

"We should really wait for everyone," Luke said.

"He'll catch up." Ashley didn't look back.

BANG! BANG!

As they moved, more shots rang out, sending a branch crashing to the ground near them.

"I think you're both fucking wrong!" Raspberry yelled from afar.

Luke and Ashley quickly dropped back down. "Look!" Luke exclaimed with a finger forward.

Through the collection of trees stood a man, pistol in hand. A grin stretched across his face from cheek to cheek, his eyes drowning in death.

Ashley surveyed her surroundings, her mind racing. Elias was gone, lost in the chaos. Dwelling on him was futile now. Her gaze locked onto the man ahead. She was unarmed and vulnerable. Her eyes darted to a branch—just out of reach. She considered tackling him from behind, but the odds were slim.

"Ashley, what's the plan?" Luke hastened over to her.

Ashley snapped back, "He's far enough away, we should run."

"What about Raspberry?" Luke asked.

"He can't even wa-"

BANG! BANG! BANG!

More rounds zipped past, their whiz now deafening. Too close for comfort. The tree Ashley had taken cover behind erupted in a shower of debris, sending her crashing to the ground. Luke shielded his face and darted left. As Ashley sprawled on the grass, she crawled toward a fallen tree trunk, using it as cover. When she finally peeked over, Luke was gone. Standing ahead, a man with a lingering, manic grin gripped a gun—like a loon, reckless and unfazed. She knew, without a doubt, he was out of his mind.

A bead of sweat trickled down her cheek as her eyes remained locked on the advancing threat. Her mind spun with countless scenarios, each playing out in what felt like an eternity. Should she grab the branch to her left? What if she hid and tackled him over the fallen tree? Was it worth the risk of reaching for the pistol? The image of her head being blown off flashed repeatedly, haunting her thoughts. She cycled through every possibility, her sweat turning into a torrential downpour as fear washed over her.

Then she heard it. The click of the firearm. The pin finding out there wasn't a casing to hit. No more chain reaction, just the sound of an empty magazine hitting the ground.

She lowered her right hand onto the downed tree, thrust her body over the obstacle, and engaged her quads to their fullest extent. Her arms pulled on air and her eyes locked on. Just meters away, the loon pulled out another magazine and drove it upwards. As the magazine entered the handle and a round entered the chamber, she froze.

Breathing rapidly, she stood face to face with the creep. She witnessed his beige outfit and its asylum logo. His blood covered skin. She saw the evil in his eyes. Her beating heart ceased.

The pistol was readied to her face. Ashley stared down the barrel and thought of nothing else.

WHAM!

Blood sprayed from the back of the man's head as he dropped to his knees. His body collapsed in front of her. Standing over him, breathing heavily, was Elias, wielding a thick branch. His breath came in ragged waves as he stood, staring down at the maniac.

Ashley blinked, taking a step back. "Elias? Elias!" She rushed to him, wrapping her arms around his frail body. "Thank you!" She noticed his blank eyes, the vacancy that lingered there. "Elias, are you okay?"

He didn't respond. He was a statue, motionless, with eyes fixed in a distant trance.

"Ashley!" Luke yelled, approaching the two. He noticed Elias standing over the loon. "Did he do that?"

"Where's Raspberry?" Ashley asked.

"I thought you weren't concerned with him," Luke scoffed.

"Yeah, fuck me right," Raspberry muttered. "I'm still dying here, you know."

"Come on. Let's get out of here," Ashley motioned for everyone to follow. Luke attended to Elias, prying him away from the scene.

It wouldn't be long before the four were reunited side by side. The group moved on, the tension still heavy in the air. Ashley, a little on edge, slowed down as they approached another stretch of white tiles. The towering structure, reaching toward the sky, seemed endless. She scanned it from left to right, but the path remained as shrouded as ever.

"Wait..." Ashley's eyes caught something.

Broken branches. Trodden grass. She gestured for them to follow. They came upon a narrow breach in the barrier, wide enough to suggest escape. Its edges were worn but promised a way forward.

"Looks like I found a way out of here. Let's go." Ashley went in first, followed by a broken Raspberry and Elias.

The doctor paused and noticed the trail left behind. "Are you sure this is safe?"

"Does it matter at this point? We need to hurry. Get in." She pressed on into the all-too-familiar hallways of white, glistening with unusual cleanliness in a place of grimy death.

Raspberry's blood drenched the tiles as he limped over them. Ashley couldn't help but admire his indomitable will, despite his condition.

The wall instantly receded behind them.

"I'll never get used to that," said Ashley, watching the seamless white tile slot back into place behind Luke with a quiet hiss. The echo of the wall's closure hovered in the air like an unfinished sentence. The corridor's antiseptic gleam cast their shadows long and uneasy.

Luke turned to Ashley with fire behind his eyes. "You froze back there," he said, voice low and needlelike. "If Elias hadn't shown up, you'd be dead. We'd all be dead!"

Ashley kept her arms crossed. "You're the one to talk. Don't lecture me about freezing."

"I was trying to circle behind him," Luke snapped. "You didn't have a plan. You just stood there, waiting to die."

Elias remained silent, his gaze distant, focused somewhere far beyond them.

Ashley stepped forward, eyes narrow. "Okay, so what's *your* plan then?" Her shoulders rolled back and her chest puffed.

"Maybe, my plan is not trusting someone who can't hold her nerve," Luke shot back. "Or did you forget Raspberry's still leaking like a sieve?"

Raspberry grunted. "Please, by all means, continue fighting while I die standing."

Ashley turned her head and exhaled sharply. "Fine. Then follow me or don't. I don't care anymore."

Elias, wordlessly, moved first. The others reluctantly followed.

They walked deeper into the hallway. The silence between them amplified. Even Raspberry, usually full of complaints, stayed quiet. Elias walked like a man already lost, and Luke's glances at Ashley spoke volumes.

They walked on until something caught Raspberry's eye.

"Wait, look," Raspberry pointed to the floor.

Faint streaks of red led away from them. A trail of blood, faint but unmistakable. It wasn't fresh, but it was deliberate, human.

Ashley crouched down. "Blood?"

"And footprints," Raspberry added.

"Looks like whoever came through here was in a hurry." Luke observed the trail.

"Another blood-ridden villain? Great." Raspberry clenched his jaw.

Ashley stood up, "Let's go."

They followed the trail in silence. It weaved slightly left, occasionally vanishing and reappearing like a glitch in reality.

The corridor's brightness subtly shifted as they walked—imperceptible at first, until a wider section opened before them. There, to the left, embedded deep in the wall, was a pane of glass taller than a man and three times as wide. It framed a scene of bizarre, pulsing blue arcs of energy. These arcs danced between metallic prongs, rotating in concentric rings around an empty center. The inner rim shimmered, like disturbed water reflecting static light. No switches, no labels, just structures twisted together in a strange ballet of light and energy.

Ashley took a step forward, mesmerized. "What the hell is this?"

Raspberry gasped and shifted his weight to his good leg, "Looks like the bastard child of a generator and a church window."

Luke stepped closer, squinting at the interior mechanics. "I don't see any power cables or maintenance access. Just… energy."

Ashley stood still, arms crossed. The subtle thrum of the structure made her skin crawl. It wasn't just a machine. It felt *aware*.

Raspberry pointed with a grimy finger. "If Nick were here, he'd probably know what this is."

The words fell into the air and stayed there. Ashley's mouth twitched. She looked away from the wall and back down the corridor. For a second, her mind wandered, not to Nick, but to James. His stubborn idealism. The way he kept trying to protect people even when he was just as scared as the rest of them. His constant questioning. She crushed the thought.

"We should move." Ashley stepped forward.

"You sure? You've been staring into that glass like it's about to answer you," Luke said, his tone bordering mockery.

Ashley turned her eyes on him. "And you look like you got discharged from a haunted hospital."

Luke raised his eyebrows.

"Nice scrubs, by the way. Really instills confidence," she snarked.

Raspberry smirked behind her. Luke frowned and looked down at his pale blue pants, the dried blood and grime soaking the hem.

Ashley took one last glance at the machine, then turned her back to it completely. "Let's press on."

Behind her, Elias waited near the edge of the corridor, eyes locked not on the wall but somewhere far beyond it. Somewhere far beyond anything they could conceive. He hadn't said a word since the blow. The blow had silenced more than the shooter. They moved on, but none of them truly left the machine behind. It shivered once more as they disappeared down the hall.

The group continued, guided by Ashley and the corridor's endless stretch. Behind them, the glass wall faded into memory—just another anomaly among countless others. They walked in silence for some time. Even Raspberry held his tongue, limping with steady rhythm. He left one hand on the wall to keep from tipping. Elias remained mute, eyes low. His breath came slow and shallow, like the violence had cracked something inside. Luke stole glances at Ashley, occasionally shifting his eyes to Elias. The air was heavy with thoughts no one dared speak. Then came a sound faint and distant. Not the usual hum. Not footsteps either. Something deeper. Rhythmic. Mechanical.

Ashley raised a hand, signaling them to stop.

There, ahead on the wall, was a strange shift in the lighting. The tiles curved inward slightly, as if the hallway were bending, swallowing itself. The blood trail they'd been following had vanished. Abruptly. A wet handprint marked the wall.

Raspberry broke the silence. "Did... did someone *climb* out?"

Before anyone could answer, a single fluorescent panel overhead flickered, then went out. Then another. Then all of them. Darkness swallowed the hallway.

"Well shit," Raspberry huffed.

[CH.19]

THE
LAST
SCREAM

The machine loomed like a cathedral of cruelty. Towering before them, it clanked and hissed, its serpentine belts weaving through iron cogs and brass lungs. Pipes throbbed with pressure, venting steam from unseen depths. The air buzzed with a reverberation so constant, so low, it wasn't heard—it was *felt*. It crawled below the skin and whispered to the marrow.

Nick stared, his vision warped from breaking his only pair of glasses. The dull hum of the engine vibrated in his teeth.

"It's this. It has to be this," Nick muttered, his voice tinged with both certainty and desperation.

James stood beside him, stunned by the structure's scale. The contraption looked alive. Arterial belts coiled through rusted gears, valves hissing in intervals like sighs. The rubber belt in the center pulsed ever so slightly, as if it were a vein. Its architecture was absurd—both divine and deranged, like a steam-powered altar. Somewhere inside, he could feel it pulsing, thumping, breathing. The sound. The same sonic parasite that had plagued them from the start. He knew this was what Nick was looking for.

"The SmartArk," James said in awe of the machine remembering the message from the hologram. "You really think this is keeping us from remembering? Do you really think this will help us? Help Ashley?" He trailed off into his thoughts once more.

If they wanted us to not know then why would we have this chance to know? The hologram said this was intentional. Is this… can we stop this?

"All I know is that these cultists don't know who they're messing with. The Collective or whatever they want to call themselves. This tribulation nightmare isn't going to stop me." Nick's hand revealed a broken piece of glass. Slowly, deliberately, he pulled out the shard and held the jagged edge under the dimming lights, like the tooth of some extinct predator.

"This thing's a nervous system," Nick said. "You sever the right piece… maybe it collapses. The SmartArk won't be so smart soon."

"You're really going to stab it with your glasses?" James' voice cracked slightly, disbelief written all over his face.

Nick smirked. "Do you have any other suggestions?"

James stepped forward, concern in his voice. "What if this sets off another trap? What if more people die?"

Nick's smile faded. "Then it's already too late." He turned back toward the machine and approached the rubber belt. It was wide, slick, and fast, a central artery spinning in hypnotic rhythm. He raised the shard and a deep shiver ran through the floor. James backed away without thinking. Nick counted to himself—three, two, one—he paused only for a split-second, then plunged the glass into the belt.

The world screamed.

A shockwave detonated outward, ripping through the atmosphere. The lights snapped into a strobe, and the shrill—inhuman and infinite—punched into their skulls. James hit the floor. Blood sprayed from his nose and ears as he clutched the sides of his head, shouting into his own palms.

Nick staggered backward. The lens had lodged deep, tearing the belt, and with it, the rhythm. Sparks spat in every direction as one of the engine's outer coils snapped. But the noise persisted. High-pitched. Piercing. Primeval. The shriek of a dying god.

Across the Ark, unseen yet palpable, cries of torturous suffering rushed through the air. In the distance, something shattered, followed by the sounds of bodies collapsing, and convulsing in pain. A chorus of torment resounded throughout the facility.

Back in the chamber, Nick stumbled into a metal railing, clutching his hand. His palm had split open when the shard bounced back, slicing his skin into a perfect crescent wound. Blood streamed from between his fingers, warm and steady. It didn't stop him.

"The motor!" Nick yelled through gritted teeth, voice worn.

Nick seized a nearby pipe that had flown off, a thick rusted piece of steel, and charged toward the center housing. His fingers, slick with blood, slipped on the grip. He gathered his strength before unleashing a brutal swing.

CRACK!

He struck the housing again.

CLANG! WHAM!

He delivered a flurry of brutal blows. Dust and rivets scattered. Gears stuttered and jerked. The machine groaned. James crawled forward now, vision blurred, every inch of him shaking.

"AH!" James pointed. "THERE, THE PANEL!" He was still struggling to breathe, reaching with a trembling hand.

A section had warped open from the pressure. Inside, a snarl of wires hissed with electrical discharge. James plunged his right hand in and yanked. The heat scalded his skin. He stared at the snarled sinew of severed circuitry. The machine shrieked one last time. Then… silence.

It wasn't just quiet. It was colossal. Terrifying. Complete. The belts halted. The lights faded. The room, for the first time, exhaled as though it had been holding its breath for eternity.

Nick dropped to one knee, his chest heaving, blood dripping freely from his fingers. James leaned back against the wall, shaking, barely able to stay upright.

"Did we do it?" James asked, voice hoarse and hollow.

Nick didn't look up. "I think—" he caught his breath, lips cracked, "—we broke it."

The silence lingered, heavy and haunted. The machine slouched in stillness, ribs cracked open, its cycle broken. But the Ark was not dead. Not yet. The stillness clung like a second skin—sticky, suffocating. James could hear the blood in his own head now. Every breath rasped against the back of his throat like sandpaper. The machine no longer moaned, but the room still vibrated, as if the memory of its sound refused to die.

"What if this wasn't it?" James said faintly.

Nick turned to him, breath still heaving. "You mean, this machine did nothing?"

"No," James muttered, shaking his head. "I mean… if this were some kind of controlled experiment, why would we be able to sabotage it?"

"They seem like scientists, James. They observe, not interfere."

"How can you be so sure?"

"How can you, James?" Nick sighed and lowered himself to the floor.

He knelt, cradling his hand. Blood dripped in soft patterns onto the tile. His palm was a mess—skin peeled back in a crescent flap, the wound pulsing with every beat of his heart. The glass had bitten deep.

"We'll have to wrap it," James said, moving toward him, still wary of the now crippled machine. "You'll get sepsis."

Nick didn't answer. He stared at the thing as if it might get back up and strike. A low groan echoed from somewhere behind the walls. The room shifted, imperceptibly. James froze. "Did you feel that?"

Nick nodded. "It's adjusting."

Something in the air changed. A stale breeze rolled through the chamber. It was warm. Above them, the lights twitched, not in panic but confusion. The room had lost its rhythm. James glanced at the belts, now hanging limp. The wires he'd torn lay like entrails across the floor. Still, part of him expected the machine to twitch again. To recoil. To retaliate. Nothing came.

Nick sat back against a white tiled wall, his legs stretched, his bloody hand now wrapped in his shirt. "If this was keeping us from our thoughts… it's finished now."

James shook his head, eyes darting. "Then why does it feel like we're still trapped?"

A soft hiss escaped a nearby pipe. One final exhale. One last ghost of pressure easing through the broken system. For the first time since they'd woken in this place, the primal scream was at rest. Not replaced. Not reduced. Gone. And somehow, that was worse.

I hope Ash is alive. Who knows what kind of damage we've done, or who we've pissed off. James started pacing.

Nick rested his head back and let out a deep exhale. "James, just rest for a moment, will ya mate. I need to catch my breath."

He was too restless, energized with panic. "What if we've made things worse, Nick?"

"You and your questions. We're fighting back, aren't we? You said you wanted to remember, right?"

"How do we know it was this?" James' left arm wavered in the direction of the broken engine. "What if there's more than one?"

Nick didn't answer right away. James ran a hand through his hair, pulling at the roots, trying to ground himself. His thoughts were scattered, like someone had knocked the shelf over and left the mess behind. "There could be dozens," he continued, "hundreds. For all we know, this is just a decoy."

Nick raised an eyebrow, not disagreeing. "Doesn't change the fact we killed this one. And if that's the case, someone's pissed, eh?" He motioned to the sparking carcass.

James stepped closer to the broken panel, peering into the remains of severed wires and scorched gears. "Do you feel different?"

Nick exhaled, letting his head fall back again. "I feel like I've been cooked alive and hit by a truck."

"No, I mean… do you *remember* anything?"

That brought a pause. Nick's brow furrowed. He closed his eyes. Nothing.

"Not yet," he said, voice little more than a whisper.

James kicked a loose bolt across the room. It clinked twice and rolled into a shadow. "So now what? We wait to see if our minds crawl back on their own?"

Nick chuckled dryly, "Yeah, mate. That or we grow new ones."

James finally slid down against the wall, exhausted. The machine's silhouette stretched across the floor like the corpse of some fallen beast, ribs exposed, steam bleeding out in soft trails. "Goddammit," he scoffed before finally closing his eyes.

I guess I'll wait.

[CH.20]

W H E R E
S H A D O W S
L U R K

The cop followed like a phantom; eyes fixed on the figures ahead. Ashton, Cora, and Sam appeared as little more than silhouettes, their figures almost indistinguishable despite the white tiles flooding the hallway with harsh light. They trudged deeper into the endless, oppressive corridors of the Ark.

The officer's breath was shallow and restricted; his body low and silent. A shadow. He didn't dare close the distance too much. Instead, he watched. Perhaps staying behind and gathering more resources was the better option. What did it matter? His gut told him to follow. The man leading this group was too suspicious. Maybe he was the resource.

"Damn it!" A low grunt escaped Sam as he limped, his left leg dragging behind him. His face twisted in pain as he clutched his side.

Cora's voice dropped to a whisper, "Still hurting?"

Sam winced as he shifted, his face drawn. "Yeah. I didn't feel it until we got clear. Something tore into me." He didn't know what it was. He just knew it hurt.

From a distance, the cop studied a tile at his feet, where dried specks of blood dotted the path. Sam was bleeding. The hostile man exhaled harshly before lifting his gaze ahead.

Far along the corridor, Ashton didn't break stride. "Keep up," he demanded, not looking back. Sam and Cora followed him regardless.

The hallway twisted unnaturally, its design not meant for navigation but endurance. Ashton moved with purpose, pausing briefly at each junction, his eyes scanning the walls, deciphering signs no one else could read.

"Why are we going this way?" Cora asked, her tone skeptical.

Ashton's response was dry. "Because every other way leads to a dead end."

"Have you been here before?" she pressed.

He paused, one eye twitching slightly, then moved forward again. "How could I? You heard what the Collective said, we were all brought here."

Cora said nothing. Neither did Sam. Before them stretched an enormous doorway framed by a wall that shimmered slightly, like a mirage. Beyond it, the hallway gave way to a yawning open chamber. It was darker here. The usual light from the walls faded as the room expanded. The brightness had been swallowed whole.

The cop edged closer, taking cover behind a crooked wall segment. His eyes narrowed.

The room stretched impossibly high, a dizzying array of walkways and metal platforms crisscrossing in chaotic tiers. The ceilings were lost in obscurity, and below, grated ramps spiraled down to seemingly nowhere. Sections of the floor shifted, grinding into place with deliberate rotations, each movement punctuated by slow, rhythmic clicks. The lighting was patchy and uneven, coming from unseen sources above and below, creating long shadows and disorienting depth.

Cora and Sam stalled at the threshold.

"What is this place?" Sam asked.

Ashton stepped inside without answering. The inimical man remained in the darkness, studying the structure. His gut clenched, warning him this place was designed for something—an arena, a trap, a test. Ashton walked in like he already knew which path wouldn't collapse beneath him.

Ashton paused, his head snapping slightly to one side.

There was silence.

He turned his ear toward the corridor they'd come through, nostrils flaring like a hound catching a scent. Cora stopped, and Sam followed with a wince spreading across his face.

"Something wrong?" Cora whispered. Sam said nothing.

The officer pressed himself into the shade of the archway, body locked in a crouch. His heart drummed while his breath remained still. There wasn't much cover. The ambient glow from the corridor thinned just enough to make him a part of the wall.

Ashton's head snapped, "You hear that?"

Cora and Sam looked at each other. The cop's pulse quickened. He pressed himself flat against the tiled wall, melting into the narrow line of black cast by a support beam.

"I didn't hear anything," Cora said.

"Probably just this place," Sam offered, weakly.

Ashton didn't move. He watched the doorway ahead, then warily glanced back the way they came. His gaze remained for a breath too long. The officer's fingers slid toward the pistol at his hip.

Then Ashton turned forward again, lips quivering. "Step where I step," he said, continuing ahead. He exhaled sharply through his nose. "Keep close."

Sam and Cora obeyed, trailing his every movement. Sam limped harder now, gritting his teeth, while Cora kept glancing at the bridges above them and the floors below.

"I don't like this." Her voice was faint. "Feels wrong."

"It is wrong," Sam mumbled, "but we don't have a choice, do we?"

The cop crept along the perimeter, keeping to the cover of night—listening, watching, waiting. Ashton stopped near a metal console embedded in one of the walls. He stared at it.

He didn't touch it, not yet. Then, almost to himself, he said, "It should still work."

Cora caught it. "What should still work?"

Ashton turned slowly. "Nothing. Just keep moving."

The brute caught his lie.

The grated floor under their feet trembled. Sam stopped short.

"You feel that?" Sam asked, voice tight.

Cora turned, her face pale in the strange low lighting, and said, "It's vibrating."

Ashton halted mid-step. His hand hovered above a panel on the wall. The bridge shifted under his boots with a subtle lurch, a tremor, as if something colossal had exhaled deep far below, reverberating through the structure.

Then it hit.

A low drone crawled into the room, bleeding in through the walls like a tide of pressure. The sound didn't arrive; it *grew*, like it had always been there and only now decided to wake up. The cop felt it first. A sharp pinch in his teeth, like metal grinding metal. His ears buzzed with interference. Then the pressure surged.

Cora screamed.

The sound became a roar, an all-consuming, inhuman shriek that carved through the brain and rattled the bones. Everyone dropped. Sam clutched his head and fell to his knees. Cora collapsed beside him, writhing, her fingernails dragging along the bridge as she tried to anchor herself to something, anything. Blood began to seep from her ears.

Ashton stayed standing. One hand held onto the console, the other clutching the side of his skull. His jaw clenched, eyes rolling upward. He didn't cry out. Not even as blood welled in the corners of his eyes.

The cop's vision blurred. He slammed his back into the wall and gritted his teeth. A yell built in his throat but never made it out. His head pounded, sinuses imploded, and black veins itched across the skin of his arms. Behind his clenched lids, lightning danced.

Somewhere above the trio, something snapped. A far-off crash echoed from a catwalk several stories high. Pieces fell, scattering debris. The grated floor shifted. Sam cried out as a bolt of metal shot from a wall like a javelin and clanged just inches from where he'd been crawling. Just as quickly as it came, it ended. The sound cut. No fade out. No release. Now it was void.

The silence afterward was a deafening absence. Cora gasped in shallow gulps of air. Sam wept softly—still holding his head, still unsure if he was alive or already gone. Ashton, red-eyed and trembling, finally lowered his hand from the console. He looked down at them both, no sympathy in his stare.

Ashton's voice was a rasp. "Get up. We move now."

Cora blinked at him. "What the fuck was that!?"

Ashton didn't answer. He turned from the console, took a shaky step forward, then another. He didn't look back.

The officer, still concealed in murk, wiped the blood from under his nose. His thoughts came slow, distorted, until one surfaced: *That wasn't random*. Something had changed. He took a step backward into the dark, his hand finding the cold surface of the tiled wall. He needed to stay hidden. Just another shadow in a corridor riddled with them. The world tilted. His knees buckled.

The hallway swam, folding in on itself in impossible angles. The cop's hands reached for something that wasn't there. The blackness rushed forward. He fell. No cry. No warning. His body dropped to the floor behind a cluster of debris. The moment passed unnoticed.

As the others disappeared into the mechanical labyrinth ahead, the officer lay still. Half in light, half in dark. His pistol slipped from his fingers, clattering softly against the tiles.

For the first time since awakening in the Ark, he found himself at rest, slipping into unconsciousness.

[CH.21]

//:System Error //
[MEMORY LOG RETRIEVED]
Subject: 457-JOHN

//:May 24, 1992 //
//:CHICAGO, IL //

The coffee was bitter. John didn't care.

He sat at the chipped kitchen table, the edges of last night's takeout box curling inward. The apartment smelled like sweat, stale cigarettes, and mold that refused to die. His service pistol rested on the table between him and the woman crying across from him. Her lip was split. A dark, spreading bruise painted her cheek.

"You done?" he asked flatly, eyes fixed on the peeling linoleum floor.

She didn't answer. She trembled. Her hands clutched her shirt, knuckles white. Her face wet.

"Then leave."

John didn't raise his voice. He didn't have to. That's what made it worse. His words weren't threats; they were facts. Final. As though her being here any longer would disrupt his day more than hers. He finally looked at her, expressionless.

She stood up. No suitcase. No shoes. Just shame and silence. She left the apartment like a ghost. The door didn't slam behind her. John took a sip of the black coffee and looked out the window. Below, the city groaned with life—sirens, horns, trash swept into corners by gusts of alley wind. He saw a patrol car glide by. He didn't wave. They wouldn't wave back.

The department was watching him. He knew that. They had to. Too many complaints. Too many bruises left on suspects who resisted. None of it stuck. Internal Affairs couldn't prove what they didn't want to.

John played the part when he needed to. Clean uniform. Dead eyes. Good aim. That was enough for most of his precinct. He didn't laugh at their jokes. Didn't go to the bars after shift. He didn't need friends. He didn't need much.

That morning, his locker had been broken into. Nothing stolen. Just disturbed. The note inside said: "Do you think you're untouchable?" He crumpled it and tossed it before the ink could dry on his palm.

By noon, he was back on patrol. A domestic call in South Side. Screaming. Broken glass. The usual. John didn't turn on his lights. Didn't radio dispatch. He parked two blocks down and walked the rest. The building looked abandoned. Cracks in the concrete. A child's shoe in the gutter. Inside, it smelled like mildew and rot. He made it up to the third floor. The door was open. Blood was fresh on the carpet. A man stood in the kitchen holding a knife. The woman was already on the ground.

John didn't hesitate. The gunshot barely echoed.

The man slumped. Still breathing, maybe. John stepped over him and crouched by the woman. Her eyes fluttered. Alive.

He stared at her a long time. Not with concern. Not with relief. Only observation. He debated whether to call the coroner or the ambulance. Before he could decide, another officer had made it into the building, pistol ready. He lowered it once he saw John, a tall tower in the room. Inimical indeed.

The other officer was Torres, a rookie. "Should we call it in?" He hesitated.

John didn't answer. He looked around the kitchen, noted the scattered beer cans, the broken picture frame, the toddler-sized shoes by the fridge. He looked at the woman again, now weeping silently, rocking in place. Weak.

"Domestic report," John said flatly. "He got aggressive. I intervened. He slipped."

Torres nodded, uncertain. John always wrote his own narratives.

In his patrol car an hour later, John sat staring out at Lake Michigan. His knuckles ached. A storm was brewing, dark clouds stretching over the skyline like a bruise. He didn't feel guilt. Guilt was a luxury. He hadn't felt guilt since he was twelve.

What he did feel, as he lit a cigarette and leaned into the seat, was watched. He glanced in the rearview mirror. Nothing there. The feeling persisted, a constant pressure under his chest. And then it came. No light. No sound. Gravity turned inside out and his eyes widened; his lungs emptied.

And then, John was gone, as if he had never been there.

[CH.22]

T H E
P R I C E
O F
S U R V I V A L

The room hadn't changed. Even with the machine gutted and groaning no more, the air inside still felt thick with something—a stench, or a residue, like the stink of something long dead. James sat against the far wall, his shirt half-drenched in dried blood, gaze locked on the still belts and split wires. Nick lay nearby, sprawled but breathing. His bandaged hand rested on his stomach. Nothing had come. No alarms. No drones. No reinforcements. Maybe the machine was more symbolic than functional. Maybe it was the heart of something spiritual, not mechanical. Or maybe, they were just ants who'd gnawed on a power line and no one upstairs had noticed. James wanted to believe they'd made a difference. The room told a different story.

A click echoed from behind them.

James sat up sharply. Across the room, one of the smooth tiled walls hissed open—not violently, not like a trap, like an invitation. A long vertical crack split the surface, then receded. Beyond the opening was a narrow corridor bathed in a dull blue glow. It hadn't been there before. It had no right to be there now.

"Well looks like someone noticed," Nick grinned, his voice cutting through the stillness.

"Looks like a way out. Come on buddy." James helped him to his feet.

They ventured out the open slot in the wall. James started rolling ideas around in his head. Useless thoughts that kept him occupied. He still wondered if they even changed things at all. Nick, in contrast, embraced the pain of his wound and cinched down his shirt, ensuring no more blood poured out. Then the wall behind them fell into place, locking them away from the contraption once and for all.

It was a sign Nick took to forget all about it and press on. James couldn't though. He still couldn't shake the thought of Ashley, the tunnels, of Sean, the bat, the field, the shots. It wouldn't end.

James pressed forward, eyes scanning every inch of the corridor. The glow of the tiles around them seemed bleaker here, less alive. The walls didn't hum the way they used to. They breathed, softly.

Nick limped beside him; one hand pressed to his shirt-wrapped wound. Blood still seeped through the fabric in occasional spurts. He didn't complain.

James finally spoke, voice low. "Remember what that hologram said? About becoming our 'true selves'. About regressing?"

Nick gave a slight nod, eyes still forward.

James continued, "He said we were chosen. Disciples. Called to prove something. Like this is some divine science project and we're the moldy petri dish."

Nick huffed a dry breath through his nose. "And yet somehow we're still walking."

"Yeah. But to what end?" James shook his head. "They took our memories. Sent us crawling through their Goddamn maze. And when we broke their machine… nothing. Just a door. Like it's all part of their equation."

Nick grunted. "Maybe it is. Or maybe we pissed off the wrong god."

James scoffed, but it wasn't a laugh. "Either way, I think we just made it worse."

Nick looked over, his tone quieter. "You think too much."

"And you don't think enough," James shot back. "We could be walking straight into another trial right now. Another test. I'm not a fucking rat."

Nick slowed, holding his wounded hand tighter. "You want out?"

James grew quiet.

"Then keep walking," Nick said, "Or curl up and wait for them to recycle you."

James forced himself forward again, but his mind remained behind, tangled in the memory of that grinning projection, of the voice that knew his name.

In time, James, you will learn what is necessary...

He swallowed. "They called me out, Nick. That man, he knew me."

"You're clearly a favorite," Nick said sarcastically, lips curling despite his pain.

James stopped walking for a moment. "How can you remain so... so optimistic? How are you built for this?" His voice trembled slightly, half bitterness, half awe.

Nick looked away, his features hardening under the flickering glow. Then he turned back, meeting James' eyes.

"Maybe I was." His voice dropped, low and honest. "But the truth is, I don't know who I am. And neither do you. So don't start assigning virtues to strangers just because they seem braver than you feel."

The silence between them stretched, not in tension but truth.

They walked in peace for a while after that. Their footsteps bounced off the smooth lit walls, a cadence of exhaustion and quiet dread. The corridor narrowed, then widened, angling slightly downward. The tiles began to change—subtly at first, from seamless ceramic to fine, grainy concrete.

Then the floor buckled.

James shouted, grabbing for the wall as the tiles underneath them dropped like a collapsing shelf. Both men slid, tumbling through a sudden chute. A spiraling, metal-lined funnel that scraped their arms and twisted their descent. They landed hard. The impact knocked the breath from James' chest. He rolled to his side, coughing.

The lighting had changed here. No longer blue. It was a dim yellow, almost sepia-toned. The air buzzed faintly—not like the machine's hum before, but something more localized. The room was rectangular; its walls lined with mismatched industrial panels and vents. Cables hung loose like tangled veins. In the center was a crude metal platform surrounded by four large square tiles set in a pattern. The floor around those were patterned with smaller tiles, like a giant checkerboard.

Nick pulled himself up, grimacing, "We're not in the hallway anymore."

James looked around, "What the hell is this?"

Then they heard it. A mechanical *clunk*, followed by a hiss of vented air. Something behind one of the walls shifted, gears grinding behind plated steel. The door they'd fallen through had sealed above them. Gone as if it had never existed.

"Trap," Nick said simply.

James nodded, dread coiling like smoke in his gut. He moved toward the strange platform cautiously. The moment his foot touched one of the smaller square tiles, it lit up. Green. A low tone buzzed, too low to be a siren but loud enough to be a warning. One of the other tiles across the room flickered to red, followed by a beep.

A loud *thunk* followed. From above, a steel spike jutted from the ceiling and pierced into the far away floor with a hiss. James flinched and fell back towards Nick, "Okay, button makes spike come out. Noted."

Nick held back. "Don't move. Let's think."

He reminisced about the room he encountered with Raspberry, when he witnessed a spike protrude through the foot of the suited man. The patterns. The algorithm he had discovered. Now though, there were hundreds of tiny tiles. The floor shifted, enough to make them stumble. The buzz deepened. Not fast. Not violently. The room spun, and the duo were now on the other side.

James stepped back, hands slightly raised. "Okay, so red tiles bad. And the fucking room spins." He murmured, "I think I liked the machine room better."

Nick crouched, examining the corners, remaining still. "Pressure sensors maybe. It's pattern based. Guess wrong, it triggers something. Hard part is we move so I can't tell if the tiles switch."

James felt the still walls closing in. The air had a weight to it now, like it was pressing down on him. Nick was still muttering numbers under his breath, eyes scanning the rotating floor.

"The spikes trigger on the far wall, never the side you're on. That's something at least.

But it changes. The moment we think we know the layout—"

"—it shifts," James finished, voice low. His pulse drummed in his ears.

Then, without warning, a door-sized panel across the room hissed open. James flinched. A man stepped through the opening barefoot and slow. His face was bruised, eyes sunken, mouth shut like it had been sewn by silence itself. He held a crude bat in one hand, dripping with blood. His posture was casual, almost serene, but the calm concealed a sharp purpose.

Nick stiffened. "Who the hell?"

James went pale. He saw the bat and after that, every swing. The force that bashed an innocent man's face in. The random rage from the stranger he saved.

Sean didn't speak. He didn't look at either of them. He simply stepped forward, scanning the grid in his bloodied leather jacket. Not for escape. For more blood. The bat hung in his grip, steady, confident.

James found himself trapped in place. He knew that stance. He remembered the fire. The cage. The look in Sean's eyes back then, wild and desperate. This was different. This was methodical. Sean took one step forward. A tile lit up underfoot.

Nick's eyes widened. "Don't move!"

Too late. Another red tile lit up behind them. A spike jutted from the ceiling with a hiss, missing James by inches. The floor rotated again, shifting the positions of each square-tile.

Sean didn't even flinch. He adjusted his angle and kept walking.

James snapped out of it. "He's trying to kill us!"

"No," Nick said. "He's trying to survive." He dropped into a prone position, staying back near a wall.

Sean stepped again. Another tile lit green. James forced himself to stop moving and read the grid. Four red tiles flanked the platform's far edge. A cluster of green ran diagonally from where he stood toward Sean's position. The room's rotation had shifted everything two squares clockwise since they'd entered. He filed it away.

Nick shouted. "James, you need to stay across from him. Press whatever tile is adjacent to his position!"

James didn't wait. He advanced across the grid, syncing his steps with Sean's. A green tile ignited with every step he took. Sean slowed, his grip tightening on the bat as he raised it slightly. James held up hands, not in surrender, but in an effort to maintain balance. "Don't," he said calmly, "You don't even know me."

Sean didn't respond. He lunged.

James narrowly slipped aside, the first swing slicing past his shoulder. The bat cracked into a tile and the wall across the room erupted with another spike.

James rolled sideways, caught his footing, and rose. "SEAN!"

No response. Only breath. Only motion.

Nick was rooted, caught between action and paralysis. "James, he's not in there."

The game was clear now, force the other to stand on the opposite-end. Kill by proxy. Sean didn't need rage. The system was doing the killing for him.

There's no way. He doesn't even care about the tiles. He's too close!

James dodged again and lunged forward, this time toward Sean. He slammed his shoulder into the larger man's ribs. The impact sent both of them skidding across the platform, their bodies scraping over the tile. Red, green, red—each square lighting up in rapid succession. The disorienting spin of the room was now a constant, spinning faster and faster.

Nick was outcast to the other side. Spikes rushed toward him. He kept moving, rolling left and right in an attempt to close the distance between him and the two gladiators.

Sean snarled, still wordless, and raised the bat again. James caught his wrist and punched him in the side of the throat. Sean choked, reeled, and swung again. It grazed James' shoulder.

"I saved you," James hissed, teeth bared. "I dragged you out of the fire!" His plea was useless.

Sean didn't seem to hear.

Another swing. Another dodge. James struck back. Harder. He felt something inside him snap. Not physically, but something old and dormant. He wasn't just defending himself anymore. He was fighting. He was *choosing* to hurt. Blood from Sean's nose sprayed against the glowing walls. Another spike hissed from the side. A foot too far from Nick. Someone would die soon.

Nick shouted from across the room. "James! You have to end it! You have to take him out!"

James stood, panting, body shaking with fatigue. Sean remained fixed on him, dazed, his lips quivering. There were no words, no emotions, only the same unyielding violence in his expression. James glanced at the grid and then back to Sean. He ducked once more under the swing of the bat, his movements fluid. And then, without restraint, sent a left kick straight into Sean's face, causing him to stumble. Without missing a beat, James followed up with a heavy push from his right foot to Sean's chest. The force of it lifted Sean's body, sending him backward and gaining some distance between them. No more restraint. Only relentless action.

James jumped back, landing on a small tile. Green. He looked over to the square under Sean. Red. A massive spike descended from the ceiling as Sean struggled to regain his footing. The metal prong pierced his skull and caved in his torso. Blood erupted outward, splattering across the room. James blinked, feeling the spray, his face now drenched. Nick was motionless. The bat rolled across the floor, coming to a rest, while Sean's lifeless body remained pinned under the spike. There was no mercy. The spike refused to retreat.

It stayed lodged in Sean's skull like a final accusation. The room was still, no more spinning, no more buzzes or clicks or grinding.

Just the faint hum of ambient circuitry and the smell of blood and ruptured tissue. James trembled, shoulders rising and falling with each breath. The bat rested at his feet now. *Stupid thing.* Brutal. Simple. It looked smaller than before. Everything did.

Nick finally moved, creeping forward from his position near the wall. His steps were cautious, but not because of the trap. He was watching James. The smaller tiles no longer lit up. The spikes had stopped.

"You okay?" he asked.

James didn't answer. He was still staring at Sean's mangled form, one eye glassed over by a film of red. The man he had saved. The man he had *killed*.

Nick took a few more steps, navigating the tiles carefully, now that the room was still.

"I didn't have a choice," James sobbed, his voice barely audible. "It was him or me."

"I know," Nick said.

James turned to him. "I didn't want to. I swear to God, Nick..."

Nick nodded. "That's what makes you different."

There was a silence that followed, not accusing, not forgiving, merely honest. Then the low hum returned. It was softer now. James looked down. The center platform began to glow. A faint orange circle spiraled out from the middle, lighting up the surrounding four large tiles in a new pattern.

Nick stepped toward it cautiously. "It's not over."

James looked back down at Sean's body. He didn't move.

"Hey," Nick said, a little firmer. "Come on. If this is a test, we're not done yet."

James inhaled slowly and forced his feet to move. Together, they approached the center platform. A low rhythm accompanied each step. When they reached the edge, the four tiles in the exact center finally glowed white.

"Pressure plate," Nick guessed. "Final confirmation maybe."

James exhaled and stepped forward. The moment his foot pressed one of the large tiles, the lights blinked once, then again. And then, with a hiss, the far wall folded inward, revealing a dark passage. No announcement. No fanfare. Just a way forward.

James turned to Nick. "You coming?"

Nick nodded. "Yeah. I'm not letting you have all the trauma."

They left Sean behind, the spike still standing, like a grim monument to a life no one cared to understand. The room dimmed behind them and the platform powered down, fading into the background like another obstacle in the endless maze. Another corridor. Another trial. Yet something had shifted in James. His steps weren't faster, nor slower, but heavier. Like he'd lost something he hadn't realized he still possessed. For the first time, his mind fell silent. His face was ashen.

Nick, his bloody hand resting on James' shoulder, silently shared in the heaviness of the moment. "You did what you had to. We all do."

"This is what they wanted." James looked down before stepping into the corridor.

"It is, but it doesn't have to stay that way." Nick let him go and marched through the opening. Back into the seamless infinite white tiled halls. Steel doors patterned down the sides. An all-too-familiar place at this point. He hated it. So did James.

The corridor felt emptier than before. Quieter, too. Even the Ark itself had recoiled from what had taken place. James walked behind Nick, eyes still flicking back to the path they'd left behind, half expecting to see Sean standing again, spike and all. But the body remained still. No movement. Nothing followed.

They walked for what felt like several minutes, each step resonating with the consequence of what had been done. The tile underfoot was slick in places, too polished. The walls were featureless again, bright white and humming low. That hum… it never left. It was part of the Ark now. Part of them.

Nick's steps slowed. James noticed, remaining quiet. He kept his speed steady until Nick's shoulder dipped, and his limp worsened.

"Nick?" James asked.

Nick's jaw tightened, a muscle twitching under the strain. "I'm good," he sighed, pressing his hand to his side. The bandage had nearly soaked through.

James reached out, bracing him, "You're bleeding again."

"No shit," he smirked. The humor didn't land. His pupils were dilated. The color was draining fast from his face.

They took a few more steps. Then Nick crumpled. Badly this time. James caught him by the arm, hardly keeping him upright. "Hey, Nick come on!"

Nick shook his head, trying to fight off the agony. "Guess… guess I pushed it too far." His knees buckled.

James lowered him delicately to the floor. "Breathe. Stay with me."

Nick's eyes fluttered. "You remember when I said I was built for this?" he rasped.

"Yeah?"

Nick gave the faintest smile. "I think I was wrong."

He went limp and his eyes rolled back as consciousness left him.

In an instant, James had his hands on Nick's chest, feeling for life. There—a rise and fall. Weak, but enough.

"Fuck." He spun around, eyes scanning the never-ending corridor, "God damn it. Not now."

He pressed his back against the wall beside Nick, his breath shallow as his eyes searched for any sign of movement. Nothing happened. No walls opened. No traps triggered. Only a heavy hush filled the air. With Nick unconscious at his side, James was left unsure of what to do next.

[CH.23]

//:System Error //
[MEMORY LOG RETRIEVED]
Subject: 386-NICK

//:August 5, 2097 //
//:London, GB //

The sky above London was never black anymore. It simmered with a violet aura, a restless cocktail of data towers, neon haze, and ghost satellites. Nick used to love the skyline—once. Before the war. Before the curfews. Before firewalls replaced fences and hunger queues stretched longer than download speeds.

He stood atop the fractured edge of Tower One, peering down through a smog-burned atmosphere. Beneath him: a city under siege by silence. People didn't riot anymore. They queued, quietly. They rationed. They obeyed.

Pushing his glasses up to the bridge of his nose, Nick adjusted the terminal strapped to his arm—an obsolete piece by modern standards, but modified beyond recognition. His fingers danced in the air, manipulating ghost keys only he could see. Every move sent data crawling through abandoned cables, hunting the endpoint.

They'd called it the Eden Directive. A full-spectrum lockdown protocol to consolidate power under a single adaptive AI. Parliament didn't vote. It wasn't built to be voted on. It was built to survive at any cost. And it had, with terrifying success.

Nick had watched it happen. Cities ringfenced by surveillance. Dissent algorithmically erased. Free thought demoted to an error code. When the hunger started, the AI kept feeding the stock markets while children in the suburbs starved. So he struck back.

He breached the grid at 3:07 a.m. A time chosen for silence. The master node was buried in the old London Archives, disguised as a historical preservation server. No one expected an anarchist to aim for history.

The final code string flashed in his vision. A recursive data cascade that would collapse the Eden Directive's core. He had written it with unsteady hands, alone in an abandoned flat with power siphoned from a neighbor's solar array.

"This is for the ones you didn't feed," he had whispered.

He executed the command.

At first, nothing happened. Then came the power failures. Dozens. Then thousands. The sky pulsed. The city exhaled. For one second, it looked like freedom. Then came the reports.

Power grids across Europe crashed. Refrigeration systems in emergency shelters failed. Data vaults corrupted. Medical drones lost protocol. A heatwave followed. Within forty-eight hours, millions died. Not from the AI, but from the vacuum Nick left in its place. The chaos of sudden freedom. He hadn't killed them. Not directly. But he might as well have.

When the black-ops vans came, he didn't run. He walked into the light of their weapons and said, "Do what you have to." They didn't kill him. Not then. That would've made him a martyr. Instead, they took him somewhere deep. Somewhere cold.

With a bag over his head, he reflected on his first attempt to hide. He had spent three days in a crawlspace concealed in an abandoned loft in Shoreditch, eating freeze-dried rations and watching the network unravel from a cracked datapad. He thought maybe he could disappear. But the others would've found him. The other hackers he once aligned with weren't friends, they were opportunists. Trading coordinates for crypto. That's why he gave in. None of them could do what he did. They didn't have the strength or the smarts. He had tried to rally them before, to unify the last remaining minds willing to fight the machine from inside, but even they had limits. Morals wavered when credits were on the table. Loyalty eroded behind anonymized usernames and VPNs.

He had outgrown them. Not in arrogance, but in purpose. They were reactionaries. Nick had been a catalyst. And now, shackled in silence, bag over his head, waiting for whatever came next, he didn't regret it. He regretted nothing, except how many he hadn't saved.

The van smelled of rubber and sweat. The agents didn't speak. He had memorized their boots, the scrape of hard soles against steel floor. He'd imagined a trial, even a death sentence. That never came. Instead, they drove for hours. Then a change. No more city sounds. Just the hum of isolation.

They dragged him out, footsteps echoing in an underground facility. Concrete. Metal. When the bag finally came off, all he saw were white walls, a single chair, and a camera lens blinking in the corner. Without his glasses it was difficult to see. He managed. After being greeted by an agent and briefed, he was left alone. The blur in his vision became white light. Blindness. When the agent returned, Nick had vanished.

[CH.24]

FRAGMENTS
OF
REALITY

James adjusted Nick on his back for the fourth time in as many minutes. The incapacitated and pale man was dead-weight now. His injured side leaked warmth, pressing into the contour of James' shoulder. It was a constant reminder telling James he couldn't stop, no matter how much he felt he couldn't carry on. He kept moving despite everything, as the white corridor extended into infinity, lined with locked steel doors and humming with that ever-present, low-frequency tone.

He had stopped calling Nick's name after the first few turns. There was no point anymore. His own voice bounced off the sterilized walls. The wet smack of his boots on the tile amplified the throb of blood in his ears. Occasionally, the tiles seemed to shimmer, like water under glass. James blinked it away.

"Get a grip," he said to himself, shifting Nick.

The corridor didn't feel right. It hadn't for a while now. The light flickered inconsistently. Too wild. Too vacant. And every so often, the hum dropped a half-step, like the Ark was glitching.

And Sean. God, Sean. Every time James closed his eyes, he saw the spike, the red tile, the wet burst of bone. He hadn't meant to. He hadn't wanted to. He told himself that over and over, and still the man's blank expression followed him down every corridor.

James stopped. Up ahead, a door was open. Just one, slightly ajar in a sea of sealed steel. He stepped inside.

The room was nearly bare—no furniture, no panel, just tiled walls. A mirror hung across from the entrance. *That's out of place.* James eased Nick down against the wall and approached it cautiously. It wasn't like the other reflective surfaces in the Ark. This one held depth. It thrummed under the surface, almost sentient—aware it was being watched.

He stared at his reflection, trying to recognize himself. Pale. Haggard. The blood on his cheek had dried to a dark smear. His eyes were wrong. Older. There was something behind them now, something that hadn't been there in the tunnels, or the forest, or the early hours of confusion. Something feral.

He sat down in front of the mirror.

"What am I even doing?" he asked aloud. "Trying to survive? Trying to escape? For who?"

His reflection didn't answer. James exhaled, letting his head fall against the tile behind him. "They said we'd find our true selves. If this is mine… maybe I don't want to meet him."

The silence in the room felt alive. He blinked, and for a moment—just a second—his reflection smiled. But he hadn't. Electricity coursed through his spine and snapped him upright as he backed away from the mirror. When he looked again, the reflection was still. Stoic. Only him. The smile hadn't faded, James realized. It was never his to begin with. It just waited. He turned, picked up Nick's limp form, and stepped out of the room.

Except, when he turned, he didn't step back into the corridor. Instead, he stepped into the Sanctuary. Impossible. No shift. No sound. No warning. One moment it was white tiles and a mirror—now it was open air and overgrown grass. The makeshift stars above still shined. Tree limbs fluttered in a wind that didn't belong. It was quiet. Too quiet. James' breath caught in his throat.

Bodies.

Not in piles. They were scattered and stacked over each other, half-covered by debris. Familiar faces contorted with inflexible expressions of fear. It seemed their minds had left before their bodies. The grass was streaked with dark, flaking stains. They huddled around a circle of ashes. One of them had managed to make a fire.

James staggered forward, heart racing. "What the hell happened here?"

"RAH!" A blood-curdling cry ripped through the air, shattering the silence.

A man appeared. Filthy and shirtless, he had arms scratched with crude symbols. He shuffled from behind one of the broken trees, eyes wide and mouth mumbling incoherent syllables. His teeth were stained. His fingers twitched. James flinched when the man sporadically charged his way. A look of mania smeared across his face.

James shifted Nick, keeping one arm free. The man stopped inches away.

"You hear them too?" he breathed.

James didn't answer.

"They sing sometimes," the man continued, voice rising. "In the walls. In the fucking sky. Can't sleep, you know. Can't—CAN'T SLEEP!"

James took a step back.

The man's eyes rolled. Then, without warning, he laughed. A full-bodied broken laugh before turning and sprinting toward the edge of the Sanctuary. He disappeared into the tree line shouting, "The memories! The memories make it worse! Make it stop. Make me sleep!"

James couldn't move as the silence rushed back in. The breeze picked up, stirring the leaves. He turned in a slow circle, trying to find something human in the wreckage of corpses.

Nothing.

Ahead he noticed an opening in the forest. James carried Nick toward it. What lay beyond the tree line was worse. An open field, maybe once a clearing, now stained. Almost a hundred bodies, twisted in impossible ways, littered the ground. Some half-buried. Some with faces he swore he knew. Ashley. Sean. Luke. They weren't real. He knew that. He had to know that. He fell to his knees. Blood soaked his pants. He couldn't breathe. He just screamed. No one heard it.

WHY! So much violence. So much DEATH! He struck his forehead with a fist, trembling.

"People aren't like this. Are they?" he asked out loud.

James looked to Nick's unconscious body. "Please wake up. I can't do this alone. These people… we don't deserve to suffer."

Tears splashed on the bloody grass as his eyes carved graves for the fallen. "Th-these fucking monsters. This fucking Collective. Stupid religious tyrants. God damn you."

James sat there a while. Desolate. His breath shallow. The silence pressed against his eardrums like pressure under water. Then, for a moment, he heard it.

"James."

He locked in place, unable to move.

"James."

It was no more than a breath, but unmistakable. A voice he couldn't place. Male, maybe. Or female. It came from nowhere and everywhere. He turned toward the sound, toward the far side of the field.

There was no one there.

Still, something compelled him. A magnetic pull behind the ribs. James stood with effort, lifting Nick with renewed determination, though his muscles bellowed. His eyes fixed on the trees beyond the corpses.

"You want me broken," he said aloud. "You want me mad?"

His voice didn't echo. The Ark had swallowed it whole.

"Die, James." The whisper lingered. "Nick. Sean."

It paused, then one more name came. "Ashley."

His eyes zipped left to right, and his ears turned outward.

"Ashley."

"NO!" He hollered.

And then something inside him shifted. James gritted his teeth and pressed forward, each step over the corpses another refusal. The voice shifted behind him, stretched thin like smoke. He didn't look back. He didn't have to.

It reached out to him again, "You killed James."

"No. That's not me." James pressed on through the field of corpses, tripping over one as he carried Nick. "You're wrong."

"Subject 333… special… we're watching you." The whisper gouged.

"I'm nothing like them. They don't know me!" James reluctantly continued through, ignoring the strung-out organs and bullet holes in skulls and torsos.

He had reached the tree line across the grassland. The whisper reached out once more.

"You can't stop it, James."

This time he didn't reply. With a sharp inhale, he spun around. The corpses were gone.

Every last one. No blood. No rot. Just grass, swaying gently in the artificial breeze.

[CH.25]

SHATTERED MINDS

The energetic scream had knocked them off their feet.

Ashley's ears still rang from the concussion blast that had swept through the facility hours, maybe just minutes ago. There was no use in checking her watch. She didn't care. It was impossible to measure time anymore. The floor had groaned beneath them, the walls had thrummed like a struck bell, and then all had gone still again. She wiped the blood from her nose before her body shook. Rattled both inside and out.

The others were damaged too. Bloody. Disoriented. They had regrouped in the dim corridor just outside the pulse's epicenter, some of them vomiting from vertigo, others just lying still, waiting for the buzzing in their skulls to fade. Ashley had pressed her palms to the wall, trying to feel the Ark's rhythms. There was nothing there. No thrum. No pulse, not even a faint vibration. It was like touching the skin of a dead man. A cold stillness sank into her chest, deeper than fear. The silence felt final.

"Something broke, something deep." Elias stayed under his breath—eyes rolling, he walked ahead.

Now, as they moved forward, the corridor felt different. Quieter. Heavier somehow. It stretched ahead endlessly. The passageway's light was blinding. Ashley led the group with measured steps, each footfall resounding softly behind her. Luke flanked her right, Raspberry to her left, and Elias followed close behind, glancing over his shoulder now and then like he expected the walls to shift.

Blood smeared the tiled floor in odd patterns, scattered drops here and there like breadcrumbs from something wounded and limping. The sight kept their minds tense and fingers curled.

Ashley held up her hand. "There," she whispered.

A man lay slumped against the right wall, limbs askew, one boot twisted behind him. He looked less like a person and more like a discarded marionette. A shotgun was strapped around his torso and a handgun at his side. He remained lifeless, positioned right under the archway of a large opening at the end of the hall.

Raspberry approached on edge. "Is he dead?"

Luke knelt and checked his pulse. "No. Breathing. Weak, but steady."

Raspberry grew eager. "Then let's end it. Before he wakes up."

Ashley shook her head. "We're not butchers. Just disarm him and let's keep moving."

Elias stripped John of his shotgun, a sidearm, and a half-empty pack of rations. Luke checked his pulse again. "He's definitely not dead. He might wake up soon."

"Then we should go." Ashley tightened her backpack strap and reached for the pistol Elias handed her. She checked the magazine before cocking the weapon. Elias secured the shotgun around his shoulder after checking the chamber.

They moved past the unconscious form and into the arched chamber beyond. The moment they stepped through, the environment chilled. It was vast. Home to towering levels of grated walkways, shifting platforms, and hydraulic bridges that creaked softly in the distance. The ceiling was lost in darkness. The lights were blinking like stars above a mechanical abyss.

Ashley led them to a low vantage point behind one of the upper-level grates. It was far enough away from the unconscious man. His body was a silhouette now. The distant rattle of metal made Ashley drop. The others followed suit. Down one floor, they could hear commotion. Quickly, Ashley crept along the bridge to the other side. The light was broken up by each bridge that extended in diagonal directions. Shadows cast here and there. Large boxes and hanging chains littered some of the floors like a warehouse.

From here, they could see the main floor. On it, they saw a man in the center of the open platform, shirtless and rail-thin. His skin was marked in dark script, words written in his own blood or someone else's. His arms were spread wide like a preacher.

"ASHTON STOP THIS!" A man howled below. It had been Ashton, Cora, and Sam. Folks Ashley was fortunate not to have met. She wasn't so fortunate now.

Cora was upright against a tall pipe, bound at the wrists, her eyes bloodshot and panicked. Sam was curled on the floor beside her, one ankle badly broken and cut. His face was bruised and slick with tears.

"They said the Ark would show us who we really are," Ashton intoned, voice thick with rapture. "And I have seen the shape of my soul." He twirled a rusted pipe in one hand and turned toward the ceiling. "The Collective watches. They whisper in dreams. In waves. I've been reborn."

Ashley's breath caught. Luke clenched his jaw. Raspberry looked pale. Elias readied his shotgun.

"He's gone," Raspberry murmured. "Gone completely." At this point he completely neglected his wound. Whether it was from shock or because madness drowned out the pain, now it was as if it never existed.

Ashton walked slowly to Sam and lowered the pipe. The lights stuttered in uneven bursts.

"You think this is pain?" he said gently. "Pain is the rusting of purpose. Pain is silence in the presence of truth."

The pipe came down, narrowly missing his skull. Sam whimpered.

"What do we do?" Raspberry hissed.

Ashley's fingers hovered over the trigger. "We don't rush it."

Her eyes swept the grated levels and the edge of the nearest descent point. The expanse could have six stories and at least four visible bridges. The main floor, which appeared in the middle, had no walkways. She could make it down. She could run. Leave them behind. Rappel three floors, disappear under the platform's supports and vanish into the unknown. They chose to follow her. She owed them nothing.

But still, Luke trusted her. Raspberry, despite his pain, had kept up without complaint, and Elias had covered her back when she was almost shot in the face. There was a time, not long ago, when she'd barked orders in the tunnels, rationed water, and kept the group sane. When she used to believe in leading. In helping.

Now? That certainty had fractured. Everything good she'd tried to protect had been drowned by the Ark's storm of disorder. Maybe this is who she was now. Someone who knew when to cut and run. Someone who didn't wait to be swallowed whole.

"Do you two have any idea how long I've been down here?" Ashton's sermon broke Ashley from her thoughts.

Raspberry perched behind her shoulder while Elias and Luke stood further into the shadows. All four looked down at the show.

"Why are you doing this?" Cora cried, while tears streamed down her cheeks.

"Why do we do anything? That's the point. For His Grace or whatever the fuck they want to call it." Ashton raised the rebar to Cora's chin, his voice dripping with derision. "You think this is madness?" He kicked Sam, sending him sprawling to the ground. Vomit burst from his mouth, splattering through the grated floor below. Ashton's smile twisted. "But it's not. It's clarity. I've been purified in this place. Scraped raw until all the lies were gone. You don't see it yet, but you will. You all will."

He looked skyward, eyes distant. "The Ark doesn't make mistakes. Every room, every scream… it's scripture. And we're here to obey just as you fools followed me. Because of what? Fear? Obedience? You are tools, nothing more."

Sam coughed up phlegm, trying to speak, "We're innocent!"

Another kick to the abdomen shut him up. "No one here is innocent," Ashton proclaimed.

Raspberry leaned back from the edge above. "He's lost it."

On the third floor, Ashley, Luke, and Raspberry watched the turmoil unfold below.

"He's stalling," Ashley muttered to herself.

Luke, hearing her, asked, "For what?" He turned back to the bridge and froze. The cop was gone. His voice dropped to a low, urgent tone. "Ashley!"

Ashley turned to him, following his gaze.

Across the expanse, where the man with weapons up for grabs had been, there was now only empty tile. The silhouette had vanished. They all stood motionless and stunned.

"Shit!" Ashley cursed, her voice sharp.

A new sound pierced through the chamber. Metal clinking between each grate, a chain unbound.

"WHO IS THAT?" Ashton demanded. "WHO'S THERE?"

"HELP US, PLEASE!" Cora bawled, her voice strained and ragged.

Ashton answered with a savage swing of the rebar, striking her bound body. Blood spewed across the floor and over his arms, dousing him in crimson. Sam let out a choking sob and collapsed in anguish. Cora's head lolled, her skull fractured beyond recognition. A ruin of flesh and bone.

The clatter of metal intensified. Rattling chains echoed through the structure like a warning bell. Elias had already backed away. Ashley caught it—just barely. The old man's eyes weren't wide with fear. They were narrow. Focused. He looked once at John below, then once at Ashley, and something passed across his face that she couldn't name. Not panic. Not guilt. Recognition. Then the shadows took him, and he was gone without a word. A survival instinct had overridden his soul. Or something else entirely.

Raspberry dropped to the floor, limbs quivering like a rattlesnake's tail. Ashley squared her stance and raised her pistol, jaw tight with focus. Luke held steady at her side, eyes darting between the noise and the figure of Ashton below.

And then—he stepped into view.

John.

His eyes were open now, glassy and empty, yet sharp. There was a hollow precision to his movements, like he was following commands written into his spine. The chain dragged behind him, links scraping and snapping against the metal with every step. His shirt was torn and his mouth bled. He didn't care.

Ashton turned, pipe raised. "You! You're not part of this. This isn't your sacrament!"

John didn't stop. He didn't speak. He moved like a machine.

The first swing was wide—Ashton sidestepped it—but the second struck him hard in the ribs. The pipe clattered as Ashton stumbled. Sam whimpered beside him.

Ashley had her sights on John, but her fingers couldn't move. A chill rolled through her. James had mentioned, back in the tunnels, about the possibility of a cop among them. Someone broken. Someone dangerous. And now, seeing John—bloody, relentless, precise—she knew. This was him. The one James feared. The one who had haunted their escape. And she had walked right past him, let him live. Her breath hitched. For a moment, guilt eclipsed the terror. James had seen this coming and she had ignored it. All those events unfolded once more in her mind—the way James risked his life for her, the way she had easily left him behind.

John dropped the chain and grabbed Ashton by the throat. He followed up by slamming him into the grated floor.

The others observed from above. "How did he get down there without us noticing?" Raspberry moaned.

"He's a ghost," Luke muttered, his eyes widening, as if the very fabric of reality had unraveled before him.

"You think you're the saint or the sinner?" the inimical man sneered, standing over Ashton with an unsettling calm.

"How'd you get down here?" Ashton's voice cracked, panic set in as he crawled backwards.

In an instant, John lunged. His fists slammed into Ashton's head, each blow harder than the last, pounding his skull against the hard, unforgiving floor. The metallic clang of impact reverberated. Blood pooled around them, mingling with Sam's vomit, dripping through the grated floor in a grotesque cascade.

Luke took a step forward. "We should stop him. Wait, where's Elias?" Luke turned to count heads. In doing so he noticed Ashley was missing as well.

Down below them, John stood upright, breathing hard. Ashton lay still. John retrieved the chain and dangled it over the zealot. He slung the steel links around Ashton's neck. With one yank and a snap, his neck broke.

Ashley saw it from above, clear as day. Her breath caught as she watched John's arms tense and the sickening crack that followed. She didn't need confirmation. Ashton was dead.

Executed. And John… John had done it without flinching. For a split second, Ashley caved. This was it, the brutal truth James had warned her about. Her hand hovered near the rope on her bag, her instincts torn between action and paralysis. The image of John—ruthless, unwavering—etched itself into her mind. Was this the future waiting for all of them? Her breath hitched again. Whether it was horror or self-preservation, she made her decision.

More metal clanking rang out from above. John glanced up and saw Ashley struggling to pull herself off the ledge, the rope tethered firmly into the grated floor. Her legs quivered while her grip slipped, though her determination remained unshaken.

She was too late.

John turned and looked directly at her, smiling.

Ashley's stomach dropped. That smile didn't belong to a man. It was a monster's grin, and it shattered any illusion of control she thought she had. In that moment, she remembered the times she had stood strong—keeping the lead, making the impossible decisions back when they still believed there was a way out. But now, here, faced with something inhuman wearing a man's face, all of that resolve evaporated. Nothing mattered now, except her own safety.

Luke tried calling out in time, "Ashley! Where are you going!?"

Before descending, she looked across to him, "I'm sorry Luke. I can't."

She let go of the edge and quickly descended, story after story, aiming for the bottom floor. John walked over and picked up the piece of metal pipe Ashton carried earlier and raised it high. His eyes followed her down as he counted in his head. Ashley's rope whipped taut, two stories short of the floor. She hung for a second, vulnerable. Then the pipe came. With bullseye aim, the steel struck her forehead, and she let go of the rope. Her body fell past the remaining stories and her back slammed against the ground. No more slack. No more good luck.

Luke's face grew dark. He couldn't find Elias, who had the only other weapon and a useless Raspberry laid helpless on the floor. He had caved in to panic. John took note of Luke's position now. He started pulling himself up the thick chain, hand over hand, like a creature bred for ascent. The distance between them was closing fast. In sheer terror Luke ran into the darkness while Ashley drifted off. The world tilted. Black swallowed her pain. She felt something strange overcome her. Not fear, but failure. Her eyes finally shut.

She was out.

[CH.26]

//:System Error //

[MEMORY LOG RETRIEVED]

Subject: 390-ASHLEY

//:July 7, 2016 //
//:Mt. Rainier, WA //

The thick fog pressed around them as the group trudged uphill. Mud clung to their boots and the sky above threatened another storm. They were less than twenty-five hundred feet from the summit.

Ashley led, her breath steady despite the climb, eyes locked forward. She was the captain. The compass. She had led expeditions up Rainier every summer for the past six years. Each summit built her streak, her credibility, her shot at Everest. She couldn't afford to fail now, not over a little rain.

Behind her, Peter slipped and cursed. "Can we take a break?" he called.

Ashley didn't stop. "You can drink water while you walk."

The others exchanged glances. Two rookies from Phoenix. The last pair were newlyweds from Michigan—overpacked and underprepared. Ashley maintained her stride ahead of the others.

"We're less than half a mile," she said over her shoulder. "We push to the summit, then take the flatter slope down. We won't need ropes."

Another voice chimed in. "Ashley, the weather's turning. Maybe we should head back."

Ashley paused, turning to scan their faces. They were soaked and winded. Soft.

In her mind, she heard the mockery that would come if she failed to summit. The gossip at the center. The chuckles from the others who'd seen her as competition. Samantha. That bitch. Her and her perfect record. Everest slipping further away.

If they can't handle the climate, they shouldn't have requested me. They paid for this trip—every one of them—and I'm not about to lose my streak because they're afraid of a little weather. If I give in now, they'll just call me weak. A failure. I need this.

She swallowed her frustration, hardening her expression.

"Fine," she said, trying to mask her irritation. "Head back to the signposts. Hang out near the bear bins. There's another group down that trail. You can rendezvous with them. Radio's on channel three. I'll call it in."

"You're going to summit alone?" one of them asked.

"You're welcome to join," Ashley replied. "I'm finishing this regardless."

They hesitated. She didn't. Turning from them, she radioed base to confirm her group's detour, then started up the slope alone.

Rain lashed sideways, then cleared, then lashed again. The fog thickened. Still, she moved like clockwork. Her body knew the rhythm.

An hour and a half later, she reached the summit. Clouds blanketed the horizon, hiding the world below. She let out a long breath, soaking it in. It was hers. She had done it again.

She didn't linger though.

On the descent, the mountain began to change. The clouds darkened, shifting fast as if pulled by invisible strings. The air thickened with the tang of ionized metal, bitter as old iron and singed copper, biting at the back of her throat with each breath. Wind barreled through narrow ravines, rattling loose shale. Distant thunder rumbled beyond the ridgeline, its resonance off. Too deep. Too sluggish.

Needles of rain returned, slicing at her cheeks and jacket. Each step felt heavier. The world narrowed to just her breath, her boots, and the slick, treacherous path. Fog swelled upward from the trees, no longer drifting but crawling, deliberate and low. A warning.

Ashley's chest tightened. She increased her stride.

She reached the base of the slope near the signposts and paused.

The campsite was gone.

In its place: shredded branches, mangled gear, and earth gouged into unnatural shapes. A boot jutted from the mud. A torn sleeping bag flapped against a tree. She ran. Called names. No response. The ridge had given way.

Not a massive landslide, but enough. Enough to bury them. To erase them. She found Peter's bag wrapped in vines. A torn jacket half-submerged in clay. No bodies. Just absence.

Ashley dropped to her knees, chest heaving. No sound came. Her hands sank into the soil. She had reached the summit. They had not.

When the rangers found her hours later, she was seated beside a washed-out tent. Her face buried in her mud-covered hands. She reported the timeline, the weather, the choice they made. She spoke like a professional. Efficient.

She didn't mention how badly she had needed that summit though. She didn't say she'd heard the storm and dismissed it. Or that, in some small part of her, she'd believed they couldn't hold her back.

She only told them what they needed. And that's all she told herself. As the ranger helped her to her feet, the fog grew unnaturally dense. A high-pitched ringing started in her ears. Her fingers twitched. The fog didn't drift. It beckoned.

She didn't see the horizon fade or the trees blur. She only thought, *I left them.* Then the world stuttered. Ashley vanished mid-step, swallowed by something just beyond human understanding. In that moment she was gone.

[CH.27]

L O S T
A N D
F O U N D

Drip. Drip. Drip.

The sound pried Ashley from the depths of her sleep.

Cold. Damp. Her eyes fluttered open to a dim, green-tinged darkness. The ceiling above her was cracked and rusted, a web of ancient pipes weeping condensation. Something soft cushioned her back. Blankets. Real ones. Not tile or steel.

She tried to sit up. Pain lanced through her shoulder.

"Easy now," a voice came from nearby, low and soothing.

Ashley turned. A silhouette hunched near a small, flickering lantern. The man looked more like a pile of laundry than a person—tattered clothes, wild hair, eyes sunken but sharp. He handed her a metal cup. Water.

"You were out a long time," he said. "Thought you'd died."

Ashley drank. The water was cool, clean. She coughed once, then looked around. The room was narrow and cluttered, walls lined with salvaged junk: wires, broken panels, worn boots, ration boxes, what looked like a half-burned pillow. It was hidden, tucked between cracked partitions and shrouded in shade. A pocket between dimensions.

"Where am I?" she asked.

"Somewhere safe. For now." He shifted, joints cracking. "This place… it's got corners. If you know where to look, you can hide in 'em."

Ashley blinked. Her head throbbed, memory fogged. There had been shouting. Chains. Blood. John.

"Elias? Is that you?" she asked, her voice, carrying both relief and confusion. He'd vanished during the chaos—now here he was, a spectre, pulling her back from the edge.

"You were near the service bridge. Sprawled out like roadkill. Lucky you didn't bleed out. Saw the whole thing from a vent shaft. Waited 'til the noise stopped. Dragged you here."

"How long have you been here?" Her hands gripped her head, fingers threading through her hair in a frantic search for clarity.

He scratched his beard. "Time's funny in this place. Years, maybe. Maybe more. Long enough to know how to stay alive. Long enough to stop expecting rescue."

"No, I meant from when you left us."

"Oh, not too long after that man showed up. Large fellow he was."

"I didn't know you could speak so clearly."

"When Luke found me, I was a bit hazy. That evil ringing never gets old. It boggles the mind. Seems like someone managed to shut it off. Never seen that before."

"James," the name slipped from her lips, soft and fragile, like a breath that had barely escaped.

"Good fellow he was. Shame he had to split."

"Yeah, it is." Ashley tried to stand. "The others… what happened to them?"

"Luke ran, and the man in the suit—Berry or whatever his name was—he just stayed there like a scared animal. You need to recover, miss. Nasty fall that was." Elias gestured to a corner with scavenged supplies and a battered map, marked with symbols.

Ashley stared at the diagram. "You've been charting this place."

"As best I can. Most corridors rearrange. But some pockets, they stay. I've left caches. Food. Batteries. Even medicine. Not much, but enough. Scattered them here and there."

She walked toward the map, still limping. Her reflection appeared in a fractured mirror nearby, mud-streaked, blood at her temple, eyes alight with a mix of weariness and fury.

She touched the glass. *I left them.*

Elias watched her quietly.

"I remembered something," she turned to Elias. "Before this… I-I left people behind. It cost them their lives. I can't do that again."

"We've all done bad things here. That's what they do. The Collective. They drag people like us in here. Bad folks, broken ones. For their God. Or whatever name they give it."

Ashley was upright. She took a deep breath. The air smelled like copper and dust. Her eyes met Elias'. "I never thanked you. For saving our lives from that man in the Sanctuary."

"Oh, that. Yeah, I guess I lost myself a bit, didn't I?"

"None of us would have made it without you."

"Neither would I without you, miss," Elias smiled.

Ashley felt a spark of hope. A refreshing feeling that she hadn't felt in a long time. She looked back down to the map. "What happened to that cop?"

"Oh. I stayed away from that, couldn't see him from where I was. Waited for the silence before I retrieved you."

"I don't blame you."

She went for another sip of water and then ate some rations that had been lying on the floor. The space was tight. Not bad for a hole in the wall. Dark but cozy. She embraced some blankets. "What do you know about the SmartArk?"

"This hellish building? Only what I already told you. It rearranges itself but some things don't move. Every place gotta have staff you know."

"Have you ever been into the areas that don't change?"

"Maybe once or twice, every time they either zap me with that damn sound or force me out. Think I ran into some others once. Nearly died then. Nearly die all the time."

"Think you can lead me there?"

"I can try." Elias shuffled toward a corner and retrieved a small pile of items. "Figured you'd want these back."

He handed her the familiar weight of her backpack, scuffed but intact. From inside, she pulled out her flashlight. The battery was still good. She clicked the beam on.

"Lucky flashlight." She gave a faint smile. "Feels good to have it again."

Looking down she noticed her watch had broken. It didn't matter now. Time had become irrelevant. She was just happy to have her gear back.

"I also found this." The reflection of unyielding steel caught her eyes. Elias found the pistol they had recovered from John's unconscious body.

Ashley holstered the pistol in her pants and slung the pack over her shoulders. "Glad no one else found that." She raised the flashlight. Its beam cut a clean line through the gloom.

They moved toward the exit of the hideaway, crouching through a narrow crawlspace lined with wires. The facility beyond was quiet. Too quiet.

As they stepped into the corridor, Elias muttered to himself before securing the shotgun to his torso. He was a resourceful man. Now

Ashley wouldn't take that for granted anymore. She erased the thought of leaving James behind— or tried to. It didn't shake cleanly. It clung the way guilt does, not loud but persistent, a low note under everything else. He hadn't asked her to stay. He hadn't even looked betrayed. He'd just watched her go, and that was almost worse. Maybe she could find him again. Maybe they could get out. Maybe.

Elias moved first, lifting a hanging cloth from a corner and revealing a narrow service crawlspace. They ducked through, weaving between rusted piping and warm conduit, until the path widened into a sloped passage that fed directly into a familiar chamber. The layered room yawned out before them.

Ashley slipped the flashlight into the strap loop on her backpack and adjusted the shoulder harness. Pain pulsed beneath her ribs, yet clarity pressed through the fog of exhaustion. She stopped at the threshold's edge.

The mechanical abyss hadn't changed. Grated walkways stretched out in tiers like spiderwebs, hydraulic bridges sagged or half-shifted, groaning occasionally in the stale air. But the silence was different. Its stillness had substance now. The residue of violence.

Ashley descended a level. Her eyes combing the shadows. Blood trailed along one of the grated floors. A smear. A patch. A handprint.

Her breath caught. There, farther across the chamber, was the spot she'd last seen Sam. There was no body now. Just a stain. A memory. Elias stayed a few steps back, giving her room.

"They're gone," she whispered, "All of them."

He didn't answer right away. Just watched her face.

"I was right there," she added, her voice brittle, "And I ran."

"You survived," Elias said. "There's no shame in survival."

Ashley didn't respond. Instead, she knelt, brushing her fingers against the dried blood. "I don't think survival is enough anymore. Not when it means leaving people behind. Not when it means walking over the ones who stayed behind."

A long moment passed before Elias spoke again. "This room wasn't always like this. Years ago, it was cleaner. Humming louder. They'd run simulations here. Tests."

Ashley looked up at him, "Tests?"

"Group dynamics. Trust and betrayal. They'd feed us lies, set traps, wipe memories between rounds. I figured it out piece by piece." He shook his head. "Didn't matter. By the time I understood it, I'd already done things I couldn't undo."

Ashley stood, facing him fully now. "What kind of things?"

His eyes were dark, "There was a woman once. Strong like you. Took charge. Got people moving. She reminded me of someone I lost a long time ago. And I let her die."

"Why?"

"They promised me a way out. Said if I cooperated, if I proved that I could make the right choice… I'd be free."

Ashley sighed, "And?"

"I've been here ever since."

They stood in silence. The chamber groaned. Ashley looked away. The weight of it settled somewhere behind her sternum—not pity, something closer to recognition. She thought of her own group left scattered across the place. Of the choices she'd dressed up as logic. Of the ranger helping her to her feet on the mountain while she recited only what they needed to hear. Elias hadn't done anything she hadn't. Her teeth gritted. "Then let's make sure this place never forgets her."

Elias nodded. "We need to get to the bottom."

She adjusted her bag and moved toward the next descending bridge. Staying beside Elias, she kept watch and clung to her sidearm. Ashley said nothing as they walked. Not because she didn't want to, but because Elias led the way with such conviction that interrupting felt wrong. The corridors no longer buzzed—only the soft creak of pipes and the occasional drip danced through the empty halls.

Elias walked with purpose, limping slightly. His feet were in no rush. He moved like someone who had memorized the pulses of a living machine.

Ashley followed. For once, she followed.

She gripped her pistol tighter than necessary and kept her backpack light against her shoulders. Her torch flashed across doorframes, rusted bolts, and dried bloodstains. A piece of someone's shirt hung like a flag from a bent pipe. Probably that psycho Ashton's.

"Do you always know where you're going?" she asked after a long silence.

Elias didn't stop walking. "Nope," he said. "But I know where I've been. And sometimes, that's enough."

They reached the edge of the multi-tiered chamber. Her flashlight cut a slow arc through the room. Everything looked still, but not untouched.

Ashley took the lead now, stepping carefully to the grated floor, her boots clicking lightly with each step. The metal trembled faintly around them.

"Over there," Elias said, pointing.

Near one of the disconnected ramps, by the remnants of a handrail, a pair of worn canvas shoes sat neatly together, half-soaked in dried blood.

Ashley's breath caught, "Raspberry?"

She approached them with creeping intent. One shoe had been slashed along the side, the sole nearly detached. The other, a hole through the top and bottom. The injury he had sustained with Nick. The one he miraculously pushed through. Not easy to do with a hole in your foot. Raspberry was a trooper. She thought he'd never make it as far as he did. If only she had done better.

She crouched, reaching out, pausing only briefly before touching them. Still warm. Not from life, from being here too long. Absorbing the temperature of this place. Of death.

Elias crouched beside her and investigated. "Lot of blood there."

Ashley turned her head stiffly. "I was surprised he kept up for so long."

She picked one shoe up and then stopped, staring into the blackened pit beyond the ledge. "He was scared. Always scared. But he never ran. I don't know how he kept moving, but he did. And I… I let him down."

Elias cleared his throat.

Ashley placed the shoe gently beside the other. "I wonder where he is now."

They stayed there for a while, just standing in the dark. Pondering the thought of the building consuming the man. They both shook the thought. Then Ashley asked, "Who were you before this?"

Elias leaned back against a support beam, arms crossed. His face was unreadable in the dim light.

"A coward," he said. "A drunk. Worked in security for a pharmaceutical company, before I was a paramedic. I lost people. Too many. Didn't handle it well."

Ashley looked over at him.

"I got bitter," he continued. "Mean. Took it out on others. Thought the world owed me peace. Then I woke up here." He gestured toward the ceiling. "Guess they didn't agree."

She gave a deliberate nod, feeling the burden of his words. The air between them felt thick, as if the truth of it all had settled on their shoulders, too heavy to move.

"But that's not the end of it," Elias added. "Being brought here doesn't mean you're done. I've survived this long not because I'm good, but because I decided I would no longer be what I was."

Ashley's voice was soft yet firm. "You're not a coward. You've come this far. That counts for something."

Elias chuckled dryly.

They surveyed the room, the emptiness no longer an alien presence—it had settled in as a constant companion. A weighty one, pressing heavily against her chest with every step. The air felt dense, charged, as though the tide was on the verge of rising. She could sense it, creeping ever closer.

Ashley straightened her shoulders, pushing the past aside for now. "Let's keep moving." The words were final.

Elias nodded, adjusting the shotgun with a steady hand. Without another word, he took the lead and Ashley followed. There was no turning back now.

[CH.28]

A
NEW
DIRECTION

The sound of water trickling over stone echoed through the hollow grove. James crouched near the edge of a shallow stream, his hands shaking as they dipped beneath the surface. The water was clear—unnaturally so—almost crystalline as it passed over the moss-covered rocks. It shimmered in the dusky light that filtered through the false canopy above, casting fractured reflections across his scarred knuckles.

He brought the water to his lips. Cool. Clean. But the taste brought no comfort. James lowered his eyes again to the surface. A face stared back—his own. Less familiar than ever. Pale. Gaunt. Eyes sunken with fatigue and something deeper. His lips were chapped. Dried blood still crusted under one nostril.

He touched his cheek. *Is this who I am now?*

The image rippled as the water shifted, distorting his features into something monstrous. He flinched and pulled back.

Behind him, the artificial forest swayed gently. But there was no wind. The impossible world fell silent and there was a long, settling hush.

He sat down on a stone, elbows on his knees, staring into nothing. The field of corpses had vanished, swallowed by the dreamlike illusion of the Sanctuary. The memory lingered, the feeling of Sean's blood on his hands still raw. The Sanctuary, once a surreal reprieve, had turned into a graveyard. It didn't matter if it was real. The consequences were the same.

You killed him. The words replayed inside his skull. Unspoken. Impossible to ignore.

James exhaled slowly, his breath catching as he pressed his palms to his eyes. He hadn't meant to. He *had* meant to. Both were true.

He had no idea how long he sat like that—minutes, hours, days. Time bent in here. The water kept flowing. The walls hummed faintly. Inside him, nothing moved. He looked up again, to the trees that weren't trees. Plastic. Synthetic. The illusion of life, like him. A hollow version of himself, adrift in mind and body.

Turning to Nick, he saw his slumped form. He had laid him in a patch of soft grass, whatever comfort he could give, even in unconsciousness. James wondered if he'd ever wake up. Was it a coma? Or something worse? Everyone who helped him disappeared eventually. Faded out, one by one. Abandoned again, he rested.

The voice returned. *"JAMES."*

His eyelids lowered and his head met his palms. Deep breaths filled his lungs. A sigh opened his eyes. He pressed his hands to the stone. Hard. Frigid. Like him.

His mind looped back to the tunnel, the stream of water he followed, the beautiful woman he found. The man he failed to save. The man he had saved… and killed. The thoughts looped, again and again.

"Subject 333… we've been watching you."

"GODDAMMIT!" he erupted, hurling a loose rock into the stream. His breath quickened. His eyes snapped wide. *I'm not going to make it, am I? Not like this.*

Then a sound stirred behind him—a low grunt, muffled movement against fabric.

He rose, heart hammering, and turned.

Nick ached, shifting on the patch of grass. His face twitched, eyelids fluttering as if fighting off a dream. Then a cough, wet and shallow, yet real.

James raced toward him. "Nick?"

Another breath. Nick's eyes blinked open. For a moment, they were empty, unfocused. Then they snapped toward James, and something behind them ignited recognition. Not fear. Not confusion. Just… awareness.

"Took you long enough," Nick rasped.

James dropped to one knee beside him, relief breaking through the fog in his chest. "You're awake. Jesus. I thought—"

"You thought I was gone?" Nick tried to sit up but hissed and held his side. "I've felt worse. Not by much."

James helped him upright. "You've been out for days. Or hours. I don't even know anymore."

Nick blinked, looking past James to the synthetic trees and glowing underbrush. "The Sanctuary. How'd we make it back here?" He paused. "You carried me?"

"Yeah," James muttered. "I didn't know what else to do."

Nick gave a faint nod. "You did the right thing. You saved my life."

James looked away. "Better than the alternative, right?"

The stream babbled nearby, undisturbed.

Nick's eyes found James again, "That man with the bat?"

James didn't answer.

"I saw it before I blacked out," Nick spoke softly, "There was no other option."

James clenched his fists; his nails cut into his palms. "It shouldn't have come down to that. It was… it was like something else took over. Like I'd already decided. And I can't tell if that was a survival instinct or who I really am."

Nick didn't speak. He watched him.

"I keep seeing it," James added, "Him choking on blood. The look in his eyes. I—" He shook his head. "I don't know if I can come back from it."

Nick offered, "This place was built to break us. Every corridor, every sound, every missing piece of memory—it's all a pressure test. They want to see what we'll become when we're cornered."

James turned toward him. "Yeah, the Collective." He looked down in dismay. "Masters molding monsters."

Nick didn't answer immediately. His eyes drifted to the treetops above them, where soft light filtered down like a memory he couldn't shake.

James noticed something different in Nick's eyes. "You know something, don't you."

Nick met his gaze. "I do."

A silence stretched between them.

James narrowed his eyes. "What is it?"

Nick exhaled, his tone low. "It's… nothing you need to hear."

James took a step forward. "That's not your call."

"It is if I'm trying to keep you alive," Nick pushed back. "Some of what I remember… it's not just information. It's pain. And if I dump it all on you now, it might make things worse for you. I've seen it happen before— memories flood in and people shatter. They give up. Or worse."

James opened his mouth, then closed it. He looked away.

"You're carrying enough already, James." Nick chose his words with precision. "Guilt. Doubt. Rage. I'm not hiding the truth to control you. I'm doing it because you need to survive. We both do."

James didn't respond at first. He turned back to the stream, watching the water curl around stones like it had somewhere to go.

"Just tell me one thing then," he said quietly, staring into his own reflection. "Do we have a chance?"

Nick stepped beside him, gaze steady. "If we don't quit? Yeah. There's always a chance."

James nodded once. It wasn't peace. But it was something close. He stood and offered Nick a hand. "Then let's make our next move."

Nick took James' hand. They rose together, as if the weight of it all had barely lifted.

Nick didn't let go right away. His hand rested briefly on James' shoulder. "Thank you," he said. "For carrying me. For not leaving me behind."

James shrugged it off with quiet humility. "Seemed like the least I could do."

"No," Nick said. "Most people wouldn't have done that."

A silence passed between them, thick with unspoken recognition.

"I keep wondering where they are," James said. "Ashley. Raspberry. Even Luke and Elias, if they made it."

Nick followed his stare out toward the forest. Its stillness offered no clues. He thought back to Raspberry—where he saved him from drowning, the torn leg, the spike through the foot. The blood. Always blood.

"I want to believe they're alive," James added. "That they've handled things better than we have."

"They made their decision. We have to live with that just as they do, mate." Nick stared into the hollowed eyes of James. "Now we have to keep making ours."

"I want to stop this," James said, voice stern.

Nick smiled. "Glad to hear you say that."

They stood there dwarfed by fabricated trees, alone in a manufactured wilderness.

"I've been thinking," Nick continued. "This place… whatever it is… it's more advanced than anything I've ever seen. The architecture, the seamless integration of control systems… it's not just some underground facility."

James tilted his head. "What are you saying?"

Nick held back, weighing each word as he spoke. "I think… we're not where we think we are. Or *when*."

James' brow furrowed. "You think we're in the future?"

"I don't know how far. But the tech here… memory suppression, environmental control, neural resonance feedback? It's decades ahead of what I knew. Even advanced AI wasn't this clean. This precise."

James looked shaken. "You've seen a place like this?"

Nick wagged his head. "Not even close."

They paused, letting it hit them.

"The SmartArk," Nick spoke gently, "It's too advanced."

"Isn't that obvious?"

They both paused for a moment to think, taking the time to recollect the hologram's briefing before bloodshed had ensued.

Nick's chin rose, "There's bound to be access tunnels. Corridors that link deeper levels."

"We don't have anything," James said. "No food. No weapons. No map."

"Then we improvise," Nick said, tapping his temple. "The architecture shifts in tandem with cognitive behavior."

"Isn't that what the hologram said?"

Nick smirked. "More or less. If we will it, it changes."

James frowned, the memory flashing in front of him—pressing his hand to the wall, watching it open. "That's how I got us out last time."

"You didn't know where you were going," Nick said. "But you still moved forward. Strong will on you, mate." He laughed and clapped his hands.

James crossed his arms. "So what, we just think our way to freedom?"

"I wish it were that simple." Nick's tone sobered. "But it means something. We adapt to the Ark… and-"

"It adapts to us?"

Nick nodded. "That's the idea."

James was calm for a moment, then turned to face the tall surrounding trees. Their surreal leaves shimmered faintly, lit by a soft glow from somewhere above.

"That doesn't tell us how to get out," he said.

"No," Nick agreed. "But maybe it tells us where to start."

They stood there wounded and empty-handed, but no longer aimless.

James let out a breath and looked down the winding path ahead.

"Alright," he said. "Let's change the rules."

[CH.29]

E C H O E S
O F
T H E
P A S T

They descended stealthily. Each floor of the layered room behind them had been a memory—faint screams, broken railings, twisted metal—Ashley felt all of it pressing down from above. The bridges grew narrower the deeper they went, until at last, they reached the bottom level. It was an empty, echoing basin of metal grating and darkness, too far down for light to reach.

From there, the corridor revealed itself. It was massive.

A white tiled passage ran perpendicular to the open pit of the layered chamber, stretching to infinity in either direction. The walls pulsed faintly with artificial light, and each tile on the floor gleamed like it had never been touched by human hands. Immaculate. Inhuman. Terrifying in its precision.

Elias pointed, slowing her. "There," he whispered.

Ashley followed his gaze and saw it.

A wide, wet streak tore across the white floor. A smear of blood dragging along the corridor's edge, veering slightly before disappearing around a distant corner.

She didn't speak. Neither did he.

"I've seen markings like that before," Elias finally said. His voice was low, gravelly with memory. "Years ago, maybe more. Blood like that doesn't dry properly here. It keeps its shine. Stains the mind more than the tile."

Ashley crouched down, brushing her fingers across the edge of the smear. Still tacky. "It's fresh."

Elias scanned the walls. "I think this corridor might lead to the administration sector. If the old maps were right… it was always deeper. Further in."

She nodded, standing. Her breath misted slightly in the cold, lifeless air. Her grip tightened around the pistol.

They began moving, stepping lightly along the corridor's edge. Ashley kept an eye on the blood trail as it curved around the corner, her pulse quickening with each step. Elias followed the curve.

"Is this the way?" she asked.

"Unfortunately," Elias answered grimly.

The hallway ahead narrowed slightly. The lighting buzzed above, flickering in a rhythmic pulse that seemed almost intentional.

Ashley turned to him. "What exactly are we walking into?"

Elias sighed. "Knowing this place? You can't ever be sure."

They rounded the corner. The blood trail thickened.

What had once been a single dragging smear widened into erratic splashes—arcs along the wall, half-formed handprints sliding out of shape. Light bled across the room, pale and pitiless. It showed everything. Even the footprints staggered near the edge of the trail, evidence of a struggle. Someone had fought. Someone had begged.

Ashley tightened her grip further, knuckles white. Her finger rested along the trigger. Elias walked slower now, every step deliberate. Shotgun ready.

"Suffering." His voice was nearly lost in the buzzing light.

The corridor tilted slightly, or seemed to. Geometry warped the deeper they went. Shadows cast by nothing. Ceiling panels hummed like static on a television. The blood turned darker where it pooled, oxidized against the sterile air.

A few more steps and the corridor opened into a small alcove where the trail ended.

Ashley was stunned.

A body lay slumped against the wall. Twisted. Vomit clung to his chin and chest. One arm was broken at the elbow, bent backward. A jagged piece of rusted rebar jutted from his lower abdomen, pinning him like an insect. A wide lake of blood and bile had soaked the floor.

It was Sam. Someone must have finished him off after Ashton's skull was crushed.

Elias exhaled behind her, "Christ."

Ashley knelt, inspecting him without a touch. The eyes were half-lidded, the pupils clouded. A strange expression still clung to his face—apprehension and disbelief caught mid-moment. A cry that hadn't finished.

"He was awake when it happened," she breathed. "He felt it."

Elias scanned the walls, then the body. "This isn't just rage," he said. "It's execution."

"That cop?" Ashley's skin prickled, a chill moved up her arm like static.

"Hm," Elias narrowed his eyes. "A man without a soul."

She stood, swallowing the bile that crept up her throat. The blood on the rebar still glistened. Her stomach turned, not just from the smell, but from the dampness in the air.

"He tortured him," she said, "dragged him this far alive. Why?"

Elias gave a solemn nod, "We should keep going."

Ashley glanced further down the corridor. It continued—darker now, tighter. She didn't want to move forward, though there was no choice anymore.

"Okay, we keep moving." Her back straightened.

Elias gave the body one last glance, then stepped ahead to lead.

They moved past the carcass in silence.

Each step rang sharper now, as if the corridor were narrowing behind them, pushing them forward, deeper. The tiles remained immaculate, but the light faltered, carrying a weight that pressed against the skin. Shadows fell in strange angles, like the architecture itself had begun to lean inward.

Ashley's jaw tensed. The blood trail was behind them now, but it lingered in the back of her mind. She kept the pistol low and ready, scanning every seam and corner.

"There should be a chamber up ahead," Elias said, his voice hushed but steady. "If this place still runs on the old designs, we'll hit a convergence point soon."

Ashley glanced sideways. "And if we don't?"

He stared ahead, expression unreadable. "I'll leave that part up to you."

A sharp *click* sounded off down the corridor.

They stopped.

Ashley raised her pistol while Elias slung the shotgun to his front and released the safety.

Ashley's voice was a breath. "Are we just hearing things?"

"Could be nothing," Elias said.

She was scared to take a chance.

They pressed on, footsteps slower now, drawn forward by the rhythmic buzz above and the sense that something waited at the edge of perception.

Eventually, the tile under their feet changed. The surface dulled. It was matte and industrial. A faint line stretched along the base of each wall, almost like rails. Ahead, the corridor widened.

They reached the chamber.

A single glass wall cut across the room, seamless and high. Behind it lay a different world: rows of deactivated workstations, clean desk spaces, and long black monitors mounted to the walls. Everything was powered down, except for one screen in the center.

It glowed, steady and soft, displaying slow-moving lines of unfamiliar text.

Ashley halted just short of the glass. "There's no entry point. No door. No handle."

Elias studied the wall. "This separates us from them."

Ashley turned to him. "Can we shoot through it?"

He shook his head. "The way this place is? That glass is probably steel."

She frowned, eyes narrowing at the display. "Then maybe I'll just ask politely."

She stepped forward, staring into the glass as if daring it to answer her. Her reflection glared back, subtly warped, like everything else in this place. She didn't touch it. She didn't blink.

And then—a quiet mechanical shift.

A seam materialized at ankle height, then rapidly drove upwards, causing a section of the window to recede with a faint mechanical hiss. The air shifted, thickening as the pressure in the room changed.

Elias looked over at her. "Aren't you special."

"Gee, thanks."

They stepped through together, passing into the control space. Ashley moved between the silent terminals like relics on display, untouched and waiting to be discovered.

All the monitors were black except one. The screen glowed a dull green. As Ashley approached, she noticed a cursor blinking in the top right corner. It began typing on its own.

```
//:USER RECOGNIZED //
//:WELCOME
//:SUBJECT: 390
```

Ashley hardened mid-step. She tucked the pistol into her waistband and lowered herself into the nearby chair. She hadn't touched anything.

Elias stood behind her and examined the screen. The shotgun nestled in his arms.

Ashley stared at the monitor. Her own reflection rippled in its surface.

"It knows me," she said.

The screen stayed blank for a breath, except for the blinking cursor. Then more words appeared.

```
//:MEMORY CORRUPTION: PARTIAL //
//:ACCESSING BACKUP THOUGHT STREAM
//:DONE
```

Ashley leaned forward. "Thought stream?"

The text began to scroll again. Faster now.

FIVE LITTLE MONKEYS
JUMPING ON THE BED
ONE FELL OFF
AND BUMPED HIS HEAD

She blinked. "What?"

Elias squinted, trying to make out the text.

"Five monkeys," she murmured to herself.

MAMA CALLED THE DOCTOR
AND THE DOCTOR SAID

Her hands slowly curled into fists. The words struck. A memory surfaced from so deep, entombed in decades of dust and dread.

"No more monkeys jumping on the bed," she said softly.

"It's a nursery rhyme," Elias added, glancing at her.

The air thickened. The glow of the monitor deepened, as if the light itself had drawn a breath and held it.

Ashley stood abruptly, her voice hoarse. "It can't be."

She turned away from the screen. It reached for her.

"I don't understand," she whispered.

The cursor flashed—once, twice—then it resumed typing.

WOULD YOU LIKE TO CONTINUE?
Y/N

She hesitated.

"Don't touch it," Elias warned, voice low and firm.

But her hand was already lifting, guided by something deeper than thought. Not brave. Not reckless. Just… drawn.

"I need to know."

She pressed the key.

Y

The moment she did, a wave of force flooded through her eyes. The terminal stopped typing. A video overtook the screen.

A childhood bedroom. A window streaked with condensation. Someone's soft voice whispering her name.

Ashley took a step back, color draining from her face. "That's not possible…"

Elias stepped beside her. "Ashley, what is this?"

She didn't answer.

The footage continued.

A girl—eight years old—climbed down from a window. Her mother entered, humming the rhyme. The young girl scrambled back onto the bed as the older woman began folding laundry.

"Ashley," her mother said gently, "What did I tell you about climbing through that window?"

"I'm sorry, Mama," young Ashley replied.

Then a man's voice roared in the distance. Slurred. Unsteady.

"ASHLEY! WHAT DID I TELL YOU ABOUT LISTENING TO YOUR MOTHER!?"

A figure barreled into frame. The door slammed open. He held a belt, stumbling through the door.

"George, stop. She didn't do anything," her mother pleaded.

"MOVE!"

He threw the mother to the side of the room. She wailed as her body fell to the ground. Young Ashley crawled under the bed, screaming.

"NO! NO!"

A flash of black went by Ashley's shoulder and the screen cracked. The monitor burst into a violent spray of sparks, lightning flaring from its frame. Evocation ended. Elias swung the shotgun back to his side. Tears ran down her face, while smoke filled the air.

"We're done here," Elias said, his voice flat as he stared at the fractured, sputtering screen.

Sobs tore through her body as she collapsed to her knees.

Elias dropped beside her, one hand steady on her shoulder, the other still gripping the shotgun. "I'm sorry you had to see that."

"How? How is that possible?" Her face fell into her palms. The floor was drenched underneath her.

Her breath caught, chest cinched tight, like something unseen had curled around her lungs and squeezed. The ruined monitor fizzled out with one last electronic gasp, the screen fading into a final, empty black. It looked like an eye closing.

She didn't move.

Elias remained beside her, reserved. His hand on her shoulder stayed firm. Not comforting, just present. There was no comfort left in a place like this.

"Come on. Stand up," he said, raising her to his level.

Ashley wiped at her face, but the tears wouldn't stop. "How would they know that? That's not possible."

Elias hovered nearby, watching her. Then his eyes swept the room. "I'm sorry, Ashley. We need to go now."

Ashley caught her breath. He embraced her and led her to the far end of the room. Traversing between the dead monitors, they all powered on at once. The video resumed.

Ashley stopped in her tracks, her mouth falling open. Dozens of screens now displayed the same nightmare: the bedroom, the belt, the whimpering. Over and over.

He covered her eyes and escorted her forward. Her ears rang as they passed screen after screen, the audio distorted and warped by the speakers, like memories shouting in space. Her eyes flooded.

"Keep moving," Elias assured her. "Ignore it."

Ashley faltered, her vision clouded by more than just his hand.

They reached the far end. Elias raised a boot and kicked the final doorway open with a metal clang.

They passed through into another corridor—square, austere, suffocating. The walls here were bare concrete, lit by strips of harsh lights patterned across the ceiling. Along both sides, paired steel doors ran the length of the hall like cells in a prison. It stretched on and on into what looked like forever.

Elias pulled her forward.

"We're getting out of that room," he said, "Far away. Come on."

Ashley let herself be moved, hardly aware of her own feet. Behind them, the room they'd left drew silent. She didn't look back.

The corridor pressed in around them. Too clean. Too symmetrical. Each steel door passed like a drumbeat, each footstep echoing like they were walking through the hollow bones of something long dead.

Ashley's breathing evened out. Her legs ached, but she didn't complain. Elias stayed close, always a step ahead, scanning every corner, every shadow.

The hallway stretched on longer than it should have. Then, without warning, it ended.

A double-wide door loomed ahead. No markings. No keypad. Just blank steel. Elias reached out. It slid open before he touched it. They stepped through and stopped.

The space before them was massive. A circular room with no visible ceiling, no seams in the walls. Smooth, matte gray extended up into a void. The floor was identical—flat, undisturbed concrete. No fixtures. No furniture. No exits. Nothing.

Ashley turned in place, her footsteps barely making a sound. "What is this?"

Elias stepped in beside her, his voice cautious. "A dead end."

Their words dissolved into the air, consumed by the flawless acoustics of the space. Even the usual hum of the facility seemed to halt in this place. No blinding lights from above. No flickering screens. No watchful eyes. The room was empty.

Ashley walked a few steps further in. A familiar feeling crawled up her legs, then spine, then neck. "Oh no."

Before she could finish a thought, a vertical seam split wide across the landscape, seamlessly parting into the surrounding frame. Something stepped out.

It was a man. Short. Rigid. Wrong in every detail. Edging closer, he moved with a disturbing calm, barefoot across the clean floor. His skin was pale, the color of old bone. As he came closer, the details sharpened. His uniform was beige, wrinkled and torn in places, clinging to a body too still to be alive. Blood dripped faintly behind him, giving way to the silence.

Then she saw it. His face. The damage. The left side of his skull was caved in, a horrifying depression like someone had slammed a cinder block into it. Impossibly, he grinned. A savage, gleeful grin stretched across a face that had no business moving at all.

The face was unmistakable.

She recoiled. "Elias," her voice broke. "That's the man who was shooting at us in the Sanctuary."

"That's not possible." He pressed forward, shotgun shouldered. Aim ready. Elias positioned himself in front of her.

"It's him!"

The man stopped a few yards away. Head tilted. The smile never wavered. His eyes were empty. Not dead—just hollow.

Without pause, Elias fired.

The blast echoed in the chamber like thunder, but the man darted to the side with inhuman reflexes. His hand moved fast, pulling a handgun from behind his back. He fired three times.

Ashley hit the floor hard, diving into a prone position.

Then a stillness settled in.

Everyone remained a statue. Ashley looked up to Elias. He was like stone. Motionless. The expression on his face was blank. His eyes protruded and his mouth dropped. The shotgun kept its aim outward until his body dropped.

"NO!" she screeched. Her voice tore out of her throat, raw. Water returned to the ground. "ELIAS!"

Blood spread beneath him, dark and quick. Two holes smoked in his chest, the last of his breath already gone. His hand gave a small, final twitch before stilling completely.

Across the room, Dunn straightened his back.

"Well well, little lady," he drawled, voice slick with amusement. "That was fun."

Ashley, palpitating, stared at him. Her heart thundered in her chest, drowning everything else out.

Dunn tilted his head; the same grin carved deep into his ruined face. Blood oozed from his crushed skull. "Ya wanna have some more fun?"

Ashley scrambled to her feet, raising the pistol with both hands.

"Whoa now," Dunn chuckled, "No need to rush things. Not with a pretty face like that."

"Fuck you!" she hissed, finger tightening on the trigger.

"Little edge on ya. I like that." He took a step forward, lowering his weapon like it was useless. "Come on. Do it. Try."

Tears blurred into sweat. Her blinking sped. He was right there. One shot—just one.

He raised his arms in a crucifixion pose, fingers curling into mock claws. "C'mon now, shoot me."

310

Her vision doubled. Her jaw clenched. He's so close she couldn't miss.

"You're weak," he spat. "So goddamn sad. Did I hurt your feelings, killing your little friend?"

Her finger twitched on the trigger.

Scchhh

A seam hissed open to their right. Another wall panel. A rectangular gap emerged silently from the gray.

"Hello?" Dunn called out. His grin never faltered.

Ashley's stance broke. Still aiming, just distracted. The darkness beyond the opening pulled at her like gravity.

BANG! BANG!

Ashley flinched and pivoted. Dunn staggered, one bullet tearing through his thigh, the other into his hip. He stumbled but stayed upright.

Then a figure stepped through the opening. Tall. Steady. Clad in a Soviet uniform, the red star gleaming dimly on his shoulder.

Without breaking stride or aim, he fired again.

BANG!

The shot hit center mass. Dunn's grin caved inward. A thick spray of black-red matter exploded from his abdomen. His insides spilled onto the floor with a grotesque splatter as his body dropped.

Ashley stood in shock. Muscles incapable of moving.

The Russian approached, lowering his weapon only after he stood over Dunn's writhing form.

"Скатертью дорога," he grumbled in disgust, spitting on the dying man. Then he turned to Ashley, expression neutral. "Good riddance," he said, accent thick.

Ashley lifted her hands, her pistol hanging loosely from one finger.

The Russian nodded toward the open passageway.

"Go."

She stopped just long enough to take in Dunn's ruin. Then her eyes found Elias.

He was exactly where he'd fallen. Shotgun still angled outward like he hadn't finished yet. Like he was still trying. The blood had spread further than she expected— dark, quiet, and unhurried. She had seen enough blood in this place to stop noticing it. She noticed this.

She didn't say anything. There was nothing left that words could do. She just looked at him for one second—one real second—and then she ran.

Past the corpse. Past the Soviet. Into whatever came next. Behind her, the final rounds of the magazine fired in deliberate rhythm.

The sound reverberated out into the corridor. She flinched violently and her pistol dropped at her feet.

Ashley didn't look back. She ran.

The corridor stretched endlessly. Her boots slammed against tile, each step faster than the last. She didn't care where it led. She only knew she had to get far away. From Dunn. From Elias' body. From the room of monitors and childhood nightmares.

Her lungs burned. Her vision blurred. Her mind unraveled by the second.

This isn't real. This can't be real.

The pain in her legs was very real. The sweat pooling at her collarbone. The blood that still soaked her hands. The tears. The shrieks tearing out of her skull.

You're in a nightmare. You never woke up.

She turned a corner, sharp and reckless, nearly slipping on the smooth concrete floor. Her shoulder slammed into the wall, but she kept moving. Always moving. *Need to keep moving.* As long as she ran, she didn't have to think.

Then she heard it.

A voice. Muffled. Strained. Little more than a breath, yet undeniable.

"Ashley…"

She went numb.

"Over here…"

Her breath caught in her throat. The voice drifted from behind a sealed door to her left, flush with the wall. She pressed her ear against it.

"Ashley… please…"

She pushed. It gave.

Inside was a washed-out light draped over the sterile examination room. Medical trays lined the counter. A cracked mirror hung on the far side. The air felt still. In the corner, slumped against the wall, was Luke.

His clothes were torn, face gaunt, eyes sunken deep into his head. He looked like he hadn't slept in days. Or weeks. Maybe longer. His eyes found hers.

"I remember," his voice was dry, cracking even more as the words came out.

Ashley stepped cautiously inside. "Luke?"

He was frantic. He was small. "I remember everything."

She stopped a few feet from him. "What are you talking about? What happened?"

"I was a doctor. Before all this. Before… the Ark. They said I could help. That I could fix people." His voice was strange now, empty and crazed. "I didn't mean to do it. I shouldn't have."

Ashley's heart thudded. "Luke, who did this to you? How'd you get here?"

His head shook, "So many lives. I needed the money, Ashley."

She was rooted to her spot, overwhelmed by a sense of awe that held her in place.

"I was wrong. I'm sorry. They signed on for the procedures. I couldn't stop myself. Oh God."

Ashley inched closer, unsure if she was comforting him or interrogating him. "What are you talking about?"

"You deserve to know. You always did. You were stronger than any of us. Please Ashley. Please."

He looked up at her and reached for her right cheek.

"I'm sorry," he cried, "For all of it."

She backed away, eyes stern and brows low. Watching him wither away in madness. She couldn't take anymore. She turned away too slow.

A sharp crack clashed across the side of her skull. Her vision shattered into white. The floor rushed up to meet her.

And then—darkness.

Boots dragged her body away. Luke didn't move. He just watched and bawled. Repeating himself as she was swallowed by darkness.

[CH.30]

THROUGH
THE
VEIL

They moved fast.

The water behind them rippled over stone, the last breath of the stream they'd left behind. Now, only their footsteps moved through the damp grass, soft and unsteady.

James scanned the dark ahead, his pulse still elevated from everything they'd survived. The forest grew thick. Briers tore at his arms as he pried the brush apart. He didn't have time to worry about petty thorns.

Nick walked directly behind, holding a line formation. His hand lightly pressed to his ribs. He hadn't spoken since they left the water. The few gulps of fluid he'd taken worsened the pain in his side. The pain of the gouged hand, however, faded like his broken toe had.

"You good?" James asked, not looking back.

Nick took a breath before speaking. "As good as you can be after nearly dying five times."

"We should hurry," James pressed on. His hand caught a hard batch of thorns. "Ouch." After a single glance, he shook it off.

The woodlands were deep and sparse between each field and meadow. There was no way to tell how vast the Sanctuary truly was. James thought back to the first time he arrived in this room. The awe. The shock. His mind wandered back to Sean. The sixteen hits with a bat. Then to the circle of prisoners and the damned holographic message.

"You think that column is still in the meadow?"

Nick whisked through a vine. "I don't see why it wouldn't be."

They navigated through a thicket of trees, their shadows elongating like jagged teeth in the dark. The canopy above devoured the meager light the Ark allowed, plunging them deeper into the suffocating blackness.

Nick grunted as a branch scraped his side. "Feels like this place is getting tighter."

"It's messing with us. It always does," James reminded him.

After another twenty yards, the woods thinned. Their shoes bent grass as they emerged onto sloped terrain. Then, there it was. The clearing. Wide and hollow, like the eye of a storm.

The same meadow where the hologram had first appeared, where blood soaked the grass in a perfect circle. Most of it had dried by now. Dark smears, broken weapons. Torn fabric and littered bodies. Real ones. James stepped carefully around the edges. Nick paused behind him, catching his breath.

Still standing in the middle of the field was the column. Dead. Inert. Flawless.

"I don't like it when things are quiet in this place," Nick said, eyeing the structure.

James approached it slowly. "No power. No glow."

"It's probably activated elsewhere," Nick implied.

James stopped in front of the column to examine it. He had never been this close to the device. The material looked foreign and unreal. Not quite metal, not quite stone. It held a strange sheen, like liquid captured mid-motion. It was patterned with cryptic, overlapping designs that didn't seem carved so much as *grown*. The lines followed no symmetry he could recognize—fractal, recursive, almost biological in shape. It felt ancient, like a relic excavated from the edge of reality.

Even standing still, the obelisk seemed to shift, like it resisted being perceived. James let his eyes flicker and saw the patterns realign ever so slightly, as if they had moved when he wasn't looking. The air near it was sharp. Not from any breeze—from presence. Like standing near a monument meant for something not human. He found himself holding his breath.

"Hey!" he shouted at it. "You like watching us? Like studying us? Where the hell are you, you son of a bitch." James kicked the device, regrettably. His foot recoiled and was met with two palms. Toes throbbed while he hopped around in agony, clutching his shoe.

Nick sighed. "You're yelling at a rock."

James took a step back, trying to piece together what kind of intelligence could've created something so cryptic, so ancient. Nick remained a few steps behind, eyes narrowed, not in wonder but in calculation.

"I've seen blueprints in my time," Nick confessed, "Military tech, prototype architecture, energy conduits mapped for AI interfacing… but nothing like this." He walked a slow half-circle around the column, hands on his hips, breathing shallow. "This is peculiar." He said it with his face inches away.

"It's like it's vibrating without moving," Nick breathed, eyes darting along the jagged filaments etched into the alloy. "This isn't just decorative. It's… coded."

James shook out his foot, wincing. "Coded?"

Nick tapped gently near one of the seams. "These grooves aren't just for show. They repeat. Fractal patterns. Self-replicating, impossible technology."

"Not so impossible if I'm staring right at it," James said.

Nick didn't respond at first. He circled once more, gaze darting between fascination and unease. Without his glasses his vision blurred but his hands made up for it. The column remained inert, as though daring them to comprehend it. He pressed at one of the seams, pushing and pulling in subtle ways. Nothing reacted.

"I'll be honest with you James, I don't think we're getting any answers from it."

"Shit," James scoffed, taking a step back. "Waste of time. I learned more back in those stupid offices."

Nick glanced over. "What did you say mate?"

"I said *stupid offices*. We'd been in a few rooms before ending up here. Sean—the miscreant with the bat—he, uh…"

"I know who he is." Nick's tone was flat.

"Right," James said, clearing his throat. "He lockpicked some doors. I remember thinking it was ridiculous at the time. We're in this nightmare, and this guy's out here opening doors like it's some game of hide and seek."

"What did you find in there?" Nick asked, suddenly attentive.

James hesitated, trying to sort through the flood of memories—Ashley, the tile corridors, Sean's death, the blood. "Some papers. One mentioned fungus we saw growing in the tunnels, some kind of study. Another was labeled 'Smart Architecture.' Didn't mean much to me then."

Nick perked up. "Tunnels, you said?"

"Yeah. Pretty sure I woke up in one. Felt like miles of pipe and runoff. But those documents just seemed… random. Not helpful."

"They weren't random," Nick was enthusiastic, tapping his chin. "Back in my time, before I ended up here, there were whispers, rumors passed between people in my field. About Smart Architecture. Morphing blueprints. Structures that could adapt, react, even… learn. We thought it was vaporware."

"Well," James said, gesturing to the column, "you were wrong."

Nick didn't deny it. "A structure capable of evolving based on the input of human cognition—responding to thought, memory, emotion. I thought the theory was too ambitious. But here we are."

James blinked, "Man, I have no idea what you're saying." He was overwhelmed by Nick's fluency.

Nick turned, looking back at the meadow, the stillness of the column. "Why would there be tunnels, sewers, old office layouts? Why would *documents* be lying around? Unless…"

"Unless what?"

"Unless this place isn't just reacting to us. Unless it was built, maintained even. Machines can simulate all sorts of things. But they don't invent protocol. There are rules. And where there are rules—"

"—There are people making them," James finished. He stepped closer. "The Collective."

Nick gave a tight smile. "Exactly." He ran his palm along its surface, reverent. "This thing? This is a constant. It hasn't moved. It hasn't changed. Just like the Sanctuary itself. That whole environment—it's static. Everything else shifts, warps. But this? This is *anchored*."

James narrowed his eyes. "But we were in those maintenance corridors. They changed too. Rooms kept evolving."

Nick nodded. "Because those are part of the adaptive systems. But administrative layers—true infrastructure, that stuff has to remain stable. Otherwise, the whole machine breaks down. Somewhere, deeper than where we've been, is a place that doesn't change. That's where the rules are written. And maybe… just maybe—where we find whoever is responsible."

"And you think places like that are accessible?"

"Only one way to find out."

They left the column behind, its silent geometry receding into the foliage like a monument abandoned by time. As they pressed on, the grass thinned, giving way to packed earth and scattered stones. The forest, once tangled and wild, began to shift. The trees grew farther apart, their trunks unnaturally straight.

Though the direction they'd chosen was entirely random, it didn't feel that way anymore. Somewhere under the surface, he sensed a current guiding them. One way or another, the Sanctuary would greet them again—its towering walls always waiting. And if one wall could be opened, another might be too. For the first time in forever, something unfamiliar anchored itself in James' gut. Optimism.

Still, he couldn't shake the sense of unfeasibility, as if Nick's lecture had snapped him back into his usual state of mind. Always questioning. Always chasing the impossible. He walked in silence, eyes scanning the trees like instruments, searching past the leaves, past the bark, down to invisible patterns beneath it all. Microscope eyes, hunting for meaning where none was promised.

A thick fog rolled in without warning.

It came low to the ground at first, licking their ankles like a dog at their heels. Then it climbed—fast. Within moments, James and Nick were shrouded in a soupy haze that turned the forest into a wet, white blur. The temperature spiked. Thick beads clung to their faces, collecting on their eyelashes, rolling off their chins. The humidity was suffocating.

"Shit," James muttered, wiping his brow. "I can't see anything."

Nick said nothing, already familiar with how the world bent out of focus. Their footsteps grew unsure. The soft crunch of grass and twigs faded into muffled squelches. It was as though the forest had swallowed all landmarks. Their direction had shifted without their feet ever turning.

"Did we loop?" James asked. "I can't tell if we're still headed straight."

"No way to know," Nick replied. "The fog's too thick. We could've turned without noticing."

Then something took shape ahead.

A silhouette—faint at first. Large. Singular. A tree.

As they drew closer, its scale dwarfed the others around it. The trunk was wide enough to fit a car through. Its bark gnarled and coiled in unnatural twists like ropes grown wild and fused together. Branches stretched upward in absolute stillness. No birds. No insects.

James moved forward and placed his palm against the bark. It was warm.

"There's something wrong with it," he said.

The trunk bore a seam.

A split ran down its center, imperceptible until James pressed harder. With a soft click, the bark receded. Not like a door swinging open, more like the tree *unfolded*. The inside was hollow. Darkness greeted them, long and unnatural. A passage.

James stepped in. His foot hit tile.

Nick followed, one hand still wrapped near his ribs. When both bodies crossed the threshold, the bark closed. No hinges. No slam.

They turned and only a wall was behind them now. There was absolutely no trace of any sort of opening.

Nick murmured, "This wasn't an exit. It's an invitation."

Their gaze held, unspoken tension thickening between them. James knew this was it. Whatever lie beyond, whatever came his way, he was ready. A fist formed then opened. He looked down into his palm. Empty. *I wish I had a weapon*. He kept the thought to himself.

The corridor ahead stretched forward, narrow and ribbed like the inside of a throat. The walls were lined with subtle ridges and pulsed faintly with a warmth that didn't comfort. It felt alive in the worst way. The air remained clinging to their skin even with the fog gone.

James took the first step. The footstep splashed, rippling down the hall. Nick walked close behind, his breathing shallow.

"This place doesn't feel like the others," Nick said.

James nodded, eyes forward. "It's warmer here."

They pressed deeper. The further they walked, the more the space narrowed. The walls seemed to bend inward, distorting perspective, until it was impossible to tell how far they'd gone. There were no turns. No signs. Just one curve ahead and the lingering sense they were descending.

James clenched his fists again. Still nothing. No weapon. No Sean. No Elias. Just Nick, broken and bleeding. And himself—unarmed but unwilling to be helpless.

Up ahead, the corridor suddenly widened. A shape emerged in the dark metallic distance. A junction with four corners. Four aimless directions. Both men entered the intersection. Twisting heads and moving eyes wandered until they spun enough to be completely lost. Befuddled, James reached out to a wall, taking the weight off his legs for the moment.

"Which way did we come from?"

"I don't remember," Nick answered.

James looked back the way he thought they'd come. Same curved walls. Same ribbed texture. Same sickly luminescence. Every path looked identical.

"Don't tell me we're fucked?"

"Proper fucked. Been that way the entire time." Nick let out a short, pained laugh and clutched his side.

James let off the wall and listened.

"JAMES..."

The remnant voice came back to him.

"Did you hear that Nick?"

"Hear what?"

James had confirmed he was indeed losing it. He gave in, head down.

"*James…*"

It came from the left hall. He perked up and without a word he pressed into its direction. Nick didn't bother to ask, following behind the soon-to-be-deranged man. Each footstep James took was more brisk than the last. The corridor tightened, swallowing them. The lights dimmed. The deeper they ventured, the darkness thickened, swallowing the light until it transformed into a void. Total, unrelenting nothingness.

Concentrating beyond perception, James ignored the development for too long. A punch hit his gut and he frosted over. Turning back to Nick forced his jaw to drop. No one was there. In the belly of black, he called out.

"Nick!" His lungs throbbed. "Nick where'd you go!"

Disoriented, he twirled. "Come on, man. Don't do this." He was right there. The corridor had swallowed him whole. James patted his own body—chest, legs. Still solid. Still here. Still real. His heart was trying to break free.

"NICK!"

Silence.

Then hands gripped his shoulders. Light rushed back into the corridor. The darkness retreated.

"I'm right here James," came the calm voice behind him. "Been here the whole time."

James staggered forward, panting, clutching his knees. Nick stepped closer, eyebrows knit with concern.

"You alright, mate?"

From hyperventilation to deep, jagged breaths, James steadied himself. *SMACK! He* slapped his own cheek twice.

Stay awake. Stay present. Don't vanish like they did. Just keep moving.

His feet began again, slow and uneven. One step followed by another. Forward—whatever forward meant anymore. Then it came. A scream. Far off. Human. Raw.

"Help!"

Nick and James locked eyes.

"Please tell me you heard that," James said.

Nick gave a single nod.

Another cry, closer this time, desperate, high-pitched, and ruptured by something wet.

SNAP!

It was a sickening crack, like bone splintered by merciless pressure. Returning silence brewed. The two wasted no more time. They ran.

No signal, no plan—just inertia. Their feet slammed against tile, all caution forgotten. The corridor blurred around them. White streaks gave way to that of gray. The lights overhead strobed in a rhythm that stoked the fire of their fear.

The further they sprinted, the more the hall changed. Clockwork. The seamless white walls fractured, and the concrete became more permanent until it reached a full evolution. Hairline cracks split the walls. The air turned dry, as if they'd passed through a membrane between spaces. All too familiar metal doors patterned each side of the walls. Only this time they bore descriptions on the front. Neither had time to read them.

In the middle of a full sprint, both men, side by side, leaped into emptiness. Without warning the floor dropped and down they went.

[CH.31]

BENEATH THE SURFACE

They hit the ground hard, welcomed by cold, unwelcoming gray. James rolled to absorb the fall while Nick landed with a pained grunt, clutching his torso the instant his shoulder hit the floor.

For a long second, neither of them moved.

James coughed, forcing air into his chest again. "You good?" he wheezed.

Nick groaned, curling onto his side. "Define good."

They lay there in the dark, surrounded by the low hum of unseen machines, listening to the electric breath of something vast and hidden around them. Slowly, James pushed himself to his feet. His palms scraped against textured flooring—corrugated, stained. Beneath one hand, he felt something crusted and flaking.

When his eyes adjusted, he saw it. The room wasn't just concrete. It was filthy. The floor was layered with dust and splattered with something long dried. Faint red lines trailed to the far wall like forgotten veins.

Nick eased himself upright, biting back a wince. "Where are we now?"

James scanned the space. "Nowhere good."

A door stood ajar on the far end of the chamber, metallic and half-bent inward. It looked like something had forced its way through, or out. Beyond it, the pathway narrowed and sloped gradually downward. James inhaled and helped Nick stand.

They entered together.

The air changed immediately. Stale. Dead. As ancient as the obelisk. It wasn't long before James halted his momentum.

They saw it slumped in the corner, partially hidden behind an open ventilation panel. A figure with limp arms and contorted legs. Both neared, each step heavier than the last.

It was a body.

James crouched, and under the grime and blood, he recognized the clothes. The blue tie. The hollowed face.

"Raspberry," he gasped. The name caught in his throat. Words refused to follow.

Nick moved up behind him. He paused when he saw the corpse.

"Shit." He dropped to a knee beside James. His eyes didn't blink.

James reached forward, brushing aside part of the collar. The chest had caved inward from blunt force. Ribs shattered. Limbs twisted unnaturally. The hole still in his foot was accentuated by the absence of shoes.

"Poor guy," James said, masking his face. The stench was unholy.

Nick was silent for a while before speaking again. "I saved his life once."

James regarded him.

Nick spoke quietly, pupils still fixed. "First moments here. Two rooms. One filled with chains. The other similar to the room where we encountered Sean. We survived both. Barely." His voice was soft, "Didn't know if I liked him, didn't know if he liked me. But we didn't need to."

James looked back at the corpse. "What kind of man do you think he was?"

Nick hung back. "The kind who didn't deserve to end up like this."

The sight evoked the brief time he called him Rasp. How he was covered in blood and still carried on. How fitting it was for a man with his name.

Time stretched thin, like fabric on the verge of tearing.

"How'd he end up like this?" James pondered. "And if he's here, where is everyone else?"

Nick didn't answer. They both knew the truth. You don't end up like this by accident. Not in a place like this.

Suddenly a howl, isolated and coarse, muffled through layers of concrete.

Unmistakable. *Ashley.* The thought surfaced to reality.

"ASHLEY!"

Without a word, they broke into a full sprint. A gait so hard, the reverb sprang off the walls like spears, nudging them into the abyss. James tore through the corridor with raw instinct. No plan. Just motion.

The hall veered left, then right. Its angles too smooth, too deliberate. Pipes clung to the ceiling like alloy nerves, dripping condensation that slapped the concrete with each passed step. Lights flashed above red, then white, then dead altogether.

"Keep up!" James shouted, though he didn't need to. Nick was right behind him, limping but undeterred.

Another scream—closer now.

They rounded a final bend and slammed into a halt. Ahead of them was a corridor choked by debris—metal girders and thick steel panels half-fallen from the ceiling. Whatever lay beyond had been intentionally barricaded or destroyed.

James ran to it, scanning the crumpled wreckage. "We can find a way through."

Nick limped up beside him; his eyes already assessed the blockage. "There's no time to look for one."

James threw his shoulder into the mess, rattling it. Too tight. Too heavy. His hands scraped over rusted edges. No way in. He saw figures move through the crevices but couldn't ascertain what or who they were. "God dammit." Enraged, knuckles crashed into steel, over and over until his knuckles split. "Mother FUCKER!" He kicked wild.

Nick stepped in. "James stop it." His voice anchored.

Chest heavy, eyes teary, James wept.

Nick intervened. "Stop, James." He tugged him backwards.

Fists dripping, James sagged against the debris. His breath came in broken waves. Red mist clouded the edges of his vision.

"There's gotta be another way," Nick said under his breath, scanning the passage's edge. "There always is."

James wiped his face, smearing blood and sweat into a single brutal stroke. He looked up and saw it. Not an exit. Not quite. But something strange.

Off to the side, partially hidden behind a slanted support beam, was a small square recess in the wall. It was clean-cut and intentional. The material around it wasn't concrete, it was tile. White tile. Impossibly white. Untouched by the grime of the rest of the facility.

"I think I found something," James said, breathing out steadily.

Nick followed his line of sight. Together, they drew near. The recess was just tall enough to crawl into, but it narrowed quickly, funneling into another chamber beyond.

At once they entered. On the other side was a room of diamond perfection. A flawless cube. Every surface, from the floor, walls, and ceiling, was comprised of back-lit panels arranged in mathematical symmetry. A sourceless light emitted from a haunting, soulless power.

The epitome of surreal. Alien in nature. A compressed void.

When James brought himself upright, an invisible wall engaged, blocking the line between him and Nick. "Shit," he sparked, turning as if he could stop it. Something scraped the floor behind him. His head whipped around first, before the rest of his body could follow.

A figure stood at the center of the room.

James went still. The apparition didn't bear a single motion. It didn't twitch. It didn't breathe. It stared.

James analyzed without movement. The image of a man, wearing the same blue striped long-sleeve shirt. The same boots. The same khakis. The same cuts along the knuckles. The exact same eyes. It was a mirror in the flesh, rendered without glass. A perfect imitation. But something in the posture was off. It stood taller. Shoulders squared. Proud.

Then it smiled. Its mouth never opened.

JAMES.

It was the whisper. The oppressor.

The double circled him now, slow and fluid.

All this time, trying to piece yourself together. Trying to be human.

Its voice was his own.

You gave them everything. Your trust. Your guilt. Your pain. For what?

James clenched his fists. "YOU'RE NOT REAL." His anger verbalized.

I'm more real than you. The smile lingered. *I'm the better you. I'm everything you buried.*

Every instinct you silenced. I'm the one who could've saved them all.

James jabbed a finger at him. "You're nothing like me."

The Echo laughed, dry and mirthless. *And yet, here you are, terrified I might be.*

James trembled. "I'm not scared of you."

Oh please. I know everything about you. Even the parts you don't know.

A flash of white cursed James' eyes. He fell to his knees, blinded by scenes of misery:

Ashley bellowing in pain, blood on her hands.

Sean, eyes wide, skull caved in, whispering his name.

His younger self, curled in a hallway corner. Forgotten. Alone.

James James James.

He gritted his teeth. The Echo stepped closer.

You never had a self, you just wore one like a coat. You changed it to survive. In here, that doesn't work anymore.

"Shut your fucking mouth," James spat, blinking and regaining his sight.

The Echo walked circles around the man.

You're a vessel. Hollow. Filling yourself with other people's grief. And the worst part? The Echo leaned in, voice like ice against his skull. *You're still pretending there's something worth saving.*

James struck—sudden, desperate, a wild fury. His fist collided with flesh, but it was like punching a wall that hit back. The Echo reeled for a moment, then retaliated. The two versions of James crashed. Mirror to mirror. Fury to fury. Every blow was matched. Every attack countered.

There's no use, James. You can't defeat yourself.

He slammed the Echo into the wall, but it twisted free and grabbed him by the throat.

There's only one way to do that.

The Echo threw James to the floor.

Let go, James. Let me finish this. Let me be who you really are.

James sucked in a ragged breath, the voice rising with every vicious strike they traded.

James.

Failure.

Coward.

Let me in.

Be free.

"RAH!" James bellowed, blood flecking his lips. "I know who I am." He wiped his chin with the back of his hand.

You're a fool James.

"I've made mistakes." His hands gripped the Echo's wrists and forced them down. "But I choose who I am. Not you." He greeted him with a headbutt sending the Echo back.

The Echo's face twitched. Fractured. A ripple passed through its skin like a dropped pebble in water.

James took one final breath.

"You're not truth. You're fear."

Once more, with endless power, he drove his forehead into the Echo's. The impact rang like a bell and his vision obscured.

Both fell to a knee in unison. The Echo chuckled.

James, you can't defeat me. We're the same.

James stood, breath settling. "We'll never be the same."

He planted one foot behind him, chest leaning forward like a drawn bow. Energized, he plunged his front leg deep into the floor. His body thrust in a singular direction. Only one objective. With all the violence he could muster, James ignited himself. At bullet speed, he traveled through the Echo. The imitation absorbed his presence and James tackled through nothing but air. His pivotal speed, unstoppable. With no way to brake, he crashed into a wall.

Another white flash filled his eyes until all radiance receded. The Echo evaporated. James collapsed. His body tumbled and his eyelids closed.

In the silence that followed, in a room too perfect to be real, a blood-streaked man lay unconscious. Battered, but not broken.

[CH.32]

//:System Error //
[MEMORY LOG RETRIEVED]
Subject: 333-JAMES

//:December 20, 2008 //
//:Richmond, VA //

The air was cold and thick with dust. Afternoon light slanted through the bent blinds in dull stripes, casting shadows on the cheap carpet. A ticking clock above the fridge sounded louder than it had any right to. Nothing else stirred.

James stood in the middle of the small apartment, shoulders taut, jaw tight. His knuckles were white around the wrinkled envelope in his hand—final notice. The words were printed in all caps, black and clean, no room for mercy.

"Why now?" he said to himself. "Why today, of all goddamn days."

Across the room, a duffel bag slouched on the couch like a body. A few clothes. A notebook. A toy dinosaur. He stared at it without seeing it. His pulse didn't belong to his chest anymore. It lived in his ears, louder than the clock.

From the hallway, the soft voice of a child carried in. "Dad?"

He didn't answer right away. The name hit harder than expected. He blinked, the sound dragging him back. The girl stood in the doorway in mismatched socks and a wrinkled shirt she'd picked herself. Her curls were frizzy from sleep. She rubbed one eye.

"I'm hungry," she said simply.

James didn't look at her. Not directly. He stared past, jaw still tight. "We'll eat later."

"It's already later," she replied, with the unflinching honesty only a child could manage.

The pressure behind his eyes built, but he didn't release it. Not yet. He turned away from her, gripping the edge of the sink, his knuckles flaring. His reflection in the window looked ghostly. Pale. Distant. Someone else.

"I said later."

There was a beat between them.

"Are you mad at me?"

That was the crack.

"NO!" He snapped. Too fast. Too loud. Then his tone lowered. "I'm not mad at you, okay? Just… just go to your room. Please."

She didn't move. She didn't understand. She looked at him with those small eyes. Too wide. Too soft. The kind of gaze that pressed questions into silence.

He turned. "I said go."

Her lips quivered as she remained still.

Then James hit the counter.

She flinched, stepping back out of reflex. And that—that moment—stuck. Her small hand reached to her side, her eyes watering, not crying but absorbing. He watched her withdraw from the room like air leaving a balloon, as if every step backward took some brightness from the space.

The door to her room didn't slam. It clicked. Gentle. Final.

James stood there, heart thudding, his hand still resting where he'd struck the counter. He went back to staring at the envelope. For a long moment, the silence ruled. No clock. No street noise. Only his own guilt, taking shape in the stillness.

He didn't go after her. Not right away. Not when he should have.

It was only after the hour passed, after he'd sunk into the couch, stared at the static of the TV he never turned on, and the dusk had crept in, that something felt off.

Too quiet. Too long.

"Em?" he called out, standing.

No answer.

He moved down the hallway. The light was on in her room. The toy dinosaur sat beside the bed and the sheets were tossed aside. The window was open, but the screen was gone.

James froze.

"Emma?" His voice cracked.

He ran to the window, then outside to the fire escape. Then the alley. All empty. He hollered her name so loud his throat tore. She didn't answer.

James didn't remember climbing through the window. Only the frantic burn of the fire escape railing under his hands. The chill biting at his arms. The hollowness echoing through the alley as he shouted her name again and again, until his voice cracked and collapsed into coughing.

The neighbors heard. A light came on across the street. A door creaked open. Someone shouted down, asking if everything was okay. James didn't answer. He couldn't. He just kept running down the alley, into the road, spinning in circles as if she'd materialize if he looked hard enough.

She was gone.

When the police came, he could hardly speak. A patrol car rolled up to the curb, lights flashing, too bright for the dark that had settled inside him. He waved them over frantically, jerking his hands. No script. No story. The officer asked the usual inquiries. Age. Height. Last known clothing. Allergies. Did she have somewhere she'd go?

"She's eight," James said, "She doesn't have places to go."

They searched the area. They took down notes. Someone told him to stay calm. That it was likely nothing. "Kids wander off sometimes," they said. "She'll turn up."

But she didn't.

The next twenty-four hours were a blur of bureaucratic rhythms and emotional collapse. Officers combed the neighborhood. James stayed inside, questioned repeatedly. Every minute replayed. Every small choice. Did you leave the front door unlocked? Had she done this before? Was there trouble at home? No. No. No.

Her room was photographed. Her toothbrush collected. The toy dinosaur was bagged in a plastic sleeve, like it might confess something. And James, numb in the living room, still held the goddamned envelope—final notice—creased and sweat-stained. His life had already been unraveling; he just hadn't known it could tear clean through.

On the second day, the apartment dimmed with silence. The blinds remained closed, casting those same striped shadows across the carpet. He sat with the weight of it all. The way he hadn't hugged her goodbye. The way she had looked at him. The counter. His hand.

He replayed it so many times that he started to forget what was real.

He called out her name until it started to sound like a stranger's. Until his throat went raw and the walls stopped answering back. Then he didn't speak at all. Just sat. Hands curled like claws into the couch cushions. Watching time trickle into ash.

Eventually, someone knocked. It wasn't the police.

It was his brother, who hadn't visited in months. James didn't open the door right away.

He sat there, knowing who was behind it. Finally, he cracked it open.

"Jesus," his brother said, embracing him. "You look like hell."

James stepped aside. "She's gone."

"I heard."

His brother didn't say much else. He looked around the place and noticed how dirty it become. He found the couch and sat down.

"You need help."

James stared at the floor. "I needed five fucking minutes back."

They didn't speak again for a long time. The room stayed heavy, thick with loss.

And when night came again, James lay in Emma's bed on her tiny pillow. Her smell still there, faint and cruel. He held the wrinkled shirt she'd worn. Folded it. Unfolded it. Folded it again.

Outside, the world kept turning. Inside, James never did. He had gone back to the living room and downed a fifth. He pried open the couch cushion and pulled out a revolver. The barrel spun.

Over and over, he asked himself why. What he could have done differently. What he should have done differently. He checked the chamber. One round. He drank what was left of the whiskey before folding back. Gun meeting his temple.

He couldn't pull the trigger though. He thought too much. Cried too much. Then he closed his eyes. In that moment his world went white. He felt unmoored and removed. The revolver dropped to the floor, knocking the empty bottle over. And then James was gone.

[CH.33]

N O

G O D S

H E R E

James?

The voice was faint.

James… wake up!

It wasn't the whisper. Lower tone.

"James, come on, wake up."

Something rattled him. He drew breath like someone pulled back from the edge. A sharp sting pulsed through his ribs and spine as consciousness dragged him back to the surface. Somewhere, distantly, a voice echoed—urgent, human.

"James!"

He blinked. His vision fractured, shapes swimming into place. The white walls came into view. The void returned. Nick's face hovered over his. He had shaken James till he jolted upright.

"James, come on. We don't have time." Nick loomed over him, pale, trembling, and very alert. His voice wavered with restrained panic. "She's close. There's a way out. This way."

"Wh-what?" James was still groggy. "N-Nick? What happened?"

"I thought we were done for. The room split us up. I thought I was losing it! A few minutes went by and the wall dropped. I found you lying on the ground. What happened to you?"

"I-I…" He couldn't put the words together.

"Fuck it, doesn't matter right now. Let's get the hell out of here yeah?" Nick propped him up and allowed him to return to his feet.

James stood too quickly. The room spun. He braced himself with both palms, coughing once before steadying. His pupils dilated and the blurs cleared. Across from them was the opening. Both limped through the arch and into the recess.

The corridor ahead was shadowed, metallic, and groaning under its own age. They came forth into a vast chamber—far taller and broader than any they'd seen in the Ark. The ceiling vanished into shadows. Steel beams crisscrossed high above like a skeletal canopy, and the floor sloped gently downward, vanishing into a mess of machinery.

Pipes. Hundreds of them. Some fat, some thin. Some hissed steam or trickled foul water. They wound across the walls and overhead in tangled snarls, forming a labyrinth of chrome intestines. The sound of dripping liquid echoed endlessly. It was a factory without purpose. Alive without a heartbeat.

James pressed forward, weaving between conduits and low-hanging ducts. His body ached with every motion, adrenaline dragging him on. Nick followed close behind, his hand still clutched near his ribs.

Then—a sound.

"James…"

It was her. Her voice was fragile, like it was trying not to cry out again. Muffled. Nearby.

James whipped around. "You hear that?"

Nick nodded. "She's close."

The pipes distorted the acoustics—sounds bounced, twisted, then reappeared from the wrong direction. They turned toward it, then away. Up—then down. It was like chasing a chime through a steel jungle.

"Ashley!" James roared. "ASHLEY, WHERE ARE YOU?"

No response.

They pushed deeper, ducking under low-hung valves and squeezing through gaps barely wide enough for a shoulder. The walls had ceased to be walls; now they pressed inward as barricades, latticed with metal intestines. The air thickened with steam and heat. Breathing became harder.

Another voice. A sob.

"Help…"

It wasn't an echo. It was almost close enough to grab.

James lunged forward, bashing aside a loose panel. It screeched and clattered to the ground. Beyond it, another opening—a circular tunnel of red-lit steel, its edges slick with condensation.

They stepped through into another section of the large interior. Massive. Cylindrical. Lit from above by a mechanical aperture pulsing in intervals. In the center, surrounded by wires and restraint hooks, was a platform. On it, Ashley.

Strapped down, her head hung low, heavy with exhaustion. Deep cuts marred her arms, streaked with blood, and a crimson smear stained her lip. She was barely clinging to consciousness, a fragile flicker against the unrelenting darkness. Beside her limp body, Luke's corpse lay in a twisted heap—decayed and lifeless, just another casualty in the sea of forgotten souls.

Standing over her, shirt half-torn, eyes ablaze with lunacy was the inimical man himself. A metal melee weapon gripped firmly in his hand.

John raised his head, and whatever passed for warmth never reached his face.

Memories flashed once more in the mind of James. This time *all* of them. His life and his daughter. The tunnels and water and smell. Ashley. The fungus. The cages. The fire. The flesh. The papers. Sean. The bat. The sixteen hits. The blood. The gore. The crater left behind. The Sanctuary. The message. The chaos. The machine. The murder. The insanity. The reflection. The Echo.

He was finished with them all.
NO MORE!

James didn't scream. He didn't lunge. He took one step forward.

Each footfall exploded, a rhythm building not in haste but confidence. The ache in his legs had drowned. The blistered soles, forgotten. Every wound he'd earned in this godforsaken maze burned into resolve.

John looked at him like a man awaiting a verdict, his pupils wide with something that wasn't fear—maybe anticipation.

"I told you I'd find you," he said, his voice hoarse, as though he hadn't spoken in hours. "I bet you thought I didn't know it was you in the hallway."

James remembered the time he tackled the man with the shotgun from the beginning. Risking his life for Ashley. Certain there was no way he could see him in the cover of night. *The badge*. James remembered his presence all too well.

Nick advanced, trying to pull James back, "James think about this first."

He pushed him back. "Do what you do best, Nick, play it smart. I'll handle my end," he said, voice firmer than ever.

Ashley stirred on the platform. Her eyes fought to open while her lips formed James' name, though no sound came out.

John tilted his head, blood slick on his jawline. "She's stronger than she looks. Most of them broke hours ago. Not her. She's tough. Thought I'd let her see you die."

"It doesn't have to be like this. You're a cop. Think about what you're doing." James was never good at bargaining.

"And what do you think I'm doing?" John paced back and forth on the platform. The metal pipe in his hand resting on his shoulder. "You know I've been doing a lot of thinking."

James' chest tightened with rage. Pure. Hot. Focused. He stepped closer.

"I stayed quiet, tried to figure things out for myself. Figure out, this Collective or whatever bullshit name they give themselves." John continued, "But you know what, after a while I felt free. Not tied down by regulations. Free to be who I want. Free to do what I'm good at."

"Yeah and what's that? Being a monster like everyone else?"

John jumped down from the platform, fast and deliberate, like he was descending into a duel instead of a fight. "I'm not like everyone else. I'm worse."

As John roamed near, James held his ground. The man towered over him like a skyscraper leaning into a storm.

"You don't have to let them get to you," James reasoned.

John chortled, "I was like this before *they* ever existed."

Swiftly the metal weapon swung towards James. He tucked and rolled to the right, colliding with a crate.

John laughed maniacally, "Come on now. Don't kill yourself before we get started."

The words struck a nerve.

James grabbed a broken piece of the container and waited till John was close enough. He felt the authority hover near and propelled the plank skyward. Another roll to the left. He managed to crawl in between some vertical pipes letting out steam. A mist filled the air distorting vision.

John was too occupied with dodging the board, he failed to see where James escaped.

"Brave little man, aren't you," John said peering through the mist. "I see why she liked you." The pipe smashed into a vertical beam over James' head.

Lucky guess.

James remained hidden, crouching under hanging chains and fog. He crawled around the room looking for something loose.

John's steps were slower than rot creeping through wood. "I'm in no rush. I'll find you." Another swing crashed into a crate to the left of James. Way too close for comfort.

James moved like a shadow, chest pressed low against the floor, hands seeking anything—wire, pipe, tool. His breath burned in his throat. The steam made everything blur.

Another crash blared behind him. Sparks lit the mist for a second like lightning trapped in a bottle.

"You're just like the rest of them," John growled. "Pretending you care. Pretending you're something you're not. Pathetic coward."

James didn't answer. He found a rusted chain lodged under a panel. Heavy. Dense. Good enough. He kept it taut.

"Tell me something," John's voice warped through the smoke, "What do you think you owe these people?"

James stood slowly, chain gripped tight. "A chance," he said aloud. Not a whisper. A vow.

John tuned in. Footsteps angled. He was drawing close.

James pivoted behind a hanging cable. John passed just feet away, pipe raised.

Now.

James lurched forward, the chain arcing. It connected hard with John's forearm. The pipe clattered to the floor. John roared and swung back with the other hand, catching James square in the cheek.

They both stumbled.

James spat blood, vision shaking. He pounced for cover like an animal. "You're not free," he growled. "You can't even escape yourself." James found cover and hid.

"That's where we're different." John sniffled, his eyes rolling. "I'm not hiding from anything."

John reached into the unknown with his gorilla-like hands and grabbed James' throat. Holding him up, he brought him to his face with godlike strength. "Even myself."

He chucked his feeble body through the fog onto the steel floor. James dented ductwork and gasped for air, falling to the ground. John towered over him once more.

James looked up at the brute showing no remorse. As he looked deep into the eyes of evil, he peered left and saw movement from the platform. Nick was freeing Ashley using the pens from his pocket as a lock pick.

"You know I can't believe someone like you could survive so long." John put his boot across his throat, holding James down like he was underwater. "I can't believe the cultist fascists waste time on roaches like you."

"GAH!" James' eyes bulged. Trying to lift the boot off his neck, he squirmed. "AHH!" He couldn't breathe.

"You want freedom?" John pressed harder. "You want salvation?"

James let go of the boot and helplessly punched at his leg.

"There are no gods here." John moved all his weight onto his suffocating victim.

Then—suddenly.

"Just assholes!" A blur from behind came into his frame.

CRACK!

The beast fell to the floor. From his back stood a weary Ashley, panting harshly. Nick crept beside her. She looked to him while flipping the torch in her hand. "Lucky flashlight."

They both assisted James to his feet. Choking, he recovered. One hand motioned them back while he held his throat, trying to get the words out. Before he could, John had already recovered.

From the menace rose a demon with hell in his eyes. He batted Nick first, sending him far left, causing him to disappear in the haze. Ashley cowered back as he raised the bent pipe high.

James rushed to breathe, hand still on his throat. He reeled forward. The other palm in the air reaching to stop John. Reaching to end it. He was too far away. He was too late.

The pipe came down not once, not twice, but three rock-hard times onto Ashley. Her whimper was subtle and she fell to the floor. Before John could make his final strike, James pounced.

He gouged his thumbs over John's eyes in a fit of rage. John gasped his first cry. James then proceeded to choke him, but only for a moment. John heaved him off his body, then cupped his eyes. Trying to regain his sight, he reached for James. This time, John was too late.

James recovered Ashley's flashlight. His arm raised high then dropped, bashing the monster's face. Again, he hit. Again, he slashed. Again and again. The blood smeared over his face. Again. Another hit. One more. The gnashing of muscle and bone tore through the air. The stench of iron filled his nostrils. The taste scorched itself into his mouth. Fire brewed in his stare as the barrage continued. The flashlight bombarded evil with defiance until its last breath of light.

Exhausted, James was reduced to his knees. He remained idle over John's body, staring at the jaw that was the only thing left. His eyes didn't wander. His mind didn't think. He just delayed.

[CH.34]

AFTERMATH

Minutes passed before James had the courage to look up. He refused to accept what happened. He couldn't handle the sight.

He stood over John's twisted corpse; the flashlight still clutched in his trembling hand. Its rim was coated in gore. His breath came in shallow bursts. His grip refused to loosen. The beam flickered once, catching on the jagged edge of a broken pipe until it steadied.

He didn't remember the last time he blinked. His eyes burned trying to stay open.
He still hadn't looked.

He couldn't. Not yet. The room was too quiet now. Not the peaceful kind—no, the other kind. The kind that comes after the screaming ends. After the fight. After the damage is already done. He breathed in through his teeth, the air still thick with copper, steam, and iron.

Ashley hadn't made a sound in several minutes.

He felt her presence tugging at him, an invisible force pressing against the base of his spine. His body demanded him to look up, to find her, but the crushing fear that she was gone rooted him in place, paralyzing him with insecurity.

His legs twitched. Every instinct clawing at him to move, to look, but he stayed planted. As if by keeping his eyes on John's corpse, he could preserve the memory of her.

That hair. That face. Those hazel eyes.

"Please." His breath was dry. "Please, be alive."

His voice didn't echo. It withered.

The flashlight sagged in his hand. A deep, shuddering breath pulled through his chest. Finally, he looked up.

The beam of the flashlight jittered across the floor, catching rust, loops of wire, and the charred remains of something mechanical. His body trembled.

There she was, sprawled at the base of the platform. Her body battered and broken.

She was half-curled, one arm outstretched in his direction. Fingers splayed. Reaching. Her eyes were open and vacant. Whatever had once lived in them was gone. Her blood told the rest.

James dropped to his knees, the flashlight clattering beside him. His hands hovered inches above her shoulder, too afraid to touch her, too broken to pull away. Her shirt was soaked through, a deep wound in her side still glistening.

He didn't need to check for a pulse. He didn't need confirmation. The truth surged through him like a jolt of electricity.

"Ashley." It came out as breath, not his voice.

He finally reached forward, brushing her matted hair aside, tucking it gently behind one ear like he'd done before, back when the Ark felt like something survivable. Her skin was cooling fast. Her arm had gone rigid.

She was free at last.

Disbelief crept in. If she had never left his sight. If he had held on.

She made her choice.

James pressed his forehead to hers, wordless tears carving through grime-streaked skin. The machines around them whirred and hissed, oblivious to the scene.

"You never gave up," he mourned.

The image burned into him: her body moving, pulling, dragging itself toward him while he fought for his life. She had used what little strength she had left not to run, not to hide, but to fight.

It hadn't been enough.

James let out a sound that wasn't a shout or a sob. It was something in between, something primal. He pulled her limp form into his lap and rocked. Back and forth. Slow. Like a man trying to undo time with motion alone.

They were supposed to make it. Finding her was everything.

He did all he could, and now, she was gone.

Dead trying to save *him*.

His hands trembled—not from fear, but from the enormity of it all pressing in. Everything. The unbearable truth that this was it. No reset. No illusion.

She was gone.

And yet, James couldn't let go. His arms stayed around her, like if he held on long enough, she'd come back. Like the Ark would grant him this one mercy. But there was no mercy in this place. Only death. The worst of man.

Everything the Collective wanted came true. They knew all along what was going to happen. No matter what they thought they could do, the system ran its course. *A fucking rat.*

James' eyes watered and he continued to rock. Stroking her hair, cradling her spirit.

"I'm sorry Ashley. I'm so sorry. I should've tried harder. I should've never let you leave. You were so stubborn. So much stronger than me. I'm sorry Ash. I'm sorry."

Tears washed away the bloodstains on her face, restoring her beauty.

"You're free from this place now. Don't worry. You don't ever have to come back. You're free."

Reticence crept in and James grew still. The rocking stopped as he laid her head down to the floor. He straightened her body before rising, laying her hands across her chest. Standing over her, he mourned one last time.

COUGH! COUGH!

The sound of gagging drew his attention away.

YACK!

"Hello?" he called out.

"J-James…" the sound was small.

"Nick!?"

James hurried over to a cluster of vent pipes. "Oh my God. Nick!"

Nick's body sat upright inside of a folded cylinder of ductwork.

"It's hard to breathe-" Nick struggled. "—help."

"Hold on," James said, heart pounding. "I've got you."

The duct was folded in around Nick like a discarded tin can. His upper body was exposed, but one leg was still pinned by heavy metal warped from impact. His face was pale, streaked with sweat and dirt. Every breath came shallow and ragged.

James wedged his hands at the edge of the metal, testing its weight.

"Shit," he hissed. It was heavier than expected. He braced his feet, tightened his jaw, and heaved.

The metal gave a groan, reluctant and deep, but shifted enough for Nick to yank his leg free. He squealed as he collapsed to the side, clutching his ribs.

"You good?" James asked, panting.

Nick gave a weak nod. "Define good."

James almost laughed. Almost. It caught in his throat and died there. Too soon.

He reached down, pulling Nick up and draping the man's arm around his shoulder. Together, they staggered forward, putting the twisted pipework behind them.

"That son of a bitch," Nick muttered. "I thought he was going to finish me off. He slammed me into the ducts. Next thing I knew, I was choking on metal. I-I think my ribs are broken."

James didn't respond. His eyes drifted back—just once—toward Ashley's still form behind them. She looked smaller now in the distance. Fragile. As though she were fading into the facility's soulless design.

"I'm sorry, James," Nick said, noticing.

"She saved me," James' voice was flat.

"She died trying," Nick praised.

They continued moving.

The chamber narrowed as they approached the far wall. Steam hissed from ruptured vents. A faint blue glow pulsed through slits in the metal ahead.

"What do we do now?"

"We keep moving forward," James said, carrying him into the light.

"And which way is that mate?" Nick moaned, eyes shut.

"Whichever way we decide it is."

The duo was enveloped by the blue brightness until everything that surrounded them faded out. The closest thing to heaven they'd find was here. James stayed inside it as long as he needed to, unmoving.

Abruptly it dissolved. Soon after, they weren't in the room full of death and rage anymore. It all vanished. Now they stood on a balcony with tables and desktops. A large glass window appeared in front of them. Thick. Fortified.

James felt elevated. High in the air. He gently sat Nick down at one of the desks.

"Thanks." Nick slouched, both hands on his gut.

James neared the large glass window and peered out to the beyond. Down below was the biggest surprise of them all. After all he had seen, and all he had done, nothing could compare.

The Sanctuary unfolded far below, revealed in full. From his perch, he had the view of a god—but his only reaction was a slow turn of his head, left to right.

"Son of a bitch."

"What is it James?" Nick asked through his teeth.

"It's the Sanctuary."

"What?" Nick forced himself to stand, limping his way to James.

"A viewing station." James' head wagged.

"Impossible." Nick leaned against the glass, staring out.

"Still doesn't explain why we haven't seen anyone. Where is this Collective? The architects." James walked away and fiddled with a computer. It was dead.

"We're so beyond our time, James, I don't think you'll ever get those answers." Nick turned away from the view.

"I haven't given up hope. That's what they want us to do." James took a seat.

Nick smiled through the pain and sank into the chair next to him.

The two of them sat there a while, bathed in silence. For once they felt safe. Why not enjoy it for a little bit.

James leaned back in the chair, his spine arching along the hard plastic, staring at the ceiling. Fluorescent lights flickered, then held. His eyes followed one until it dimmed, as if even the light was tired of pretending.

Nick exhaled slowly. "Feels like the end of the world already happened."

James nodded. "Maybe it did."

They both turned toward the glass again. The Sanctuary sprawled beneath them like a diorama of failure—trees too still, walkways too clean, corpses too quiet. The illusion hadn't just been broken. It had been dissected.

"I keep thinking about her," James said softly. "How she never hesitated. Never looked back."

Nick didn't answer right away. His face stayed fixed toward the glass with his eyes closed.

"She believed in herself," James continued, "When others couldn't."

"She believed in an alternative outcome." Nick's eyes met his. "Just like you mate."

James pressed his palms into the table and stood. "Then I'll make sure that happens."

A low *click* rattled from across the room.

Both men turned. One of the far-side terminals had come to life. Its screen flashed with static, then cleared into a familiar interface.

SMARTARK OPERATIONS

James rose without a word, moving toward the console, afraid it might vanish if he waited too long. His fingers hovered over the surface. No keyboard. Only smooth glass. A cursor blinked in the corner. A prompt waited.

DO YOU WISH TO COMMUNICATE WITH ADMINISTRATIVE PANEL?
Y/N

[CH.35]

REVELATIONS

James felt as though an hour had passed by after tapping 'Y' on the monitor. The vacuum in the observation room stretched long. Too long.

James had been staring at the dead screen, unsure if the panel had even registered his touch. The only sound was Nick's labored breathing behind him, each inhale sharp and shallow.

He definitely broke his ribs.

Then, without warning, something clicked into place.

A hiss of pressurized air escaped from the far side of the room. One of the smooth metallic walls—featureless just moments ago—parted down the middle with surgical precision. From the shadowed threshold, a man emerged.

He was tall, although not particularly imposing. Dressed in a sleek black suit that shimmered slightly with a texture too smooth to be fabric. His skin was bone-white, not in a sickly way, but in a manner that rejected the notion of warmth. Skin that had never felt the touch of the sun. His eyes were wide and glassy. Not quite human. Not robotic either. Something between.

He moved like a phantom hovering over the ground.

"Subject 333," he said without inflection, eyes locking onto James. "Subject 386," he continued with a glance toward Nick.

James stood up, blood rushing to his head.

"You know who we are," he said, standing taller. Warm blood coursed through his veins. The sight of this man made him sick. Being labeled by a number really pissed him off.

The figure's lips parted in what might have been called a smile in another world.

"We know a lot about you," he paused, "James." The name cut like a blade.

"Well I'd like to know more about you, asshole." James' shoulders widened and his feet spread.

"Calm down James, let him talk." Nick remained in his seat.

The man's eyes traced between them with unsettling slowness.

"Interesting," he said to himself. "You both are quite… anomalous."

His head cocked slightly, not like a man who is curious, but like something cataloging behavior.

James narrowed his eyes. "Anomalous how?"

The man took a few small steps toward the central terminal, placing one unnaturally still hand on its corner.

"Most subjects fragment. They collapse inward—identity stripped, memory rewritten, choices corrupted. You, on the other hand…" He tapped a finger gently against the console. "You refused dissolution."

Nick gave a shallow laugh. "You hear that? We're too stubborn."

"No," the man replied. "You clung to the self with unreasonable tenacity. Especially *you,* Subject 333."

James tensed at the number.

"Your memory corruption should've taken root fully after your daughter's sequence," the man continued, tone devoid of empathy. "But your grief preserved you. Anchored you."

James stepped forward. "So that was part of it? Emma… Ashley… You *wanted* me to lose them?"

"No. We *needed* to see if you would become what we projected. Or *reject* it."

Nick leaned forward, voice sharp. "And if we had? If we'd given in? What, you harvest our DNA and spit us out as failed data?"

The man's lips twitched, not quite a smile. "You misunderstand. This wasn't to test *you.* It was to test *the Ark.* Its ability to induce natural selection of *ideal moral elasticity.*"

James' fists clenched. "You murdered hundreds of people to test *architecture*?"

"To test environment. Memory. Consequence. To determine if the mind, when placed under *truly shifting conditions,* would rewrite its own ethics."

He moved toward the glass, looking out over the Sanctuary below.

"You were not chosen for your strength. You were chosen for your *fractures*. And against all odds, you held."

James looked to Nick. "You knew this might be the endgame, didn't you?"

Nick gave a tired nod. "I didn't think we'd get to see it."

James turned back. "So what now? We've been tested, we've suffered, we've lost. Do we get to live, or do we just fade into another variable?"

The man stepped back from the window, one palm raised as the wall behind them split open.

Two pods. Sleek. Open. Waiting.

"One leads you back to the world outside," he said. "Whatever remains of it."

"And the other?" Nick asked.

The man looked between them. "Oblivion. If that is your choice."

James stepped toward the threshold. The hum of the pods grew louder in his ears. His hands were shaking.

"What would *you* choose?" James asked without turning.

The man was silent for a beat too long. "I was never given a choice."

James glanced over his shoulder. "That's the difference between us."

James picked up a chair and hurled it across the room. It passed through the man like smoke parting in the wind. His form rippled—head, torso, limbs bending unnaturally for a second— then solidified again as if nothing had touched him.

"Goddamn projections," James spat. "You're scared. You're hiding!"

The man tilted his head, expression unreadable. "Not fear. Efficiency. My presence is not required to be physical."

James stepped forward, fists clenched, fury boiling under his skin. "You stood behind glass while we bled, while they screamed, while she *died*. And now you stand here and tell me it was necessary?"

"I did not design your pain. Only observed its results."

Nick grunted from behind, steadying himself on the desk. "Oh, screw your results. You're a coward. All of you. The whole goddamn Collective."

The projection's voice remained eerily calm. "The Collective is not watching anymore."

James paused. "What?"

The man looked out the window again, into the Ark's artificial horizon. "They abandoned this sector once the data surpassed acceptable deviation. The Ark was deemed inconclusive."

"Inconclusive?" James echoed, eyes wide. "People died. *We* almost died."

"You lived. That was not part of the expected outcome."

James nearly lunged again, but Nick raised a shaky hand. "James…"

"Don't tell me to calm down Nick."

"I'm not," he wheezed. "I'm saying… we might be the only ones left. *No one's watching.* Not anymore."

The room seemed to grow heavier under that truth. The air thickened, the silence crushing their chests like stone.

James stared at the projection. "So why are *you* still here?"

The figure's image glitched. "Protocol. I am the final interface. I remain until the anomaly resolves."

James' brow furrowed. "What does that mean?"

"You have not made your choice."

The two pods behind them hummed louder, almost impatient. The one on the left gave off a faint warmth—inviting, familiar. The other, sterile. Cold. Absolute.

Nick coughed, covering the side of his mouth in blood. "He's not gonna pick for us."

James looked at the pods, then back at the man.

"I don't trust anything in this place," he said. "Not you. Not those machines. Not this choice."

The figure didn't flinch. "Then why are you still standing here?"

James refused to answer.

The hum of the pods intensified—deep, thrumming, almost alive. Steam hissed from unseen vents. The lights above flickered again, then steadied. Behind him, Nick coughed again, weaker this time, trying to stay upright.

"You want resolution," the figure said, its voice as smooth as silk. "You want meaning. But this was never about answers. It was about what you'd do without them."

James approached the pods. Slow. Cautious. Each step felt like a commitment. His hand hovered between them—warmth on one side, clinical cold on the other.

"I didn't come this far to be a variable."

"Then don't be," Nick said behind him. "Be something else."

James paused.

A flash passed through his mind—Ashley's final breath, Emma's small voice asking for food, the blood-soaked corridors, the whisper in his ear that always sounded like himself.

He lowered his hand and turned back to Nick.

"Maybe there's a third choice," he said.

The projection tilted its head. "There isn't."

James looked it in the eye. "Then, I'll make one."

And before the machine could protest, before the lights could respond, he turned away from both pods and walked straight into the darkness.

The hum faltered.

The light faded.

But James did not stop.

About the Author

Daniel Bradshaw is a lifelong admirer of the surreal, the cerebral, and the deeply unsettling. Influenced by abstract science fiction and psychological horror, he developed a passion for nonlinear storytelling and character-driven narratives that challenge perception and linger long after the final page.

Bradshaw draws inspiration from cinematic structure and philosophical themes, aiming to merge emotional depth with speculative dread. *The Ones That Walked* is his debut novel—a haunting descent into shifting realities, fractured identity, and the dark architecture of the human mind. A novel he started working on in 2015.

When he's not writing, Dan can be found sketching concepts, writing more novels, or helping others find their voice through storytelling. To follow his work or reach out, visit MindMazePublishing.com or connect via booksbybradshaw@gmail.com.